A Matter of Hope

Wendy Holley

©April 2017
Beacon Rock Publishing, LLC
This book is available in print at most online retailers.

ISBN 978-0-9973691-2-0

Cover Design by Integra Author Services LLC
Author Photo by Michael Diehl

Published by Beacon Rock Publishing, LLC.
www.beaconrockpublishing.com, Portland Oregon

*For I know the plans I have for you,
declares the Lord, plans to prosper you
and not to harm you, plans to give you
hope and a future.*

Jeremiah 29:11 (NIV)

Chapter One

Nine years earlier

Stop! Turn around. The words pressed against Hannah Brady's tongue. She stared out the windshield at the winding two-lane highway, taking her to a place she'd never been. To live with people she'd never met.

She rubbed her right arm where her father's hand had gripped as he shook her. "I catch Luke Daniels anywhere near you, I'll shoot him. You hear?"

Her heart in shreds, she gripped Luke's hand tighter. He squeezed her fingers. His thin smile an attempt to calm her fears, his blue-gray eyes encouraging, reassuring. She didn't want to leave him.

But she couldn't stay. Her father wouldn't listen. She touched her cheek, sore and bruised from her father's hand. "You'll do as I say and marry Owen Mitchell."

She shuddered. Her protesting marrying a man twice her age with three other wives was considered backtalk. A

1

punishable offense in the Brady household.

Why couldn't she have been born into a normal family? She glanced to her left at Rhett Daniels as he drove the big truck along the highway to Walla Walla. The road cut through a narrow canyon, slicing through the panhandle of Idaho along the river. Like the rushing water of the Clearwater River, she was swept along by circumstances she had no control over.

Two months ago, she'd turned seventeen. In three days, her father planned to give her away to Owen Mitchell. Not old enough to marry Luke without parental or judicial consent, her only option was to run away.

Thankfully, Mr. Daniels was sympathetic to his son's cause. He called friends in Washington, and they offered to take her in.

"Remember what we talked about." Mr. Daniels voice broke through the quiet truck cab.

She blinked away her tears. "No contact with family or friends." She could only correspond with Luke. "Tell Samantha she's the best friend in the whole world, and I'll miss her." Her throat constricted.

Luke released her hand. "I can share with Samantha whatever you write, but she can't know where you are."

Mr. Daniels glanced over at her. "It's for Samantha's safety."

"Tell your mother thank you." How she'd miss Eloise's chocolate chip oatmeal cookies and their time together in the library. "I didn't get to say goodbye to David or Katy." Worry for her brother and sister knotted her stomach.

A muscle in Luke's square jaw tightened. "No one can know, Hannah. You want your father to come after you?"

Fear tightened the muscles in her neck and shoulders. She didn't doubt her father would drag her back to Pinegrove.

When they arrived in Walla Walla, the hot June sun arched high in the sky. Gravel crunched beneath the tires as they drove to an old farmhouse surrounded by brown wheat fields. Mr. Daniels parked and opened the truck door. "I'll let them know we're here. You two can spend a few minutes together." He stepped out of the truck. "Luke, we can't stay long."

While Mr. Daniels walked to the door and disappeared inside the farmhouse, Luke opened the passenger door. "It's too hot in here." He led her to the driver's side of the truck for privacy. Then he bracketed her face in his hands and kissed her.

Her heart soared; her knees weakened. She kissed him back, and her arms wound around his neck.

His kiss left her breathless, her heart cracking. "I'm going to miss you."

His fingers threaded through her hair at the nape of her neck as he held her tight. "I love you." It wasn't the first time he'd said those precious words. Last night, they declared their commitment and devotion. An evening forever engraved in her mind.

"I know." She clung to him.

He pressed her head against him. "It's not forever."

Tears pooled in her eyes. The uncertainty of how long

they'd be apart clawed at her.

"Don't cry." His breath fanned her hair. "Once you're eighteen, I'll come back and get you."

Battling tears, she couldn't speak.

He kissed her forehead. "Then we'll get married. I promise."

Luke would fix up the old house on his grandparents' property. Once she turned eighteen, they'd get married and live on the ranch where they'd raise horses and cattle. There'd be nothing her father could do to her after she married Luke.

"I love you," she whispered.

He brushed his fingers over her cheek. "The McCredies are good people. My dad has known Joe and Paula for years. They'll take good care of you. You'll be safe here."

How could she not be thankful for the family who offered to take her in, care for her, help her escape?

A door slammed, and she flinched.

Luke glanced over her shoulder. "It's my dad." Emotion thickened his voice.

Footsteps descended. "Luke, time to leave, son."

Luke stepped back, leading her to the house. The McCredies gathered on the porch.

Mr. Daniels placed a hand on her shoulder. "This is Hannah. Hannah, this is Joe and Paula McCredie."

"Hello." She fought the tears welling up inside.

Mr. McCredie gestured to a young woman. "This here is our daughter, Katherine. I believe you two are the same age."

Really? Hannah blinked at the girl who seemed much more mature than her, her hair styled, her eyes accented with black eyeliner. Her cutoff shorts fit tight, and her white bra strap slipped out from a pink tank top. "Come on, I'll show you your room. It's next to mine."

Mrs. McCredie held out her hand. "Come inside, Hannah, where it's cooler."

Hannah brushed her fingers over her long denim skirt and tugged on the hem of the short sleeve blouse. Her clothes were frumpy, hand-me-downs. She shrank against Luke, whose palm pressed against her back, urging her forward.

"Joe, Paula, thank you." Rhett opened the driver's side door. "Luke . . ."

Luke walked backward toward the truck. "Write me. Call if you want to talk."

Mrs. McCredie touched Hannah's arm. "You must be hungry. Come inside, and I'll fix you something to eat. Would you like some iced tea?"

She couldn't watch Luke leave. Taking a deep breath, she steeled herself against the tears blurring her vision and entered the farmhouse. Her small suitcase parked at the foot of the narrow stairs. Fans pushed around the warm air. The scent of fried chicken lingered.

"I'll show you upstairs." Katherine bounded up the steps.

Numb, Hannah followed.

At the top of the stairs, Katherine swept out her arm,

presenting a bedroom in a flourish. "This is your room."

Pink roses against a cream background adorned the walls. Lace curtains fluttered in the breeze. A twin bed, yellow dresser, and small writing desk completed the simple furnishings.

"It's not much. Hope you like it."

"It's lovely." The room nicer than the one she shared with her sister and half-sister back home. Home? No. Pinegrove was no longer home.

Katherine's eyes glistened. "We're happy you're here."

Katherine—her little sister's name. The sister she left behind. Would Katy ever forgive her? Would someone be there for Katy and help her escape?

"Were you really going to have to marry some old coot?" a low rough voice rumbled from behind.

She pivoted and gaped at the teenager standing in the doorway carrying her suitcase.

"Dane." Katherine wagged a finger at him. "Don't be so rude."

"I'm just asking." He set the suitcase on the floor near the dresser.

"Yes, he's a friend of my father." An elder in the community. No one disobeyed Owen Mitchell and risked being shunned.

Dane leaned against the doorframe with his arms crossed. "Couldn't you just tell your father you didn't want to marry the old man?"

"It doesn't work that way in Pinegrove. Our fathers arrange the marriages."

Katherine braced her hands on her hips. "I saw a TV special on polygamy once."

They must think I'm a freak. Hannah bowed her head.

"Katherine, Dane, let Hannah get settled." Mrs. McCredie appeared in the doorway. "Hannah, there's chicken downstairs and a glass of tea on the table. Let me know if you need anything."

"Thank you, Mrs. McCredie."

"Call me Paula, and my husband would like you to call him Joe."

Hannah strained to smile.

Katherine pushed her brother out of the room. "I'm right next door if you need anything."

Alone, Hannah closed the door and dropped onto the bed. She covered her face with her hands and let her tears fall. How long would it be before she could be with Luke?

Chapter Two

Present Day

Luke didn't recognize the number on caller ID. But since his home and business number were the same, he answered anyway. "Bitterroot Outdoor Adventures."

"Hello, is Luke Daniels there?"

What's a kid calling him for? "Speaking."

Breathing and rustling of paper crackled across the connection. Great, a prank call. He didn't have time for this. Fences needed mending. A loose board on the barn's north side needed repair. Although snow flurries filled the morning sky, he had work to do.

"Look, kid—" He didn't hide his annoyance.

"You're Luke Daniels?"

"The one and only." He waited for the boy to say something. "And who are you?"

"My name is Lucas Brady."

Luke's heart stopped then slammed against his ribs.

Brady. The name resurrected a beautiful girl with long brown hair and big brown eyes. The girl who broke his heart when she stopped communicating with him.

Luke swallowed hard to clear the lump in his throat. "Are you related to Hannah Brady?"

"Yes, sir. She's my mom."

What did it matter to him? She'd obviously moved on. He hadn't heard from her in nine years, not that he was counting. "Why are you calling me?"

"My mom is real sick."

Hannah is sick? He gripped the back of the chair. "What's wrong with her?"

"She can't wake up."

"What do you mean?"

"She's in a coma."

Luke dropped onto the oak dining room chair. *A coma*, the words reverberated in his head. "How long has she been in a coma?"

"Almost a week."

His chest tightened. "What happened?"

"She was in a car accident."

A hundred questions hatched in his mind all at once.

"I was hoping maybe if you came and talked to her, she'd wake up."

"How old are you?" The moment the words escaped his mouth, his stomach twisted. He held his breath, waiting for the answer.

"I'm eight."

It couldn't be. Luke tried to wrap his mind around the

idea of Hannah leaving the valley pregnant with his kid. All these years he had a son, and Hannah kept him a secret.

And she named the boy after him.

His stomach dipped, and heat crawled up his neck to his face. He wiped a hand over his eyes and across his mouth. "Where are you?"

"At home. I found some letters you wrote Mom and a book from school with your picture."

She kept his letters and the yearbook he gave her.

"How did you find me?"

"Easy, I looked you up on the Internet. Your address was on the envelopes. Although you moved, you still live near where you did."

Smart kid.

"Where do you live?"

"Walla Walla. Do you know where that is?"

"Yeah." He knew where it was. The memory of the fear on her face, tears shimmering in her eyes crowded out all other thought. "What hospital is your mom in?"

"St. Mary's Medical. Are you coming?"

The hope in Lucas's voice tightened like a steel band around Luke's heart. "Yeah. I'm coming."

"Thank you." The kid's voice raised an octave.

"What's your address?"

"It's easy to find. We live on the Copper Ridge Vineyards."

A vineyard? The McCredies had a farm, but he didn't remember a vineyard. Then again, maybe she moved.

10

"Lucas?"

"My friends call me Lucky."

A tremulous smile stretched across Luke's face. "Lucky, you take care of yourself. I'll be there tomorrow afternoon."

Lucky set the phone on the kitchen counter. His heart pounded. He talked to his dad. And he was coming tomorrow.

He looked up at the ceiling. "Thank you, God."

He ran back into his mother's bedroom, where he'd scattered the stack of letters on the bed. The yearbook lay opened to a picture of his father in the lower right, his mother on the upper left of the other page.

He stared at his father's photo. Light brown hair swept back from a broad forehead. A smile stretched across his face. *Has he changed much?*

Holding a mirror, Lucky checked his reflection. Who did he take after most, his mother or his father? His father's eyes were bluish gray, like his.

Mom never said he didn't have a dad, just that they couldn't see him. She never explained why, and he hadn't asked. Grandpa and Grandma never mentioned him. Uncle Dane and Aunt Katherine didn't talk about him either.

Some of his friends didn't have a dad. The ones who did saw them on the weekends.

Lucky hadn't meant to snoop through Mom's

belongings. He was searching for something to take to the hospital to help her wake up.

From the bedside table, he picked up a picture of himself and his mother. They wore matching straw hats and smiled at the camera, holding up the fish they caught in the river.

Lucky leaned against the bed as tears stung his eyes. His heart hammered, and he sniffled.

"Please, God. Wake my mom up." His throat squeezed.

The front door opened. The wind howled. "Lucky, are you in here?" Uncle Dane called.

He wiped his eyes on his flannel shirt sleeve. "I'm here," he yelled back and tossed the picture on the bed. He hurried from the room, closing the door behind him. He'd be in big trouble for getting into Mom's things.

"Grandma is worried about you."

"I'm getting my books." He ran down the hall, grabbed his heavy backpack off the lower bunk, and dragged it into the front room.

"Storm is coming. The wind's whipping up something fierce."

Lucky shoved his arms into his coat and zipped it up.

"Here, let me carry that for you." Uncle Dane took the pack and swung it over his shoulder. "Good grief, these books weigh a ton. I can't understand how an eight-year-old is expected to read so much."

"It's 'cause I'm in fifth grade. If I were only in third grade, I wouldn't have so many books."

Uncle Dane messed his hair. "Yeah, come on Genius,

before Grandma sends a search party out after us."

The wind tugged at his coat as he hurried outside and climbed into the cab of the dark-green pickup truck. Uncle Dane drove the short distance up the drive from the cottage where he lived with his mom, to the big house his grandparents lived in. Further up the driveway, it smoothed to pavement. With the tasting room closed, there weren't any cars in the winery parking lot.

Out the window, rain blew sideways. "How long is the storm staying?"

"Through the night."

"Oh." He said a silent prayer that Luke wouldn't get caught in the storm, asking God to keep his father safe. Ever since his mom's accident, he worried about storms and icy roads.

Dane pressed the button in the overhead console raising the garage door. They pulled into the third bay, out of the wind. Lucky ran up the stairs to the house, beating Dane to the top of the steps and rushed through the door to find Grandma reading the daily newspaper.

"Goodness, Lucky, where have you been?"

"I went to get my books." He was careful not to meet his grandmother's eyes. She could always sense when he'd done something he wasn't supposed to.

She folded the paper and set it aside. "There's a storm coming."

"I know."

"Did you eat?"

He nodded. His tummy felt funny like a bunch of

grasshoppers were jumping around inside. Part of him wanted to tell Grandma about his conversation with Luke Daniels. But he feared getting in trouble for snooping in Mom's things. He wasn't sure how his grandparents would take the news that he called his dad and asked him to come.

"Well, don't just stand there. You have work to do. We don't want you to fall behind in your studies."

Sometimes she said the funniest things. How could he fall behind in his studies when he'd already jumped two grades?

Uncle Dane set his books on the table. "I spoke with your teacher, and she e-mailed your lesson plan for today."

"When can we go see Mom?"

His uncle squeezed his shoulder. "In a few hours."

He wasn't in the mood for his studies. Removing his coat, he draped it over the back of a chair then sat at the piano. He positioned his fingers and tapped out a tune. Grandma taught him how to play before he could read.

Sitting on the edge of the piano bench, he worked the pedals with his feet and played one of Mom's favorites, "Amazing Grace". When his fingers stumbled, he went back, found his place, and continued till he got it right. A few weeks ago, Mom had sung the song in church.

He kept playing, confused by his jumbled feelings. Sad because his mom lay in a hospital bed with bandages wrapped around her head and leg. It was hard to look at her hooked to tubes, wires, and blipping machines.

And yet, excitement made him jumpy. Since talking with Luke, he had a lot of questions. What if he was married and had kids? Why hadn't his parents gotten married? Why hadn't he visited him or stayed in contact? He didn't think about that when he looked up the number and called. He should've asked.

Unable to concentrate, he let his fingers pause over the keys. The letters Luke had written were nice. Some were yucky, mushy stuff. But he wrote that he loved his mom. Feeling guilty, Lucky didn't read all the letters. At some point, the letters stopped. Maybe Luke had found another woman, like Chris's dad. Or maybe his dad drank and got mean like Dwayne's dad. Now that he thought about it, he hoped he'd done the right thing. He pushed away from the piano.

Rain tapped against the windows, and wind rumbled between the buildings. If it wasn't raining, he'd run back to the house and read the rest of the letters to find out why his dad went away.

Mom had to wake up. She had to get better. In the meantime, he'd be extra good so God would hear his prayers and answer them.

Chapter Three

Luke stepped inside his brother's house. A fire crackled in the woodstove.

Irene, his sister-in-law, greeted him with a smile. "It's good to see you." She rubbed her hand over the slight bump of her belly before hurrying down the hall.

"Morning sickness all day long." Trent's voice rattled, gruff with concern.

Had Hannah suffered from morning sickness?

Trent's eyes narrowed. "Is everything all right?"

He shrugged. Where should he start? What could he say? Trent's gaze registered doubt and remained fixed on him as if trying to read his mind. Rightly so. There was a time in his past when he'd asked to come over to *talk* and had to ask his brother for a loan to keep his business going. Another time, he asked for help fixing his rig he'd wrecked. Things were different now. He didn't need money, and he paid Trent back years ago. In fact, he'd been trying to get his brother to go into business with him.

Good thing his parents weren't alive to learn he'd produced a child out of wedlock. Mom's heart would've broken for sure. She loved Hannah. She and Dad both. To say they would've been disappointed was an understatement. He couldn't imagine how he'd tell his folks. Confessing to his brother proved hard enough.

His brother settled in his big leather recliner.

"I got a call this morning." Luke hesitated as he searched for the words. "From a boy named . . . Lucas Brady." He stood in the middle of the room with his hands shoved in his denim jacket's pockets.

"Brady?" Trent sat forward. "As in Hannah Brady?"

Luke nodded.

Irene entered the room. "Hannah called you?" Hope rang in her voice.

What had Trent told his wife about Hannah?

He swallowed hard. "No, her son."

Irene sat in a rocking chair and positioned a pillow behind her back. Her eyebrows drew together as she gazed across the room at Trent.

Luke took a deep breath and released it. "He's eight years old."

Trent's forehead wrinkled as he calculated the years. His mouth dropped open. "Eight? That would mean . . ." Trent glanced at Irene then back at him.

Beneath two days' growth of whiskers, Luke's face grew hot. "I believe he's mine." There, he said it.

He never claimed to be a saint. It was one time. The

night before they took her to Walla Walla. He wanted her to know the depth of his feelings. He was young and stupid. High emotions mixed with surging hormones were a bad combination. He avoided eye contact with Trent.

"What made him call you?"

Luke wiped his hand down his face as his son's words came back to him. "Hannah is in a coma."

Irene gasped. "What happened?"

"A car accident. I don't know anything more."

Trent ran his fingers through his hair. "How did he find you?"

Luke shuffled on his feet. "He found the letters I wrote her and somehow tracked me down. He asked if I'd come see her. He hopes if I talk to her, she'll wake up."

"Poor boy," Irene whispered.

"And if she doesn't?" Trent was always the practical one.

"I don't know. That's what I need to find out. If Hannah doesn't come out of this, then what happens to my son?" Luke paced the room.

All morning he wrestled with his thoughts. No kid of his was going to be raised by others or end up in foster care. He had rights as a father, and he'd spend every dime to exercise those rights. "I'm going over there."

"When are you leaving?" Irene reached for the package of crackers on the table beside her.

"Tomorrow morning. Wade will look after the livestock. Things are quiet with the business." He dug into his Levi's pocket and removed a mail key. "Would you mind checking my mail while I'm gone?" He set the key on the coffee table.

Irene nodded. Her brown eyes reflected the shock he experienced this morning.

Trent glanced out the window. "The pass might be closed with this snow storm."

"I'll take the Interstate. It's longer, but they'll keep it clear." Fire simmered in his gut all morning. "I need answers."

"It doesn't sound like Hannah is in a place to provide answers."

"Then the McCredies can. I deserve to know why she stopped communicating with me. Why she kept my son a secret all these years." His voice rose.

Irene blinked her brown eyes and pressed her hand over her heart. "I'm sure she had her reasons." Her voice thinned.

Trent exchanged one of those marital looks with his bride. The kind that speaks a secret language only husband and wife could interpret. "Luke, you need to approach this calm like."

"I'm sorry. I didn't mean to raise my voice." He took a deep cleansing breath. "She used our family to leave. She put us in danger. She put Mom and Dad in danger."

His brother shook his head. "That's not exactly how I remember things."

"Well, it doesn't matter what you remember. I lived it." His chest burned with the effort to contain his anger.

"Your priority needs to be that boy."

Tell me something I don't know.

"I think we should pray." Irene sounded a lot like his mother.

Although he'd been raised in a Christian home, he wasn't prone to praying. He hadn't gone to a church service since he was nineteen. The last time he stepped foot inside a church was for his mother's funeral less than a year ago. What good is prayer going to do? He bowed his head anyway.

His sister-in-law led the prayer. "Dear Lord, we come to you with humble hearts asking for your will to be done. Thank you, Father, for bringing this boy into our lives. Watch over his tender heart, as he must fear for his mother. Lord, we ask that you heal Hannah. Bring her out of this darkness. Put a hedge of protection around her. Lord, as Luke travels to see Hannah and Lucas, keep him safe on these winter roads. Go before him and prepare the hearts of those he will meet, who no doubt are filled with grief and scared for Hannah. In Jesus' name."

"Amen," Luke echoed his brother. But he wasn't convinced it would make a difference.

Sympathy filled Irene's eyes. "We'll keep praying."

"Yes." Trent stood. "Keep us posted."

"I will."

Trent followed him to the door and put a hand on his shoulder. "You okay?"

Luke ventured to meet his brother's eyes, fearing condemnation or even disappointment. Instead, he saw compassion. The sight almost unraveled his thin emotions. "As okay as I can be." His throat tightened.

"Quite the shock, I can imagine."

He nodded.

"One word of advice."

He knew what his brother was going to say.

"Watch your temper."

He was a father. No matter how many times he reminded himself, he couldn't grasp the reality. A live-in-the-moment kind of a guy, he found himself thinking about the future. Making plans with what-if scenarios.

The long drive on slick roads blurred as he grappled with his thoughts.

What if Hannah doesn't come out of the coma? Then he'd bring Lucky home with him. Kids like horses and cows. A ranch was just the place for a boy to grow up. If Hannah did come through, then what? He didn't want to be a part-time dad. One of those guys who only got to see his kid two weekends a month and fought over holidays. He sure didn't want to just be a name on a monthly check either.

No, he'd be a fully participating dad. Hannah may have kept him from his son all these years, but not anymore.

He arrived in Walla Walla by midafternoon and drove straight to the hospital, saving the more difficult part for later—when he'd see his son for the first time.

Sitting in the truck, he stared at the double doors as

people came and went. Could he work up the courage to walk inside? If he ran into Joe or Paula McCredie, what should he say? Joe had been a kind, reasonable man and Paula a sweet lady.

The McCredies sent flowers to his father's funeral, but not his mother's. Mom must have notified them when Dad passed away, but they may not have known his mother was gone. Shame burned in his chest. Was he the cause of the McCredies distancing themselves from his parents?

Anger swept aside his shame. Why did they keep Hannah's secret all these years? He wiped his hand down his face as he tried to make sense of it all.

The answers lay inside.

Time to face his past. He opened the door and slid out of the truck, locked it with a push of the button on the keyless remote. He strode to the doors and paused, taking a deep breath. *Hospitals.* He swallowed a groan. He'd spent too much time in them over the past few years. First his father, then his mother.

He followed the signs to ICU and approached a nurse behind the counter. "I'm looking for Hannah Brady."

She slid her glasses up her nose. "Are you family?"

Family? "Uh, no. Well, sort of." As the father of her child, he was as good as family.

"Your name?" Her fingers poised over the keyboard.

"Luke Daniels."

She typed on the keyboard.

"You made it!" a young voice boomed in the quiet hall.

A boy with sandy-brown hair and blue-gray eyes

23

rushed toward him. Luke's heart slammed against his ribs. He knelt in front of his son and peered into his eyes—eyes matching his own. It was like looking at an image of himself at eight years old.

"I knew you'd come." Lucas beamed.

"Of course, I came." Luke swallowed hard around the lump in his throat.

"Luke Daniels?" The voice came out of his past.

He stood and held out his hand. "Hello, Mr. McCredie."

Joe shook his hand. "How did you find out?"

Lucky glanced up. "I called him, Grandpa Joe."

Joe gaped at the boy and back at Luke. He took his cowboy hat off and ran his fingers through silver-tinged hair. Confusion etched deep lines across his forehead.

"Sir, Lucky called me yesterday morning. I came as soon as I could. How is she?" He couldn't take his eyes off his son.

Joe shoved his hat back on his head. "No change, I'm afraid."

"May I see her?"

When Joe hesitated, Lucky spoke up. "Please, Grandpa."

Joe gave a curt nod. "This way."

Luke followed Joe and Lucky to a room on the right. He paused inside the doorway and stared at a woman lying in bed. Brunette hair spilled over the pillow. A tube ran from a machine into her mouth. Drawn into the room, he stood beside the bed. Bruises blotched her face, and bandages wrapped her head. White gauze swathed her hands, leaving her fingers exposed.

With his heart in his throat, he touched the cool skin of her arm. A rhythmic hiss and pulse of machines punctuated the silence.

Joe placed a hand on the boy's shoulder. "Lucky, go find your grandmother."

"But I want to stay."

"Please. Let her know Luke is here."

"Okay." Lucky's tone lifted, and he hurried out of the room.

Joe waited until Lucky left. "She hit black ice, flipped the vehicle several times. They got her out before the fire reached her."

A gaping hole opened in his heart—a hole he'd filled with building his house and his business. "How long has she been like this?"

"Six days."

Remorse gripped him. "What are the doctors saying?"

"The longer she's like this, the less likely she is to come out of it." Joe crossed his arms as if shielding his heart from the pain. "The swelling around her brain has gone down. That's good news."

Trained in search and rescue, Luke understood the severity. "Are the machines keeping her alive?"

"She can't breathe on her own." Joe's husky voice evidence of his turmoil.

"Any brain activity?" Staring at her, Luke rasped the question, his voice barely above a whisper.

25

"Yes."

He released a heavy sigh. At least one good sign.

She appeared peaceful. As if she were in a deep sleep, but the tubes and wires testified otherwise.

He couldn't stop staring at her. "Lucky thought if I came and talked to her, she might wake up."

"That's why he called you?"

Luke nodded.

"How'd he find you?"

"Apparently, he found some letters." Luke shrugged. "I didn't know I had a son until he called."

"She never told you she was pregnant." Joe's matter-of-fact tone said he knew the answer.

A deep ache filled Luke's chest. "No. She just stopped writing, stopped taking my calls."

"She was trying to start her life over. She wanted to leave all that behind."

A stab to his heart caused his breath to catch. Hannah wanted to put *him* behind her and start over without him?

"Luke?" Paula entered the room. Although a little older with her blonde hair shorter than he remembered, she'd changed very little. "I don't believe my eyes."

"Hello, Mrs. McCredie." How could he sound so normal? He burned to ask why they didn't call him, why no one told him Hannah had his kid. Why did they keep her secret? But as he stared at Hannah, broken and teetering on the edge of death, the fight knocked out of him.

Lucky stood beside the bed and pressed his little hand

over his mother's. "Mom, there's someone here for you. It's Luke."

No response. Only the rhythmic hiss and tick of the machines.

Luke put his hand on his son's back. "Give her time."

"How long can you stay?" Hope brightened Lucky's eyes.

"As long as it takes." Or until he had to say a final goodbye and take Lucky home with him.

A tentative smile turned up the corners of Lucky's mouth. "Talk to her."

His emotions were all over the place. "I don't know what to say." Anger, hurt, sadness, and regret all clamored inside.

"Tell her what you've been doing since you last saw her."

She looked the same, and yet different. Long hair, escaping the bandages, curved around her pretty face. Small creases now etched her eyes. "Can I have a few minutes alone with her?"

With hushed voices, Joe and Paula ushered Lucky out of the room.

Luke closed the door, then pulled up a chair beside the bed and sat. He placed a hand on her thin shoulder. "Hannah, why didn't you tell me? You didn't have to do this alone." He bowed his head. "I don't know if I should be mad or happy." He took a deep breath and exhaled. "I'm mad you kept Lucas from me. But I'm happy you had him. Come on, Hannah. You have to pull through this. Our son needs you."

He glanced out the window to the hall. "What's going to happen to Lucky if you don't come out of this? What did you think would happen to him if something happened to you? You should've been honest with me." Hurt thickened his voice.

He ran his rough, callused fingers over her bandaged knuckles and along her slender fingers. She was so delicate, small boned and barely five feet tall. If only she'd open her beautiful brown eyes.

Yet her long eyelashes remained against her pale cheeks. Her hair poked out from beneath the bandages and flowed over the sterile white pillowcase. Her chest rose in rhythm with the machine. He longed to hear her voice, see her smile.

"Come on, Hannah. This isn't you. You're a fighter. You're a survivor."

There's got to be something he could do to help her.

"I remember our last night together. It was so special, so good. I don't regret it. Not for a moment. I loved you so much." He sighed. "I still do."

Chapter Four

"I better come with you and show you the way home." A plea brightened Lucky's earnest eyes.

A loner by nature, Luke needed time to think. Besides, he had navigation in his rig. Surely, he could find the place—the old farmhouse burned into his memory from the day he left Hannah. But he couldn't resist Lucky's request.

Standing in the hall outside ICU, he checked for Joe's consent. Joe gave a curt nod. He owed Joe and Paula, respected the couple for the care and love they showed Hannah and Lucky. Even though they kept Lucky a secret.

Outside, snow dusted the parking lot. Tempted to take Lucky by the hand, he glanced down. Lucky's coat wasn't zipped. Luke knelt in front of the boy and fastened it.

Placing his hands on Lucky's shoulders, he battled the urge to pull the boy into an embrace. But he didn't want to scare the kid. "Warm enough?"

"Yeah."

Luke stood and, with a hand on his son's back, guided him to his truck. He opened the passenger door, and the kid climbed into the cab.

As he walked around to the driver's side, Luke glanced up at the gray sky and shivered. The air calmed as if the earth held its breath, waiting to see what would become of Hannah.

They left the parking lot, and he turned right as Lucky instructed.

Lucky's gaze bored a hole straight through his heart. "You look the same as your pictures. Older, but the same."

You look like me when I was your age. "You must have looked at the yearbook."

"I did. You and Mom went to school together. Were you in the same class?"

"No, I was one year ahead of her."

Lucky fidgeted and strained to see over the dash. "Want to see where I go to school?"

"Sure." The kid had an infectious, optimistic spirit. *He didn't get that from me.*

"We're getting close." Lucky loosened the seatbelt to sit up and see over the dash. "There it is. That's where I go to school." He pointed.

Luke slowed the truck as they passed by a church with a tall steeple and several long buildings toward the back. A sign out front read Whitman Calvary Community Church and right below it, Whitman Christian Academy.

My son goes to a Christian school?

It hadn't occurred to him Lucky wasn't going to public

30

school. His mother would've been pleased to know her grandson was getting a proper schooling.

He fumbled for something to say. "Do you like it?"

"Yeah. My teacher is really nice." Lucky adjusted the seatbelt to fit snug across his lap but kept fidgeting with the shoulder strap as it threatened to put him in a choke hold. "Turn left up here."

A blue tourism sign pointed the way to Copper Mountain Winery. "Should I just follow the signs?"

"Sure." Intense blue-gray eyes focused on him.

What did his son think of his old man? Did he measure up to his idea of a father? Did he see the resemblance?

"You're sad, aren't you?"

He glanced over at Lucky and swallowed hard around the lump in his throat. "Yeah."

"You're afraid Mom won't wake up."

He stared straight ahead, afraid to admit Hannah may not make it.

"She will. Just keep talking to her. Maybe you could tell stories of when you knew each other."

"I suppose I could try." Fear gripped his heart, fear that if Hannah didn't wake up his son would blame him. How would Lucky cope if his mother didn't come out of the coma?

"It's just up here to the left." Lucky waved toward a large wooden sign with a carved mountain crowned in copper.

"I see." Luke veered into the driveway and was about

to stop in front of the house where he'd left Hannah all those years ago, but the farmhouse now sported a sign that read Tasting Room.

"Our house is down the road."

He continued until the pavement surrendered to a gravel road. As they rounded a bend, a large timber-frame home came into view, its grand windows overlooking rolling hills of vines.

"Keep going down the hill."

They drove along the vineyard. A curve in the road and a slight hill brought them to a cottage with a front porch.

"You can park outside the garage."

He pulled onto the cement pad in front of the single-car garage. Flowerbeds surrounded the porch, but the bushes were twigs and sticks, void of any life.

Lucky jumped out and hurried to the driver's side.

Rows of grapevines stretched across the acres. The little house wedged up against a hillside and faced east.

Once Luke got out, Lucky rushed through the unlocked door. Luke stepped inside, his boots landing on a plush rug protecting oak floors. Removing his brown Stetson, he closed the door but remained rooted in the entryway. Vivid reds and yellows dominated the décor, from the checkered curtains to the pillows on the cream-colored leather couch.

Lucky climbed up onto a barstool. "Are you hungry?"

Luke shook his head.

"Can I get you something to drink?"

"Water."

Lucky jumped down and sprinted around the high bar into the small kitchen. He climbed onto the counter and fetched a glass from the cabinet, then hopped down.

"You want my help?"

"I got it." Lucky opened the refrigerator and filled the glass from a pitcher of filtered water. "Here you go."

"Thanks." His throat dry, Luke took a swallow of the cold water.

Pictures of Hannah and Lucky graced the end table and fireplace mantel, drawing him away from the front door. In the mantel picture, Hannah wore a large floppy hat and garden gloves. She held trimming shears and knelt beside Lucky, surrounded by vines heavy with grapes. Her smile stretched a mile wide. His heart ached.

"Can I take your coat?"

When Luke set the glass on the oak coffee table and peeled off his coat, Lucky draped it over the barstool. "Want to see my room?"

"Sure."

Luke followed his son down a hall to a bedroom. Bunk beds rested against the wall with a pine trunk at the foot. A small desk sat under a window.

"I sleep on top unless I'm sick, then I sleep on the bottom."

"What's in the trunk?"

"Toys." Lucky lifted the lid and took out his toys—Legos, plastic rifle, Hot Wheels, and a basketball. "My bike and fishing rod are in the garage."

"You fish?"

He rolled the basketball in his hands. "Grandpa takes me to the pond at the bottom of the hill. Sometimes Uncle Dane takes me to the river. Mom joins us if she has time. You fish, don't ya?"

Luke smiled. "Yeah. I fish quite a bit."

"We should go fishing." Lucky bounced the ball on the floor. "Whoops, sorry. I'm not supposed to dribble the ball in the house. Want to shoot some hoops?"

"Well, it's a little cold out."

"Oh, right." Lucky set the ball back in the trunk. "Come on. I'll show you the rest of the place."

They passed a bathroom on their way to the other end of the hall to the second bedroom. Luke stood in the doorway, reluctant to invade Hannah's privacy. With frilly lace curtains and a basket of silk spring flowers on the floor, the small space suited her. The feminine room, so much like Hannah.

On the red rose comforter lay a yearbook and a small stack of letters. His handwriting scrawled over the envelopes. He swallowed hard.

Lucky followed his gaze. "I hope you're not mad at me." He sat on the bed and pushed aside a red box.

"Why would I be mad?"

Lucky closed the book. "For getting into Mom's things."

"I can't be mad at you." Luke entered the room and sat beside his son. "I'm happy you called me."

"You didn't know about me, did you?"

34

"No." He couldn't lie to his son, even to protect Hannah.

Lucky swung his feet up and down, his shoes hitting the side of the bed. "I knew you were out there."

If he'd known about Lucky, things would've been different. "Did your mom tell you much about me?"

Lucky tilted his head and squinted as if trying to recall eight years of memories. "She said you liked fishing and played baseball in high school."

At least she told him something.

"She never said why we couldn't see you." Lucky slid off the bed and toyed with a red porcelain dish on the bedside table. "Do you have a wife and kids?" He spun around and faced Luke.

The question hit him square in the chest, knocking the air out of him. "No."

Lucky's little shoulders dropped. He stared at the floor. "A girlfriend?"

"No." Luke shook his head.

Lucky released a heavy sigh. "Why couldn't we visit you? Were you in the army?"

"No. I think your mom was afraid to come where I live."

"Why?"

"Did she ever tell you about her family?"

He cocked his head and narrowed his eyes. "I don't think so."

To explain to a boy his mother was raised in a cult and was going to be forced to marry a man as old as her father who already had three wives was something he didn't want to attempt.

"Well, looks like you read the letters I wrote her." He opted for a change of subject.

Lucky's eyes widened. His cheeks stained pink. "Just a few."

Luke couldn't remember what he'd written, but in case it was something inappropriate for an eight-year-old boy, he scooped them up and placed them in the small red box. After he secured the lid, he set the letters on the bedside table and hoped they'd be safe from prying young eyes.

He picked up the yearbook and flipped through the pages, scanning the encouraging words written by their friends. He and his family were the only ones who knew where she'd gone.

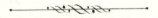

Lucky slid off the bed, relieved to know his father wasn't married and didn't have a girlfriend. So Luke could stay, or better yet, he could go visit him in Montana. Maybe his parents would get back together, get married, and they could all live together. First, he had to find a way to wake Mom up.

The phone rang, and his father flinched.

Lucky answered it on the second ring.

"You two coming up for dinner?" Grandma asked.

"Yeah, we'll be right there." He hung up the phone. "Grandma says dinner's ready."

His father wiped his hand down his face and stood.

36

Lucky walked backward down the hall. "You can sleep here tonight."

"I was going to find a hotel."

"Why? You can have the top bunk."

Luke ran his fingers through his hair. "Not sure I'd fit."

"Oh yeah, I see that." His dad was tall. Mom could fit, and sometimes she'd lie beside him until he fell asleep. They'd talk about stuff like school, his friends, and the vineyard. They'd even make the grocery list together. Sometimes, she'd quiz him about his schoolwork. If he had a bad dream or couldn't sleep, she'd sing to him.

"You can have Mom's bed."

His father looked like he swallowed a bug. "I think we better get going, or we'll be late for dinner."

Large wet flakes fell from the overcast sky as they drove up to his grandparents' house. When they walked inside, the peppery smell of crispy fried chicken greeted him. Grandpa Joe's favorite takeout.

"Is Uncle Dane coming?" He wanted Dane to meet his dad. Then again, maybe they already knew each other.

"Not tonight. It's just the four of us." Grandpa set plates around the table.

Lucky held out his hand to his father. "I'll take your coat."

"Luke, sit wherever you'd like," Grandma called from the kitchen.

Luke sat at the table's far end.

Lucky draped his coat along with his dad's over the

back of the couch, and then took a seat beside Luke.

Grandma placed the big chicken bucket in the center of the table, along with mashed potatoes, gravy, and biscuits. His grandparents held hands, and Lucky presented his hand to Luke. His father's eyebrows drew together.

"Shall we say grace?" Grandma peered across the table at Luke.

Luke grasped his hand and bowed his head. His father's hand was big and warm. Lucky didn't want to let go.

With his deep voice, Grandpa blessed the food. "Lord, we thank you for bringing Luke here. We ask that you heal Hannah. Bring her back to us, Father. Bless this meal to the nourishment of our bodies. In Jesus' name. Amen."

Grandpa passed the potatoes to his father. "So, Luke, what kind of work do you do?"

"I have a guiding business, Bitterroot Outdoor Adventures." Luke scooped potatoes onto his plate.

"He takes people fishing." Lucky reached for a flaky roll. "I saw the pictures on his website."

Grandma gave him a scoop of potatoes then poured brown gravy over them.

Luke accepted the bucket of chicken from Grandpa. "I also provide guided hunting trips, horseback riding, and camping." He set a crispy breaded breast next to the potatoes.

"Does that keep you busy?" Grandma handed the gravy to his father.

"Yeah." Luke spooned gravy over his potatoes. "I'm pretty busy, from the first part of May up to about the second week of November. I've been trying to get my brother to join me. It's getting to where I have to turn down work. I can't keep up."

Grandpa wiped his mouth with a paper napkin. "We were sorry to hear about your father passing."

Luke nodded. "Afraid his health declined quickly."

"How's your mom?" Grandma asked.

Luke lowered his head. "She passed away last year."

Both of his grandparents are gone? What were they like?

Grandma blinked several times. "I'm so sorry."

Grandpa paused with a drumstick held to his mouth. "I'm really sorry to hear that, Luke."

His dad set his fork on the plate and leaned back from the table a bit. "She had COPD."

"We knew she struggled for quite some time," Grandma whispered.

"How is Trent?" Grandpa bit into his drumstick.

Not knowing who Trent was, Lucky waited for his father's answer.

Luke peeled the meat off with his fork and scooped up potatoes and gravy. "Married a terrific lady. Her name is Irene."

"Who is Trent?"

"My older brother."

Grandma leaned forward. "Your uncle."

I have an uncle. "Where does he live?"

39

"In Stevensville, near me."

"And Samantha, how is she doing?" Grandma seemed very familiar with his father's family. "We haven't seen her since she was in grade school."

"She's finishing up college. Has a double major in music and photography."

Lucky tried a bite of chicken with potatoes, too. The crunch of the chicken skin and creamy potatoes with the spicy gravy made a good combination.

"Does Trent have children?" Grandma asked.

"Expecting their first."

Her eyes brightened. "That's wonderful."

Wanting to be part of the conversation, Lucky interjected, "Mom is an accountant. She went to college."

"She is?" The corner of Luke's mouth twitched. "She always was good with numbers."

"Hannah does our books and payroll. She designed our accounting system." Pride rang in Grandpa's voice.

"It worked so well, she took the software program and sold it to quite a few other wineries in the area," Grandma added with equal pride.

"She writes software?" Luke asked.

"Not exactly. She took an existing accounting system and customized it for our industry."

"This one here," Grandpa said, pointing at Lucky, "is following in his mother's footsteps."

"I like math. What were you good at in school?"

Luke took a drink of water. "Sports." He shrugged. "I got good grades, but I was never as smart as your mother."

"How did you meet Mom?"

Luke's eyes darkened. He set his fork down and stared at his plate. "Uh, I first saw her in the library." He raised his eyes, and the corners of his mouth curved up. "I remember the first time I saw her." He rested his arms on the table. "She was talking with my mom. Your grandmother, Eloise, was the librarian. I had to pick my mom up at work." He stared out the big window.

"What did you say to her?"

"Nothing." Luke laughed. "I was all tongue-tied. But I started going to the library a lot more."

Grandpa chuckled.

"She became close friends with my sister, Samantha, so she hung around the house a lot."

Lucky squirmed in his chair. "When did you become boyfriend and girlfriend?"

"Lucas," Grandma said in that warning tone of hers. "Eat your dinner."

"I got the courage up enough to ask her to a dance." Luke picked up his fork.

Lucky couldn't stop staring at Luke.

Grandpa reached for another roll. "Luke, you're welcome to stay here in the guestroom."

Lucky's heart jumped. "I want to sleep in my own bed." Since the accident, he'd been sleeping in the guest room, but with his dad here, he hoped they could have a sleepover at home.

"You can sleep on the couch."

"No, I want Luke to stay with me tonight."

Wendy Holley

"If it's all right with you, we could sleep in the cottage," his father said.

Yeah, his dad was cool.

Grandpa gave in with a nod. Grandma shook her head, unhappy about the arrangement. But he wanted to know more   about   his   uncle   and   aunt.

Chapter Five

Standing in the doorway to Lucky's bedroom, Luke watched his son sleep. Lucky lay on his stomach, hugging the pillow, his mouth hung open as he snored softly. In his flannel, red-and-green plaid pajamas, he seemed older than eight. Luke was no expert on kids by any stretch of the imagination, but Lucky seemed more mature than he remembered being at his age.

If he didn't get answers to the questions plaguing him, he wouldn't sleep. He put on his coat, slipped his feet into his boots by the door, and strode out into the cool, clear evening. Overhead, a canopy of stars and a three-quarter moon shone above the twisting branches of grapevines.

His breath fogged as he made his way up the gravel drive to the big house. The moon reflected off the light dusting of snow. Light emanated from the large windows overlooking the vineyard. He tromped up the steps and rang the doorbell. A guy in his early twenties answered.

"Dane, right?"

"Yeah. And you're Luke." He moved aside. "Come in."

"Thank you." Luke stepped inside onto the slate entry.

The open floorplan was perfect for entertaining. Luke buried his hands in his pockets.

"Hello, Luke, come in and sit down," Paula said. "Is Lucky sleeping?"

"He's pretty tuckered."

"It's been a big day for him."

It had been a big day for him, too.

Joe entered the room. "Won't you join us at the table?" He pulled out a mahogany chair and sat. Paula stood beside her husband. "Can we get you something to drink?"

"Something hot would be nice." He sure could use a shot of whiskey.

Dane set a cup and teakettle of hot water on an iron trivet. He added a basket of tea, apple cider, and hot cocoa mix in the middle of the table.

Luke opted for cocoa and tore the envelope open, dumping the powder mixture into a heavy ceramic mug, then filled it with hot water. He stirred it with a spoon till it dissolved to a rich creamy liquid.

"You must have a lot of questions," Joe said.

Luke folded his cold hands around the warm mug. "I don't know if you can answer them."

"We'll do our best."

Paula sat between him and Joe with her back to the windows. Dane sat across from her.

Luke unzipped his Carhartt jacket. "I guess the biggest

45

question I have is why no one told me about Lucky."

Joe folded his hands on the table. "We encouraged Hannah to tell you."

"She didn't tell us until it was obvious. I think she was afraid we'd send her away or judge her." Paula sighed. "We never judged her. We did our best to show her love and God's grace."

Luke cleared his throat. "I called, but wasn't allowed to talk with her."

Paula glanced at her husband before speaking. "It wasn't that you weren't allowed. She refused to speak with you. We urged her to tell you, to talk with you, but she was so afraid of what her father would do."

Dane sat forward. "She was terrified she'd be forced to go back to the valley, and then her father and the commune leaders would take Lucky."

"I'd never let that happen."

Joe folded his arms. "Hannah thought she was doing the best thing for her and Lucky. She had to keep him safe."

Luke's heart clenched. "I would have protected her."

"She was protecting you, too," Joe said. "Hannah told us her father threatened you."

Luke tightened his grip on the warm mug as he recalled the day Vincent Brady showed up on their property, demanding to know where Hannah was. For a long time, he avoided Pinegrove and watched his back, not trusting what old man Brady might do.

"If I'd known, I could've come here."

"And you might have led her father right to her," Dane added.

Luke combed his fingers through his hair. "When she turned eighteen, I was going to come back for her."

"But Lucky changed all of that." Paula's eyes held a plea for him to understand.

Joe rose and walked across the room down a hall.

Paula bolted from the chair. "Joe, no."

"It's time," he called over his shoulder. He returned with a large envelope. "She asked that if anything ever happened to her, we were to give this to you."

Tears shimmered in Paula's eyes. "She's not gone."

Dane leaned forward. "Mom, it's what Hannah would want."

Joe handed him the sealed envelope. Luke removed his knife from the pocket of his jeans and slit open the envelope. He shook loose a sealed ivory envelope with his name scrolled on the front and set it aside. He pulled out a stiff piece of paper and flipped it over to a birth certificate. His name, in bold type, glared up at him from the line for the father. He swallowed hard. The name given the child was Lucas Rhett Daniels. Tears sprang to his eyes.

"His middle name is my father's." The emotion welling up inside him strained his voice.

Joe nodded. "Legally, he has your last name."

"Why does he go by the last name Brady?"

Dane spoke. "Easier for school, and for a young boy to understand."

Paula stood with her arms wrapped around her

midsection, staring out the window. The moon reflected in the night's sky.

Joe sat back in his chair. "She gave us instructions if something happened to her, we were to contact you."

"Why didn't you?"

Paula crossed her arms. "Because she's hasn't passed on."

Dane cleared his throat. "The instructions were specific we were to contact you if she's . . . dead."

Paula faced him. "Please understand, Luke. She came here so hurt and broken. Gaining her trust took time. We never wanted to do anything to betray her confidence." Disappointment in her husband shadowed her eyes, and she shook her head then went into the kitchen.

"This is the right thing to do." Joe huffed. "Something you have to understand about that boy of yours. He's smart. Real smart."

Dane sat back. "Hannah took him to the college and had him tested. His IQ is in the top ten percent."

"While he's smart, he still has the emotional maturity of a boy his age," Joe added.

"He figures things out," Paula said from behind the bar. "Although he's a smart boy, he acts before thinking about the consequences."

"So he dug around in Hannah's personal belongings, found my letters, opened the yearbook, and put it all together."

"Right down to tracking you down on the Internet." Dane leaned back, lifting the chair's two front legs from

48

the floor.

"Then the little stinker kept the secret to himself." Paula came to stand behind Joe.

Luke shook his head. "He didn't get that kind of smarts from me. That came from Hannah."

Dane set his chair legs on the floor. "What is your plan?"

Luke shrugged. "For now, I hope she comes out of the coma."

"And if she doesn't?" Dane asked.

Luke's gaze swiveled from Joe to Paula to Dane. "Then I'll raise my son." He stood and grabbed the envelope. "Thank you for giving me this." His throat tightened. Was he prepared to be a father—the responsibility, time, commitment?

Yes.

If his father were still alive, he'd say it was time to man up.

These people cared for Hannah and Lucky, included them in their family. From what he'd seen of Lucky, they did a great job. "Thank you for caring for Hannah and Lucky."

"We love her like a daughter." Paula choked up. "Lucas is our grandson."

Luke understood and nodded, unable to speak. His emotions ricocheted all over the place, from hurt to anger, to fear. He needed to get out of there, find his bearings, and figure out how to help his son.

Joe followed him to the door. "You have every right to

take your son back to Montana with you. We just ask that he remain part of our lives."

Luke turned the doorknob and stepped outside. He stared down at his boots. "I wouldn't think of depriving Lucas of a relationship with you."

Back at the cottage, he sat on the couch and opened the packet, removing the certificate, a white sealed square envelope, and a photo of Hannah in the hospital holding their newborn baby.

A fuzzy head of hair topped a red-skinned Lucas. Wrapped in a white blanket, his eyes closed, he rested his head against Hannah, cradled in her arms.

"I should've been there." He set the photo on the table.

Pulling out his knife, he sliced open the small envelope and removed a letter.

Dear Luke,

If you're reading this letter, it means I've passed on. Don't be sad. I'm in Heaven where there's no more pain, sorrow, or tears.

"You are not gone." His heart heavy, he sighed.

I am so very sorry for how things turned out between us. You deserved better. Please know that I never meant to hurt you. Countless times I've thought of writing you, calling you, and telling you about your son. But fear stopped me.

First, I was afraid you would want me to go back to the valley. That's just something I couldn't do. Then I thought I'd waited too long. The more time passed, the more difficult it became to tell you. The bottom line was I feared you'd hate me. Please forgive me.

His heart ached. "I could never hate you."

I never wanted to cause you trouble. My only hope is that you can accept Lucas and that he can be part of your family.

Family? He slouched against the couch. "She thinks I'm married." But he couldn't marry. Hannah took a huge chunk of his heart. He sat forward and continued reading.

Each year I rewrite this letter on Lucas's birthday. He's eight years old now. But you should know he's not your typical eight-year-old. He's very smart, and at the pace he's going, he'll be ready for college by the time he's fifteen. He has a soft heart, so be careful how you discipline him. It's best to give him choices, even if they're the choices you'd prefer. I learned early on not to get into a battle of wills with him.

51

He's a good boy and tries hard to please. He doesn't like to be treated like a "baby." You won't catch him wearing superhero pajamas. Like you, he loves being outdoors. Joe and Paula can tell you more, and his medical records are filed in the cabinet in my office.

Luke ran his fingers through his hair and took a deep breath, releasing it slowly. From what he read, she clearly wanted Lucas with him.

The last thing I want you to know is that I love you. I've always loved you. There's never been anyone else.

A tear dropped onto the letter, blurring the blue ink. Startled by the evidence of the depth of his grief, Luke jumped to his feet, grabbed his coat, and left the cottage. Needing air, he stumbled down the gravel road along the vineyard's outer edge.

Overhead, a star studded sky surrounded a silver moon. Is God watching? "What do you want from me?" He held up his fist. "Aren't you supposed to be in control?" He swiped at the moisture on his face. "Aren't you omniscient, omnipresent, know it all? Can't you see her lying in that bed fighting for her life? Do something."

His ranting died as a wave of fear swept over him.

"Don't take her from me again." His breathing came hard, and he leaned forward, bracing his hands on his knees. "Please, Lord, my son needs his mother." Staggering into the field, he balanced himself against a wooden post. "Tell me what you want. Name your price." He glared up at the Heavens. "I'll gladly pay it."

Chapter Six

Hannah peered through the large pearlescent gate. She searched for a handle but found none. When she pushed, the gate didn't budge. Music rose above the walls, and a choir sang in the distance. "Hello, is anyone there?"

Their praises rose above the gates to a sapphire sky. There were no instruments, just voices—female soprano, contralto and men singing tenor, baritone, and bass. All in perfect harmony.

She knocked. "Hello, can someone open the gate, please?"

With a heavy heart, she sighed and turned to a white bench beneath a large old oak. She plopped onto the bench in the shade of its sprawling branches, determined to wait until someone opened the gate.

A gentle breeze stirred the floral-scented air. Bumblebees flitted from one flower to another. A caterpillar inched over the lush green grass. The buzz of a hummingbird caused her to look up. The bird hovered, studying her before zipping away.

Behind her, a rush of wind lifted the hair from her neck, and she glanced over her shoulder. The gate swung open. She stood, waiting to be let inside. A woman approached in a flowing white gown. Her azure eyes held a smile. Strands of long blonde hair caught in a gentle breeze and danced around her face.

Something . . . something familiar tugged at Hannah. She gasped. "Eloise?"

"Yes, dear, it is me."

Her heart leaped. "I'm so happy to see you."

Her friend took her by the hand. "Come, let's sit." They sat on the bench. "I've been asked to have a chat with you."

"About?"

Eloise patted her hand. "My dear Hannah, your time has not come."

"My time for what?"

Sympathy softened Eloise's eyes. "To enter the garden."

"But I want to go inside." Hannah craned her neck toward the gate, peeking beyond, her heart aching at the beauty hinted within. The trees and flowers and light— such light! Like rays of sun shining up into the sky. She wanted to sing with the others.

Peace enveloped her as she took a deep breath of the honeysuckle-scented air.

"You must go back."

She held tight her friend's hand. "Please, let me go

with you."

Eloise shook her head. "Your days are not complete."

The wind whispered through the oak branches, scattering leaves over the ground. Beyond the tree, the sky parted. Lucky sat on the couch praying. A man sat beside her son. Her heart swelled with love.

"Who is that man?" As soon as she asked, he raised his face. Hannah's heart leaped. "Luke!" She knelt in the grass. Regret stabbed her heart. "Oh, Luke."

Eloise knelt beside her. "My son still cares for you."

Tears welled in Hannah's eyes. "But how can he? I've done terrible things."

"You only did what you believed to be right." Eloise placed a hand on her shoulder.

"I was wrong. I made a horrible mistake." Hannah buried her face in her hands.

Eloise cupped Hannah's chin, tipping her face until their eyes met. "Your only regret would be not to learn from your mistake."

"How can he ever forgive me?"

"Give Luke a chance."

Hannah peered into her friend's gentle eyes. "I'm afraid he'll hate me."

"Do not fear. Fear is a lie." Eloise held out her hand.

Hannah slipped her fingers into Eloise's and rose to her feet.

"Do you want to go to him?"

"Yes. I want to be with my son and Luke." She wiped her tears from her cheeks. "How do I get back to them?"

"Jehovah is a God of second chances." Eloise led her back to the bench.

She sat and released Eloise's hand. "Then I can go back and do what's right?"

"Of course." Eloise smiled.

She stared at Luke and Lucky, her heart heavy with longing. The gate closed behind her with a gentle click—Eloise disappeared.

"Will you pray with me for Mom?"

Luke hesitated when Lucky sat beside him on the couch. After his tirade at God last night, he wasn't sure his prayers would be welcomed. But he couldn't deny Lucky. "Okay." He sat forward. "You go first."

Lucky clasped his hands in his lap and bowed his head. "Dear God, help Mom wake up. Make the coma go away so she can come home. Heal her head and her leg. And thank you for bringing my dad here."

Luke's heart leaped at hearing Lucky call him dad.

"And, God, help my parents to get along and love each other."

Luke's breath lodged in his lungs. For his son's sake, he'd do what he could to make his prayer a reality.

"Your turn," Lucky whispered and nudged his arm.

Luke cleared his throat. "God, we ask that you heal Hannah. Help the doctors know what to do, give them wisdom and guidance." He paused, trying to think of more to say, more to ask, but he wasn't sure God even heard his prayers. Why would he even listen? He hadn't gone to church since Hannah left. Hadn't prayed in years.

"Amen," Lucky said and jumped to his feet. "Okay, I'm ready to go."

Luke stood and stretched the muscles in his back, sore from sleeping on the couch.

"Will you still be here this weekend?"

Lucky's question caught him off guard. He didn't know. If Hannah woke up, he'd stay. But if she didn't, they might be on their way to Montana. As he learned with his clients, sometimes the best way to answer a question was with a question. Get to know what the person was thinking then formulate the best response.

"Why? What's going on this weekend?"

"I was hoping we could go to church together."

The earnest appeal in his son's eyes gave him pause. He was never comfortable in church, even as a child. His parents were always on him to sit still, get rid of his gum, and be quiet. The worst part was he had to wear a stiff shirt and his best Dockers.

"We'll see about that." He ruffled Lucky's hair. "How 'bout we get going?"

"Can we stop at the doughnut shop?"

"You ate cereal and toast. Are you still hungry?"

"No. But Mom likes chocolate cake doughnuts with chocolate frosting and sprinkles."

At his puzzlement, Lucky rushed to explain. "I thought we could bring one to Mom. It might help her wake up."

Luke smiled. "Good idea." If there was any chance a

chocolate doughnut would wake Hannah, he'd buy a dozen.

Lucky strode alongside his father, through the sliding doors, and into the hospital. He tried to match his steps to his father's, but Luke's legs were long, and Lucky had to hurry to keep up. He'd like to get a pair of boots like his dad, brown lace-ups. A jacket too—brown with a hood and big pockets.

They turned the corner and entered the room. "Look." Lucky's heart leaped. "The tubes are gone."

His mother lay in the bed, peaceful and sleeping. Tubes still led to her arm from the bag hanging on the metal hook.

"She's breathing without the machines."

Luke rested his hand on Lucky's back. "That's a good sign."

Lucky set the white doughnut bag on the table beside the bed. "Hi, Mom," he whispered, standing beside the bed. "We brought you a chocolate doughnut."

She didn't respond.

His chest tightened. "Why doesn't she open her eyes?"

Luke rested his hand on his shoulder. "Stay here. I'll be right back."

"Mom, wake up, please."

His heart ached, and he bit his lower lip to keep the tears back. She's gotta wake up.

Luke returned. "The nurse says they took the tubes out last night. She doesn't need them to breathe."

"Then why doesn't she wake up?"

His father's hand rested on his shoulder. "I don't know."

God wouldn't take his mother in exchange for giving him his father, would he?

He'd been praying every day. Keeping his room clean and trying to be good.

Luke was his last hope. When he found those letters and the picture book from school, he knew he had to get him here. His dad had to wake her up. "Talk to her."

"Hannah." His father spoke, leaning over her. "Remember that day we went hiking and got caught in that thunderstorm. We were soaked by the time we reached the truck. Remember how fast the clouds rolled in? And the lightning was blinding. We were right in the midst of the storm."

"What happened?" Lucky urged his father to continue.

Luke sat and rested his hand over Hannah's. "We were probably three miles from the trailhead, and all of a sudden, the sun disappeared behind dark thunder clouds."

Hannah stared down at the creek. Water cascaded over a log, tumbled over the rocks, swirled in the rapids before breaking free to continue its journey toward the Bitterroot River.

Behind her, Luke walked through the bushes, picking

huckleberries. *He has a terrible sweet tooth.* Dirt dusted her bare toes, and tickled them. A beetle feverishly dug a hole, kicking up a small dust cloud. She stepped back and shook the dirt from her sandals. The bug worked as if it was a matter of life or death.

Luke jumped down onto the trail. "I picked you some berries." He presented a small handful of purple berries, the tips of his fingers stained and the palm of his hand dotted violet.

"Thank you." She plucked them from his hand and popped the sweet fruit in her mouth. "Check this bug out." She pointed to the little creature.

Luke glanced down. "What bug?"

The bug disappeared. "Oh, it's gone. It was digging a hole. It must have buried itself."

The light dimmed, and a stiff, cool breeze blew through the narrow canyon.

"Uh oh." Luke squinted up at the sky through the thick canopy of trees. "Think we better get back to the truck."

"Why?"

A dark thundercloud swallowed the sun. The temperature dropped, and the wind whistled through the trees.

"Because that bug knew something." He grabbed her hand. "Come on, hurry."

They jogged down the trail. Raindrops tapped the leaves and soaked the ground. Cold droplets slapped her bare arms and face. Lightning flashed, and thunder echoed. The rain came harder, stinging her skin. Mud slickened the trail, and she slipped in her sandals. She squeezed Luke's hand, and he pulled, keeping her from falling.

The trail plunged into utter darkness. A momentary flash of light illuminated the path.

One, one thousand, two, one thou—

Thunder drummed in her chest. They were in the midst of the storm, directly overhead.

"Hurry." Luke hollered above the clamor.

"I am." She wiped the rain from her face. "I can't see."

"Keep your eyes on me."

She kept her gaze on his broad back. His white T-shirt clung to his skin. "What about bears?"

"They're too smart to be out in this."

Her chest ached as she tried to catch her breath and keep up. She skidded and let out a startled cry. Luke's grasp kept her upright.

His hands encircled her waist. "You all right?"

"My sandals don't have any traction," she yelled to be heard over the storm.

"I won't let you fall. Keep moving."

Lightning intermittently illuminated their way. She swiped back her hair now pasted to her head. Her soaked blouse glued to her. The wind picked up, shaking the water from the branches. Wet and cold, she shivered.

Luke stopped, and she ran into the back of him. He reached behind, steadying her.

She couldn't see what made him stop. "What?"

He wiped his hand over his eyes. "I'm wondering if

that hillside is going to hold."

Beyond his shoulder, rivulets of water cascaded down the cliff.

"I don't want to take chances, but we've got to get out of here. Take my hand." His strong fingers gripped hers. "You ready?"

She nodded, struggling to catch her breath.

"Run as fast as you can."

"Okay."

"On the count of three." He tightened his hold. "One, two, three."

They hurried, slipping and sliding. Rocks thumped and tumbled onto the trail. Crackling branches and scraping trees echoed behind her. She didn't dare look back. Her legs threatened to buckle, and her chest hurt from trying to breathe.

He slowed to a jog. The rain lessened, and darkness gave way to light breaking through the clouds.

They reached Luke's red Chevy, and he opened the passenger door. She scrambled inside, and he slammed the door shut. He ran around the back of the truck then slid behind the wheel.

Her breathing labored, her lungs burned as she fought to catch her breath. "I'm getting your truck all wet." A puddle of water formed at her feet on the rubber mat.

"No worries. It's only water." His gaze stayed fixed on her.

"I must look like a drowned rat." She laughed.

He shook his head. "You're beautiful."

Heat infused her cheeks, and she lowered her eyes to the red vinyl seat.

"You're not mad at me for getting you out in this weather?"

"No. I could never be mad at you." Her breathing returning to normal.

Although she had not told a soul, she loved Luke Daniels. She planned to marry him some day.

Luke scooted across the bench and smoothed her wet, dripping hair back from her eyes. He cupped her face in his hands and moved closer. She leaned into him, lifting her head. His lips brushed hers with such tenderness it stole her breath. Hannah placed her hand on his upper arm as he pressed his lips to hers. The kiss, gentle, sweet, and tentative. Her heart soared. His blue-gray eyes captured hers. She could get lost in his eyes.

Lucky sat at the foot of the bed, leaning in, his elbows on his knees, listening to how his parents almost got caught in a landslide.

"We got in my truck and drove toward town. When we reached the highway, the sun came out. The storm passed. Soaked to the skin, hair plastered to her head and face, still, your mother was the most beautiful girl I've ever see." Luke stared at Hannah.

Lucky turned toward his mother, mindful to stay clear of her leg. "Mom, don't you want to go hiking again? How about horseback riding? You told me you used to ride horses." He slid off the bed and faced his father. "Do you have horses?"

"I do."

"See, Mom. We can all go riding together."

Luke rubbed his son's back. "I'll teach you to ride."

Lucky braced his arms on the mattress near his mother. His vision blurred with the tears he fought, not wanting to cry in front of his dad. He stared at her, willing her to open her eyes. "Tell her another story."

It was the only thing he could think of that would work.

His father squeezed his shoulder. "Hannah, remember how Samantha used to cover for us? I'd drive you home, and you'd sit between Sam and me. You'd sit close to me until we got near your house then scoot over. Samantha would sure like to see you again. And you'll like Trent's wife, Irene."

"What's Samantha like?"

"She's a great lady. Plays all kinds of musical instruments and sings. She takes great pictures, too." Luke's eyes brightened. "Your mom and Sam used to sing songs together."

"When can I meet her?"

Luke knelt and pulled his son into an embrace. "Soon."

Lucky wrapped his arms around his father's neck and held tight, safe in the arms of his father. The ache in his heart gave way to a sense of safety and belonging, the feeling unlike anything he'd ever known.

God, please wake my mom up and let us all be a family. There had to be a way to wake her up. Playing her favorite music from his CD player on the table beside her bed hadn't worked. Talking to her hadn't worked. Aunt Katherine's foot massages hadn't worked.

Maybe if he read her a bedtime story. No, that won't work. That puts him to sleep. He needed to . . .

His heart jumped, and he stepped back from his father's embrace. He stared at his father. Luke was handsome like a prince. The sadness in his eyes a sign that he loved his mother. What if his parents were always supposed to be together, but an evil spell was cast on them? A spell that separated them and now caused his mother to fall into a deep sleep.

What if there was only one way to wake his mother?

That's it. He knew how to wake his mother.

He placed his hand on his father's strong shoulder. "Maybe   you   should   kiss   her."

Chapter Seven

Luke gulped. Had he heard Lucky right? "Excuse me?" He purposefully didn't tell Lucky that day in the truck, soaked by the rain, was the first time he'd ever kissed Hannah. Eight-year-old boys didn't need to know such details.

"Kiss her. You know like in *Sleeping Beauty*. The prince kisses her, and she wakes up."

He was no prince, but the earnest request in his son's eyes made him consider kissing Hannah.

She lay there so peaceful. The ache in his chest threatened to swallow him. Lucky looked up at him with such expectancy, he could scarcely breathe.

The last time he had kissed her flashed in his mind. He leaned against his father's truck. It was just the two of them, saying goodbye. Inside the farmhouse were Joe, and Paula, as well as his father. The pain of having to leave her opened a deep chasm in his heart. Tears shimmered in her eyes. It was the hardest day of his life.

But not as hard if he had to say goodbye forever. If he

had to bury the mother of his son. Lucky stared at him, his wide eyes urging him to do it.

Luke bent over the bed, pressed his hand to her cheek, and moistened his lips. Pulling back, he eyed his son. "You're not going to watch, are you?"

"I'll cover my eyes."

Please do.

The pressure was worse than the first time he kissed her at the trailhead. He'd wanted to kiss her so many times before, but the timing wasn't right. He took her up the Bear Creek trailhead that day with the plan to kiss her, right there by the waterfall. But the storm interrupted. Their first kiss wasn't as romantic as he'd planned, drenched and cold in his truck.

Lucky stood with his hand over his eyes.

Leaning over her again, Luke stared at her, willing her to wake up. Careful not to press against her, he gently placed his lips on hers. His eyes slid closed. His heart flew high like that day at the trailhead. Luke pulled back and opened his eyes.

Her eyelids fluttered.

Hope flooded his veins. *Open your eyes.*

Nothing.

Had he imagined her eyes moved?

"Try again, only longer."

"Lucky, you weren't supposed to watch." He pointed to the door. "Out, please." He didn't need the pressure. Certainly didn't need an eight-year-old coaching him.

Lucky shuffled out of the room with his head down.

Probably should've been a little gentler.

Luke dropped onto the chair, took her hand in his, and bowed his head. "Please, Hannah, please wake up. Please, sweetheart, come back." His hand rested on her forearm. His thumb stroked her soft, smooth skin. He covered his eyes with the other hand, squeezing his lids shut to stem the threatening tears. "I don't know what more to do." His heart ached. "God, I don't know what you want from me."

Be still and know that I am God. The words entered his head as plainly as if they were spoken in his ear. How many times had his mother told him to be still and wait, to trust in the Lord? He didn't have that kind of blind faith—the kind of faith his brother or sister had.

"Please, God," he whispered. He didn't know what to pray. Words wouldn't come. It wasn't like he was used to praying, but he didn't even know how to voice what he was feeling. "Please, God," was all he could think to say.

The hole in his heart threatened to suck him under like quicksand. "Please, God," he groaned.

Put him in this bed, unconscious, struggling for life. Make his head bleed, his hands, and his legs. Just bring her back. *Don't take Hannah.* "Please, God."

Something brushed his temple and sifted through his hair. He raised his head and checked behind him, but he was alone. Hannah's arm moved in his grasp. Startled, he jumped. Warm brown eyes met his.

"Hannah?"

She moaned. Her cold fingers weakly gripped his.

"Hannah!" He kissed the back of her hand and pressed it to his cheek. Relief infused him and joy surged, erupting in laughter. He wanted to take her in his arms, but in her fragile state, he didn't dare.

Fear flooded her eyes, and they darted around the room. She struggled to sit up. The oxygen tubes to her nose came loose.

"No. No, honey, you're okay. Stay still." He pressed his hand on her shoulder, ever so gently. "You're all right." Seeing him must have scared her.

She tossed and turned intent on getting up. The IV tubes stretched until he feared she'd hurt herself.

He pushed her back down, trying to hold her still. "No, Hannah. Stay put."

She screamed.

"Hannah, please stop."

Needing help, he reached for the call button on the remote.

"Hannah, please." He restrained her with his hands on her upper arms.

Alarms screeched from one of the machines.

She kicked and shrieked. The blankets tangled around her legs.

"Hannah, look at me." He grabbed her hands. "You're fine."

She bowed her head, shaking it, struggling to raise her hands to her head, but he constrained them.

When she stilled, he released her hands and cupped her face. "You're going to be all right."

Her breathing heavy, she pressed her hands over his. Tears filled her caramel eyes and rolled down her cheeks.

A nurse came in behind him. "What's going on?" She silenced the machines.

"She's awake." He held Hannah's hands, unwilling to trust she wouldn't freak and endanger herself.

The nurse hovered beside him. "Hannah."

Hannah turned toward the nurse. The oxygen tube hung ajar, spraying her cheek.

"Mr. Daniels, I can handle things from here. You can leave the room."

"No." He couldn't leave her, not with her so scared.

"Mom! You're awake." Lucky rushed to the other side of the bed.

At the sight of her son, panic filled her eyes. She gave a startled cry and struggled to break free of his grip.

"Out," the nurse commanded. "Everyone out." The nurse secured straps to the bedrails.

No way was he letting them strap her down. It would only scare her more. "Lucky, son. Go get Joe and Paula." He didn't take his eyes off Hannah, only hoped his son did as he was told. If his presence was upsetting her, then he needed Joe and Paula to calm her.

"Mr. Daniels, you're going to need to leave."

"No." His tone left no room for argument. Let them call security. He wasn't leaving her side.

Hannah stopped struggling and sat back with her head against the pillow, her eyes pinched shut. Exhaustion apparently overtaking her.

He released her hands, and she pressed them to the side of her head.

The nurse held a needle and lowered it to the tube that came free from her hand. He caught the nurse's eye as she reached for Hannah's hand to reinsert the tube and shook his head. The old coot's lips thinned, and her eyes sparked.

"Hannah, sweetheart." He rubbed her arm. "Does your head hurt?"

Slowly, she nodded.

"Want something for the pain?"

She tilted her head forward in a way he interpreted as yes.

"The nurse needs your left hand."

Her eyes opened, but she stared off into the distance.

"Hannah, calm down. Come on, sweetheart. Look at me." He peeled her hands away from the bandages on her head.

Brown eyes tentatively met his. He cradled her hands between his. "You're fine. Okay?"

She trembled.

"Listen to me."

The doctor hurried into the room. "Where we at?"

"Her blood pressure is high," the nurse responded. "Heart rate is elevated."

"Everything is going to be fine," Luke assured her.

Hannah opened her mouth to speak, but her voice was a mere whisper. She held her hand to her throat.

"Need some water?" Luke asked.

"Mr. Daniels, it's best that you leave. Let us handle this," the doctor said.

Luke ignored the man and held a cup of water for Hannah.

"Just a sip," he said. "Swish it around in your mouth and swallow."

"Not too much," the nurse advised. "Or she could get sick."

"I know what I'm doing." Trained in search and rescue, many missions saving victims in shock, he knew how to handle these situations. "Easy. Okay, that's enough." He set the cup aside. "What do you want to say? Take your time." He cupped her face in his hands.

"Where? What happened?" Her voice was hoarse.

"Hannah," the doctor spoke, "there was an accident. You're in the hospital."

With his thumb, Luke wiped her tears from her cheeks.

"Her heart rate is coming down," the nurse advised.

Carefully, he took her in his arms and held her. She laid her head on his shoulder and clung to him. He rubbed his hand up and down her back. "You're okay." Her tears penetrated his shirt.

"Please don't leave me," she rasped.

"I'm not going anywhere."

"What's wrong with her?" Lucky asked when his dad finally came out of the room.

Luke knelt in front of him and placed his hands on his arms. "She's disoriented. That's all."

Lucky's heart raced. He'd never seen his mother act like that. "Like waking up from a bad dream?"

"Yeah."

"Can I see her?"

"Not yet. The doctor is examining her." His father stood. "Have you eaten lunch?"

Lucky shook his head. "I'm not hungry." His stomach queasy like that time he rode a roller coaster.

"Luke," Grandpa said. "What are they saying?"

"Not much right now. They want to run some tests."

Grandma pressed her hand over her heart. "Was she okay with seeing you?"

"Yeah, she seemed to be. She wanted me to hold her."

Grandma nodded, her eyes glimmered with relief.

Lucky hadn't considered Mom might be upset at seeing Luke. Realization snuck up on him. "It worked," he blurted.

"What worked?" Uncle Dane asked.

"The kiss." Lucky grinned up at his dad. "She woke up not long after you kissed her."

His dad ran his hands through his hair. "I don't know that had anything to do with it."

Lucky knew better. "Sure it did. She woke up didn't she?"

Luke shook his head. "I need to get some air." He strode down the hall.

Lucky joined him, practically jogging to keep up with

74

his dad's long strides. When Luke realized he was following, he slowed his pace. Once outside, Luke took out his cell phone from his coat pocket and dialed.

His father's breath fogged in the cool morning air. The sun streamed through big fluffy clouds.

"She's awake," his dad said into the phone. "Thank you for your prayers." He put his hand on Lucky's shoulder. "Lucky is here with me." He gave his shoulder a reassuring squeeze. "Would you like to talk with your uncle?"

Lucky nodded. "Hello?" he said into the phone.

"Hello, Lucky. I am looking forward to meeting you." A soothing quality laced his uncle's deep voice.

"Me, too."

"Your dad is very happy to have you in his life."

"I am, too."

"We've been praying for your mom."

"I have, too."

"You pray?"

"Every day."

"That's good. God answered your prayers."

"I knew he would."

"You have a strong faith."

He nodded, and then realized his uncle couldn't see him and said, "Yeah."

"Well, you take care. Let me talk with your dad."

"Here you go." He handed the phone to Luke.

"I know. . . . Okay. Tell everyone thank you for their prayers." Luke slipped his phone into his pocket.

Lucky squinted into the sun as he peered up at his father. "When can we go to see where you live?"

"We need to wait for your mom to get better."

"But we can go?"

Luke placed a hand on his arm. "Of course."

He couldn't wait to see where his dad lived and meet his uncle and aunts. His dad had horses, too, and they could go fishing. The best thing of all—his mom and dad are back together. *Thank you, God.*

Chapter Eight

"Can you feel that?" the doctor asked, running a prickly tool along the bottom of Hannah's foot.

The instrument tickled her foot. She jerked it away. "Yes."

He examined her eyes, probed around her head, and asked her questions like what year is it and when was her birthday.

The door opened, and a tall redheaded woman walked in.

"Katherine," Dr. Richards smiled and held out his hand for her.

Katherine gave a quick kiss on the doctor's cheek before she approached Hannah. "Hi, Hannah. I'm so relieved to see you sitting up."

Do I know her?

"John." Katherine slipped her hand inside the doctor's. "Thank you for calling me. Mom and Dad are outside. They want to see Hannah."

Mom and Dad are outside. Katherine—her sister? She's married to a doctor? Yes.

John and Katherine are married.

"I'm okay with visitors."

Katherine opened the door and let a man inside. His glossy brown eyes focused on Hannah, his smile stretched across his face, and he ran his fingers through silver streaked hair. A short woman peered from behind him. Her hand covered her mouth, and tears shimmered in her eyes.

My parents. Joy lifted her heart.

Her mother stood beside the bed and rested a hand on her arm. "Thank God," she whispered. "You're all right."

John slipped out of the room. A young man with blond hair and brown eyes entered. "Sure good to see you awake."

His name escaped her. This had to be her parents, but their names lingered on the edge of her memory. She grasped for them. The harder she tried to capture the fleeting thoughts the more they eluded her.

"Hannah, what's wrong?"

She shook her head. Her heart beat fast, and her breathing quickened.

"Hannah?" Her father took her hand.

Tears sprang to her eyes.

"I . . . I'm sorry."

Her father patted her hand. "It's okay. No reason to be sorry."

"Dane," Katherine said. "Get John."

Dane, that was his name. Her brother? Yes, it had to be. She felt love for him. Love like that for a brother.

John hurried into the room. "Hannah, breathe slowly. Nice and easy."

But she couldn't catch her breath.

Katherine reached behind her. "It's best that you step out. We may have overwhelmed her."

Hannah struggled to catch her breath.

"Breathe nice and easy." Katherine fit a mask over her mouth.

Luke rushed into the room. "What's happening?"

She grasped for him, needing him.

"She's hyperventilating."

He sat beside her and touched her cheek, rubbed his hands over her arms. "Okay, I'm here. Breathe easy. Easy." His touch soothed her tattered nerves.

John took her left wrist in his hand. "Breathe slow." He glanced at his watch.

Luke held her other hand. "That's it. Nice and easy."

She focused on Luke, his presence calming. He brushed the back of his fingers to her cheek near the mask. Her heart rate slowed. She zeroed in on his blue-gray eyes, warm, reassuring, loving.

Once she caught her breath, John removed the mask. "Hannah, can you tell me what's going on?"

Afraid to confess she couldn't remember her relatives' names, she gazed at Luke and back to John. "I . . . I couldn't remember." Her voice wavered.

"Remember what?" Luke asked.

"My parents' names. My brother's name. You're married to my sister?"

The doctor's brow wrinkled. His lips moved to speak, but no sound came out.

Luke's eyes widened. "But you remembered me?"

"Of course." She could never forget the man she loved.

A little boy poked his head into the room. "Mom?"

Mom! Her heart lurched. She stared at the little boy standing in the doorway with his hand on the knob.

"Lucky, can you give us a minute?" Luke asked.

"But. . ."

"Please."

The door closed.

"Is that our son?" she asked Luke.

He nodded.

She closed her eyes, fighting tears. What kind of a mother forgets her child? A wave of panic threatened to swamp her.

Luke wrapped her in his arms. "It'll be all right."

Her heart tore. "How come I can't remember my own child?" His embrace chased away her fear. "Do we have any others?" She released him.

"No, just Lucky."

"Lucky?" She peered into his eyes.

"You named him Lucas." Luke's thin smile held sympathy and understanding. "But he goes by Lucky."

"Can you bring him in?" Maybe if she saw him again, she'd remember.

John tucked his hand into his lab coat pocket. "If you

feel ready, Hannah. But don't push yourself."

She nodded, confirming to the doctor—to John, her brother-in-law, that she wanted to see her son.

Luke opened the door and ushered Lucky inside. With blue-gray eyes and his smile, so like his father, there was no mistaking who he took after.

"Are you feeling okay, Mom?"

She nodded.

"Mom's head hurts a little." Luke provided an explanation.

Her heart swelled with love for the boy. Memories flitted on the outskirts of her grasp. Fear swelled in her heart. He's so small, fragile. A memory danced on the outer boundaries, she tried to follow it, grab it. In a hospital . . . too early.

Weak and tired, she let go of the thought and laid back against the pillows. She held out her hand to the boy. His hand was small in hers. The love radiating in his eyes threatened her composure.

"When can you come home?" Lucky asked.

She swallowed to clear her throat. "I'm hoping soon." But where was home?

Chapter Nine

Luke set the takeout pizza on the kitchen counter. Lucky shed his coat and tossed it on a barstool. He wasn't about to chastise his son for not hanging up his coat. It'd been a tough day—for them both.

He took two plates from the cabinet, set them on the counter, and put one slice of pepperoni, olive, and mushroom on a plate and two slices on another. He could sure use a beer; his nerves were frayed. But he settled for root beer.

Lucky carried his plate to the small dining room table. "Wish we had vanilla ice cream for root beer floats."

"I'll keep that in mind for next time." Luke sat at the table and picked up a piece of warm pizza with thick dough and red sauce. The spicy scent of pepperoni awakened his stomach on the drive to the vineyard. He opened his mouth to take a big bite.

"Aren't we going to say grace?"

He cringed and set the slice on the plate. "Go ahead.

You say grace." He bowed his head.

"Dear God, thank you for waking up Mom today. Help her head to not hurt anymore and bring her home soon. Thank you for this food. Amen."

"Amen." Having skipped lunch, Luke was hungry. He sank his teeth into the doughy, spicy, greasy slice and savored it.

Lucky wiped his mouth on the sleeve of his shirt. Then his eyes grew wide. "Oops, sorry."

"For what?"

"Mom hates when I use my shirt for a napkin."

Luke held back a chuckle and handed Lucky a few paper napkins from the stack on the counter. Luke wiped his mouth with one of the thin scraps in an attempt to set a good example. Even though his mother taught him manners, he was guilty of using his sleeve many times. Must be a man thing.

After they scarfed down their meal, he sent Lucky to his room to do his homework and was finishing the dishes when a knock tapped at the door. He dried his hands on a red dishtowel, threw it over his shoulder, and then answered the door.

Dane stood on the front porch with a plastic grocery bag in one hand and raised a bottle of wine in the other. "Want to celebrate? Brought a bottle of our Syrah Reserve. Good year, took silver at the Seattle wine show."

"Come in." Luke stepped aside. "I don't normally drink wine, but sure. What's in the bag?"

"Vanilla ice cream for Lucky."

He laughed. "He was just saying how he wished he had some ice cream to make a root beer float."

"Yep, that's his favorite. And chocolate cake."

"I have a lot to learn, don't I?"

Dane grinned. "You'll get the hang of it in time."

Lucky stepped out from his room. "Hey, Uncle Dane."

"I brought ice cream."

Lucky bounced in his stocking feet. "Oh, yeah. Thank you."

"You're welcome." Dane handed the bag to Lucky, who took it into the kitchen and helped himself to a bowl.

Luke rummaged through a drawer. "I'm sure there's a corkscrew someplace in this kitchen."

"I know right where it is." Dane strode straight to the drawer, pulled out the small handheld device, and went to work opening the bottle. He took two wine glasses down from the cabinet and set them on the counter. Obviously familiar with Hannah's kitchen.

Luke glanced at Lucky's bowl heaped with ice cream. "Lucky, I think you have plenty of ice cream."

"Can I have chocolate sauce?"

"You put a scoop back, and you can have chocolate."

Lucky eyed his bowl and removed a scoop, putting it back into the carton. He was going to have to keep an eye on the kid. His eyes were bigger than his stomach.

"How's your homework coming along?"

"I'm almost done. I have to read a chapter in my book and write a review on it."

"What are you reading?"

"*The Lion The Witch And The Wardrobe.* But Mom has read it to me lots of times, so it's just skimming the chapters and writing about it."

"Isn't that taking the easy way out?"

He shrugged and bounded off back to his room with his bowl of ice cream.

Dane poured the wine and handed Luke a glass. "To Hannah and her recovery."

They lifted their glasses in a toast.

He drank the wine, surprised by its fruity flavor. "Hum, that's good."

"It's almost a port." Dane took a sip.

Luke leaned against the counter. "Are you the wine expert around here?"

"Yeah. I went to school to become a winemaker. Graduated last year."

"There's such a degree?"

Dane laughed. "There is."

Luke motioned to the living room. "Make yourself comfortable." Not that Dane hadn't done so many times before. He and Hannah probably sat in this little living room sharing a bottle of wine, talking about the vineyard and their personal life. His chest tightened.

Dane took the rocking chair. "What a day."

Luke dropped onto the couch. "The last several days have been a blur."

"Yeah, I can imagine." Dane rested back in the chair. "You're doing great with Lucky."

"Thanks. I'm not so sure, sometimes." Luke settled

85

back on the couch. "You know him pretty well."

"Yeah, well, I got eight years, although I was just a teen when he was born and then I went off to college. It hasn't been until this last year that I've spent much time with him."

"And Hannah?" he asked then stopped himself not wanting to sound like a jealous jerk. His shoulders tensed.

"Are you wondering if I have feelings for Hannah?"

He respected Dane for seeing through him and being straight up about it. "She thinks you're her brother."

"That's because that is the kind of relationship we have. I'm like a little brother to her. Katherine is like a sister . . . more like best friends."

His shoulders relaxed. "I wonder how long it's going to take for her to remember I haven't always been here?"

"Only God knows." Dane sipped his wine. "There's a lot you don't know about Hannah. Some very important things that I think will help you help her."

"Like?"

"Like the number one thing in her life."

"That's easy. It's Lucky."

Dane sat forward. "No, it's her faith."

Luke fell still. "What do you mean?"

"When she came here, she was filled with a lot of bad religion."

"Tell me about it. That commune she was raised in believes in some crazy stuff."

"Like polygamy." Dane scratched his chin. "But it was very legalistic, too. She believed God was punishing her for what happened between you two."

"What made her think that?"

Dane lowered his voice. "She almost lost Lucky."

Luke's breath lodged in his lungs. "What happened?" He kept his voice down.

Dane glanced toward the hall before speaking. "She hadn't told my parents she was pregnant until she was close to five months along. So she hadn't had any prenatal care. She was also stressed, suffering from depression, and in poor health. At about seven months, she was home alone and went into labor."

Luke set his wine glass on the table and wiped his hand over his mouth. Guilt, hurt, and anger warred within him. Guilt that he left her alone and pregnant. Hurt because she didn't tell him. Anger that she kept her secret all this time.

"Lucky was born on the bathroom floor at just shy of seven months."

"She had to have been terrified."

"My mom found her and called an ambulance. That little boy almost didn't make it." Dane kept his voice at a whisper.

"Is that why you call him Lucky?"

Dane smiled and took another sip from the glass. "He's a blessed little boy."

Luke reached into his memory, trying to put the timeline together. "Hannah stopped writing me in about three months. I called here, but she never called back."

"I remember answering the phone a few times."

"Did she get my messages?"

Dane nodded. "Every time."

Luke had no reason to doubt Dane was telling the truth. "I couldn't understand why she stopped writing, why she didn't return my calls."

"I think it was shame and guilt."

Was she that ashamed of the love they shared? Sure, they were young, but the feelings were real.

"It took years for her to realize that God doesn't punish people."

Could her guilt have caused her to cut ties with him? He crossed his ankle over his knee and sat back against the pillows lining the couch.

"My mom got her to go to church to get all that messed up religion out of her head. In time, she came to understand that Jesus took the punishment for her and that God doesn't punish those he loves."

He ran his fingers through his hair, trying to comprehend what Hannah must have been going through. Even though his son was born premature, he seemed normal . . . healthy. "Lucky seems healthy."

"He is." Dane stood and grabbed the photo of Hannah. "I've been thinking about Hannah's memory." He returned the picture.

"I think in time she'll remember everything." Hope rose in Luke's chest.

Dane sat and briefly glanced at the floor. "Odd thing is she remembers you but not Lucky. When you've been out of her life for all these years but Lucky has been a constant."

"That is odd. But I was the first person she saw when she woke up."

Dane shook his head. "I have a theory."

Luke set both feet on the floor and sat forward. "Okay, let's have it."

"I think the memories that are most painful for her are blocked."

"Leaving Montana had to be painful."

"Or was it coming here that was? And given the stress, fear, and almost losing Lucky, maybe that's why those memories are blocked."

"She thinks your parents are hers."

"Because they feel like parents and there isn't any painful memory directly attached to them. There is pain associated with her real parents." Dane swirled the wine in his glass. "From what I understand, her father was a tyrant."

"No argument there. And her mother died when she was fairly young."

"She had a rough childhood."

"I see where you're going. You might be onto something." Luke sipped from the glass, enjoying the wine's rich berry flavor. "What can we do to help her?"

"I'll have a talk with John. In case you weren't aware, her doctor is my brother-in-law."

He wasn't sure what to make of that revelation.

Dane sat forward. "Is her father as awful as he sounds?"

"He's a powerful man in Pinegrove. One of the elders. She was supposed to marry another of the elders."

"But he couldn't make her do something she didn't want to do."

"She wasn't eighteen, so he held parental rights. Besides, Vincent Brady is a mean, intimidating man. A couple weeks after we brought her here, old man Brady showed up at our house demanding to know where Hannah was. Things got pretty heated, and Brady had a pistol strapped to his hip. My dad and older brother came out with their guns drawn and told Brady to get off our land."

"He knew you had something to do with her disappearance?"

"He suspected I did, but he couldn't prove anything. We were careful not to let anyone know we were a couple. But somehow, he found out. He threatened to do me bodily harm."

Dane shook his head. "He sounds crazy."

"Some say he is. For a good year, I watched my back and stayed clear of Pinegrove. I haven't seen old man Brady in years."

"It had to be difficult leaving her home, her sister and brother, her friends. And coming here to live with us. She'd never met us before."

Luke sat up and set the goblet on the table. "We didn't have a choice. I couldn't let her marry Owen Mitchell. The plan was for her to lay low until she turned eighteen while I repaired the old house. My grandparents' property was given to my two siblings and me. But they weren't interested in working the ranch, and it had fallen into pretty bad shape."

"Quite the plan."

Luke shrugged. "But it didn't work as planned. When she stopped writing and wouldn't take my calls, I gave up." He shook his head. "I should've come back for her."

"Why didn't you?"

Luke lowered his head. "Pride, stupid pride."

Chapter Ten

Lucky lay in bed not bothering to get up. In the kitchen, cabinets closed, pans clanked, water ran. The scents of coffee, along with bacon, drifted into his room. Bacon was his favorite, but he wasn't going to be tempted.

"Lucky, time to get up," Luke called from the kitchen.

Let him holler for all he cared. He wasn't getting up. His heart hurt, and he was mad for crying himself to sleep last night.

"Lucky?" Luke entered the room. "Hey, son."

Turning his back to the door, Lucky closed his eyes, pretending to be asleep. His heart beat a little fast at hearing Luke call him son. Didn't matter. He wasn't ever getting out of bed again.

The mattress pressed down as his dad put his arms on the top bunk. "Hey, you feel okay this morning?"

Lucky shook his head.

"Too much ice cream and root beer last night?"

He shook his head again.

"I thought you could make an appearance at school today."

"I don't want to go to school."

"Well, your mom has several appointments today, and I thought I'd pick you up around lunch and take you to see her."

"I don't want to see her."

"Why not?"

"'Cause, she doesn't remember me."

His father groaned. "Where did you . . . ? Oh, you eavesdropped on Dane and me last night."

"No, I didn't." He didn't mean to.

"Lucky." Luke rolled him over to his back. "You listened in on an adult conversation."

Looking into his father's eyes, he couldn't deny it. "Not on purpose." Tears blurred his vision. Embarrassed, he put his arm over his face to hide his emotions.

"Hey, it's okay to be sad." His father pulled him close, wrapping his arms around him.

Lucky tried to swallow his tears, but the crack in his heart was too deep. "She must not love me if she can't remember me." Tears seeped from eyes.

"Not true." Luke loosened his hold and took his face in his hands. "Your mom loves you more than anything."

"She doesn't *want* to remember."

"Yes, she does. We have to understand her brain has been injured. It needs time to heal."

"It's not fair." Lucky sniffled.

"No, it's not. But we have to give her time."

93

"How much time?"

"Well, it might be like a broken arm and need lots of time, or it might be like a small cut and take hardly any time at all. We just don't know."

He sat up, and his father lifted him to the floor. "Can we help her remember? Like we helped her to wake up?"

"We can try. But we need to be patient. Extend her grace when she can't remember something."

"That sounds like something Mom would say." He wiped his eyes with his flannel pajama sleeve.

His dad smiled. "It does? Well, it's something my mom said many times to me as I was growing up." Luke placed a hand on his shoulder. "Do you think you can extend a little grace to your mom as she heals?"

"Yeah," he said with little enthusiasm.

"Okay. I think it would be nice to see your friends today. Why don't you get dressed, and I'll take you to school?"

School would be better than sitting in a hospital room with his mom who didn't even remember him. Lucky followed his dad to his mother's room.

Luke rolled one of the closet doors open. "We need to bring her a change of clothes." He stood back, staring at the clothes crammed into the closet. "Your mother has a lot of clothes. Does she wear all this?" He pushed clothing back and forth, squishing things together even more.

"Yeah."

"Help me pick something out for her." His father wrestled a brown outfit out of the closet that he'd seen his mother wear around the house. "What about this jogging suit?"

"She likes that. Most of the time she wears jeans."

"She needs something comfortable that she can do exercises in."

"That'll work." Lucky grabbed his mother's Bible from the bedside table. "We oughta bring her this, too."

"Good idea." His father opened a dresser drawer and held up girly stuff. Lucky giggled at the pained expression on his father's face. "What?"

Lucky covered his mouth to keep from laughing. "You look funny." Like he had gas and was trying to hold it in.

"I don't know what she wears." His father sighed. "Turn around—you shouldn't see these things."

He turned toward the door. "I see them when she does laundry."

The dresser drawer slammed closed.

"All right, come on before we're late."

In the truck, they drove past the dog kennel a few miles down the road, prompting a question. "Do you have a dog?" He'd always wanted a dog.

"I do. His name is Bear."

"Bear? That's a funny name for a dog."

"Not when you see him. He's part mastiff part lab, and he's big like a bear. He looked like a cub when I first got him."

"When can I meet him?"

His father's mouth twitched into a smile. "Soon. I also have a cat named Toby."

"What's he like?"

"Big orange and white cat, lazy as can be."

"What's your house like?"

"Well, it's two stories. It has three bedrooms and two bathrooms. I built it myself." His father's eyes shone. "It has a stream and a big barn for the horses. I've been building cabins on it for people to come and stay."

"What kind of people?"

"My customers who I take fishing and hunting."

"Would you take me fishing and hunting sometime?"

Luke glanced across the seat at him and broke into a big smile. "You bet."

"Do you have a big TV?"

"I do. I have to have a big television for watching football."

The more he heard about his dad's home, the more he wanted to go. As they pulled into the school parking lot, he said, "School doesn't start yet." Weren't they going to the hospital first?

"When does it start?"

"Not for another hour."

"Well, then I guess we'll head to the hospital."

Luke carried Mom's colorful flower tote bag with her clothes, slippers, shoes, and Bible as they walked down the hall. Lucky held back. Would she remember him today? Will she be upset seeing him? What if she cries?

The words his father had spoken earlier rang in his head, *extend grace*. If she can't recognize him and if her bad memories keep her from remembering him, could she still love him?

The room was empty, the bed made.

His father stared at the clean room. "Stay here."

His breakfast sat in his stomach like a rock. "Where is she?"

Luke didn't answer but strode toward the nurses' station. The nurse he talked to pointed back the way they came. Luke returned with a smile. Lucky released the breath he'd been holding.

"They moved her to a nicer room." Luke winked.

Lucky's heart beat a little fast, and he struggled to catch his breath as they walked down the halls.

Luke knocked on the open door and stepped inside. "Good morning."

Lucky peeked around his father. His mother sat up in bed, and she leaned to the side to see him and smiled. Lucky sought his father's reassurance.

His father placed a hand on his shoulder. "School doesn't start just yet, so we wanted to come by and see you." Luke's voice was cheerful, but Lucky sensed tension.

"I'm glad you did." She pulled the blankets up around her as if cold. "Come here Lucky and sit beside me." She patted the bed.

His heart leaped. She remembered him. Lucky climbed up onto the bed and sat beside her.

"We brought you a change of clothes." Luke held up the bag then set it on a chair. "When do you start rehab?"

"This afternoon. I have an appointment with another doctor sometime this morning."

Her bandages had been removed. Her once-glossy hair now dull and stuck out in little prickles where a patch of hair was partially shaved, and stitches zigzagged across her forehead.

"Does it hurt?" Lucky pointed to her head.

She nodded. "Some. I'm on medicine to help with the pain."

Luke placed her Bible on the table. "We brought you this."

"Thank you."

"When can you come home?" Lucky asked.

"Soon, I hope." She fixed her gaze on Luke. "Did you bring my ring?"

Luke looked like he'd swallowed a frog. He gulped and stared at Hannah.

"What ring, Mom?"

"My wedding ring." She lifted her hand and wiggled her fingers.

Not wanting his mother to be upset should she find out she wasn't married to Luke, Lucky rushed to answer. "Oh, it's at home."

Luke glared at him and ever so slightly shook his head.

He hurried to explain. "Yeah, it's, uh . . . in your jewelry box."

Luke covered his mouth and lowered his head.

"We can bring it next time we come."

His father's shoulders bunched.

"Thank you. If you could, please do that for me." She

took his hand in hers and smiled real big. He liked making her happy.

Lucky grinned over at his father. She didn't get upset.

This time, Luke shook his head in disapproval.

She wrapped her hand around his. "How is school going for you?"

"Oh, really good. Ms. Peters has been sending my lesson plans by e-mail, and I send her my homework. But today, Dad is going to take me to school."

"You haven't been going to school?" Concern laced her voice.

Lucky bowed his head. "No, Mom. I've been here with you . . . every day."

She hugged him. "I'm so sorry for all of this."

He wrapped his arms around her neck. "It's okay, Mom. You'll get better. Your brain just needs time to heal."

Luke held back his disappointment until they got in the truck. "Lucky, you shouldn't have lied to your mother."

Innocent eyes fixed on him. "What?"

"The ring."

"But she thinks you're married."

"We're not. What do you think is going to happen once she remembers we didn't get married?" Luke's stomach churned.

"Maybe she won't remember."

"Lucky, I don't like lies." He valued honesty and

integrity. How could his son make up such a lie so easily? Every muscle in his body tensed.

"But if you told her the truth, it might have upset her."

"I would have found a way to break it to her gently."

"What if it caused more bad memories and she forgot even more?"

He turned the key, and the engine fired to life. "One lie leads to another and another. This is not good. Does she have a ring at home?"

"I never saw her wear one."

Luke ran his fingers through his hair. "Where am I going to find a ring?"

"A jewelry store."

"I don't even know her ring size." He shook his head and glanced over at his son. "This is not good, Lucky."

Lucky sat at the far side of the truck, arms crossed . . . pouting. "I was just trying to help."

A rebuke came to mind, but he chose not to voice it. The kid had been through enough already. Somehow, he'd find a way to explain to her the truth.

He walked into the school, following Lucky to his classroom, a small room with about ten maybe twelve kids. A whiteboard dominated one wall of the typical classroom—Bible characters' pictures the only anomaly.

"Lucky, you're here." His teacher hurried to greet them. "Hi." She faced Luke. "I'm Amy Peters, and you are?"

"This is my dad. Remember, I told you about him?" Lucky took off to the other side of the room to a small gathering of kids.

What had Lucky told his teacher about him and when?

Ms. Peters blinked from behind her glasses, and her mouth moved, but nothing came out.

Attempting to defuse the situation, Luke presented his hand to shake hers. "Luke Daniels."

Recognition flashed in her eyes. So she's heard of him.

She braced her hands on her hips. "You're Luke?"

He pulled back his hand. Exactly, what did Ms. Peters know?

She glanced at Lucky and back at him. "Well, that is very clear to see."

"My mom is awake," Lucky was telling his classmates. "My dad woke her up. Just like in *Sleeping Beauty*, he kissed her and she woke up."

Luke wasn't prone to blushing, but he felt his cheeks grow hot.

"She's awake?" Ms. Peters asked.

He nodded. "But she's got some recovery to do."

"Of course. The accident was awful. In the papers and everything."

"It was in the paper?"

"Yes. Excuse me for asking, but how did you find out?"

Apparently, she knows he's not been in the picture. "Lucky called me."

"I didn't realize you two were in communication."

"We weren't. He came across some papers in Hannah's things and found me on the Internet."

"He is a smart one." She crossed her arms. "How does

Hannah feel about you being here?"

Taken back by the conversation's personal nature, he didn't know how to respond. "I'm not sure I should be discussing this."

Over her shoulder, Ms. Peters instructed the class as she ushered him out the door to the hallway. "Please open your books and read the pages written on the board." She closed the door behind them. "Hannah and I are very good friends." She faced him with her arms crossed.

"Oh, so she's told you about me?" It was best to get more information before offering an answer.

She lowered her head. "Yes, she told me she had to leave you and couldn't go back to the valley because of her family."

His jaw clenched. "She could have come back."

"Not according to Hannah. Look, I'm sure you know much more about her situation than I do, but for Hannah, it wasn't an option."

"How long have you known Hannah?"

"Six years. We're best friends."

This is Hannah's best friend. What else does she know?

"Ms. Peters, I'm here for my son and Hannah."

She cocked her head to one side. "So, that's your plan, Mr. Daniels. To come here and use this situation to your advantage. Because if it is—"

"Excuse me, Ms. Peters. My plan is to see Hannah healthy and safe and to see my son have his mother back. Not some shell of her, *all* of her." His temper rose.

"Pardon me, I'd like to say goodbye to my son."

He brushed past her into the classroom and knelt beside Lucky. "I'll pick you up later. If you need anything, you call my cell."

"Okay, I will."

He kissed the top of Lucky's head and left without another word to the teacher. The nerve of the woman. He didn't care if she was Hannah's friend or not. She didn't know the reality of the situation.

Driving around town, trying to cool off, he drove past a pawnshop. Circling back around, he parked in the lot and went inside. Used stereos stacked along dusty shelves. Guitars hung over a case crammed with cameras, cell phones, and pistols. The pungent odor of mothballs mingled with tobacco.

"What can I do you for?" the large man behind the counter asked.

"Got any rings?"

"Man or woman's?"

"Woman's."

"Wedding, engagement?" He walked to a glass counter.

"Wedding." He pressed his finger to the glass and pointed to a simple gold wedding band. "That one there."

"Sure you don't want something like this?" He pulled out a gaudy ring with diamonds and faint green stones intermingled.

"Nothing like that. Something simple."

Later, if things turned out the way he'd hope they

would, he'd buy her a nice ring. But for now, simple was best. Besides, if they had gotten married when they were young, he could've only afforded a simple gold band.

"It's plain, nothing fancy. I'd say it's about a size six or six and a half. The woman would have to be small to wear it."

Would it fit? He pinched the gold band between his fingers as guilt plagued him. He shouldn't do this—add to the lie. Yet something felt right, like it was meant to be.

"Tell you what, I got this man's ring here. I'd sell them both to you, half price for the man's."

He slid the ring on his hand. It fit perfect. Like a sign he should buy them. "Okay, I'll take them both."

He paid by credit card and tucked the rings in his jeans pocket then drove back to the hospital. His stomach in knots.

Chapter Eleven

Hannah closed the door to the small bathroom and shed the hospital gown. Her breath caught at the yellow, ugly bruises on her arms, legs, hip, and chest. More than her head got banged up in the accident; her entire body took a beating.

No wonder the doctor, John, advised her to keep taking the painkillers. In the small mirror above the sink, she checked her reflection and gasped at the sight of her hair. A half-inch patch of shaved hair marred her hairline, and hideous stitches disfigured her pale skin. Her hair hung heavy and flat, desperately needing to be washed. Dark circles rimmed her eyes, making them appear sunken. She covered a yawn with her hand. The painkillers zapped her energy and left her head fuzzy.

A row of stitches ran up the outside of her left calf. Carefully, she stepped into the loose-fitting jogging pants. She secured her bra then slipped into the soft velour jacket. It smelled clean and fresh, like a field of wildflowers. She brushed her teeth and with slow, smooth strokes, brushed her hair. Sure could use a rubber band.

In her room, she sat on a chair and pulled on a pair of fuzzy socks and wiggled her toes in sheer pleasure of the warmth they brought to her toes. Inside the bag, Luke had brought a pair of pink and gray flannel pajamas. She picked up the Bible and opened it to where the red ribbon marked a passage, probably where she left off in her morning devotional. After reading the same passage several times, she gave up and closed the book. It was no use. She couldn't concentrate. She returned the Bible to the table.

She longed to go home, sleep in her own bed, and be held by Luke. A gaping hole opened in her heart. Seized with an intense longing for the man she loved. The feeling surprised her as if they'd been apart for a long time. Time was all weird since coming out of the coma.

Her heart ached over seeing Lucky hiding behind his father this morning. The poor boy was afraid of his own mother. Rightly so, she was a frightful sight. Why did they only have Lucky and no other children?

"Hey there, you're up." Katherine glided into the room.

Her sister's cheery manner made Hannah smile.

Katherine set a leather purse at the foot of the bed. "Well, it's not the Whitman Hotel, but better than the last place."

"When can I go home?"

"John has you meeting with a psychologist who

specializes in brain injuries." She perched on the edge of the bed. "And he's consulting with a neurologist."

"More doctors?" Tired of doctors and nurses. They came and went at all hours of the night, checking on her, waking her up, poking, and asking questions.

"The parents are coming this afternoon to meet with John and discuss things."

"Think they might let me go home tomorrow?"

"What, you don't like this wonderful bed?" Katherine bounced on its edge.

"No, I miss my bed, my home."

"I hear ya, sister." Katherine smiled. "I don't know. Hey, I see you're wearing that jumpsuit you bought when we went to Seattle last year."

Seattle, she tried to recall the memory and pressed her hand to her throbbing head. Unable to reach the memory, she let it go. "Luke brought it."

Katherine wedged her hands to her hips. "What, you didn't like your gown?"

"Gowns are out of style." Hannah attempted a joke.

Katherine's gaze fell on the bedside table. "I see you have your Bible."

Hannah ran her hand over the smooth brown leather. "I can't seem to concentrate."

"That's understandable. You knocked your head pretty good." Katherine crossed her arms. "How do you feel?"

"Tired. Out of sorts. I'm not sure if it's the painkillers or my injuries."

"Probably both." She dug around in her leather bag. "I

brought you something." She pulled out a small booklet. "I thought if you had a journal to write your thoughts in—your memories—it might help."

"Thank you." Hannah took the spiral-bound journal adorned with yellow daisies. "Would you by chance have a rubber band?"

Katherine rummaged through the bag. "Let me see. I usually have stuff like that on hand for Sarah."

Sarah, who was Sarah? Sarah—John and Katherine's little girl. Relieved she remembered.

"Here you go." Her sister handed her a neon-green rubber band. "When did Luke stop by?"

She secured her hair in a ponytail. "Earlier with Lucky. Then he took Lucky to school. I think he's coming back."

"Hum." Irritation or maybe frustration flashed in Katherine's eyes.

Was there tension between Luke and Katherine?

"I've come to take you to see the psychologist." Katherine stepped out into the hallway and pushed a wheelchair her way.

"I can walk."

Katherine patted the back of the seat. "Humor me."

When Hannah settled in the chair, Katherine lowered the footrest then pushed her out into the corridor. The speed in which her sister drove made her head spin. At the door, Katherine swung the chair around and backed her into an office then spun her back around. Hannah grasped the armrests to keep her balance. Good grief, this isn't a race.

"Hello, Hannah. My name is Dr. Walberg." An older man in a charcoal suit braced on the edge of his desk. His thin gray hair slicked back, and black-rimmed glasses framed kind brown eyes. He gestured toward two leather chairs. "Would you care to sit on something more comfortable?"

Katherine flipped up the footrest. "Go ahead. The brake is set."

Hannah rose and crept to the chair nearest the door.

The doctor stood. "Thank you, Katherine. I'll ring when we're finished."

Katherine flashed an encouraging smile before wheeling the chair outside and closing the door.

Dr. Walberg came around the desk. "Now then, how are you feeling?"

Why does everyone keep asking me the same question? "Like I've been rolled, punched, and asleep for weeks."

Walberg's eyes gleamed behind his glasses. "That's good you have a sense of humor."

"Does a head injury usually cause one to lose their sense of humor?"

"Sometimes."

In that case, she could count her blessings.

He picked up a yellow pad of paper. "Do you remember the *day* of the accident?"

She searched for the answer, but nothing came to mind. "No."

109

"Do you remember the accident?"

"Was it a car accident?"

"Yes. What kind of car were you driving?"

She glanced down at her hands. What kind of a car would she drive? An SUV, no. A compact—possibly. A sedan—not sure. "I don't know."

"What time of day were you driving?"

She propped her elbow on the chair's padded arm and rested her throbbing head in her palm. "I'm not sure." When she searched for the answer, all she saw was black then a flash of light. "Nighttime?"

Was that the right answer?

"Let's try an experiment. I'm going to hold my pen and have you follow it with your eyes."

He held the pen vertically then moved it to one side and back to the other. Up, then down and back to center. "Good."

The doctor wrote on the yellow pad of paper and handed it to her. "What does it say?"

"Hello, Hannah."

"Good." He walked around to his desk and turned on a radio and took the pad from her and scribbled something then handed it back to her. "What does it say?" He snapped his fingers as if keeping the beat with the song.

She glanced at the pad then out the window as the sun streamed through the glass. The radio played a catchy tune. His fingers continued to snap. He crossed his leg and swung his foot up and down. The song changed, his fingers snapped, his foot swung—her head almost burst.

She closed her eyes and covered her ears.

The doctor knelt in front of her, removing her hands from her head. "Hannah."

She opened her eyes. Compassionate eyes peered at her through thick lenses. The music stopped, the snapping gone, the sun shrouded behind a gray cloud.

He picked up the pad from the floor and set it on her lap. "Can you tell me what that says now?"

She glanced down at the pad. "Hello, Hannah, happy to meet you."

"How's your head feel?"

"Like I'm wearing a helmet and someone is banging on it."

"I have a few more questions if that's all right with you?"

She nodded. Did she have a choice?

"Where did you grow up?"

"Montana."

"Where do you live now?"

"Uh, Montana." Was that right? Yes, it had to be. Where else would she and Luke live?

"I think that's all for now."

After Katherine was called, she wheeled her back to her room. "Dr. Walberg is the best."

Hannah didn't answer, her head swimming with people walking past, squeaks of rubber soles on the floor. The sharp, pungent scent of disinfectant stung her nose.

Upon reaching her room, she crawled onto the bed. "Can I have some water?" The base of her head throbbed, the pain moved up, encompassing her entire skull.

"Sure." Katherine poured water from a plastic picture into a paper cup and handed it to her.

Hannah took a sip and several deep breaths. Her neck and shoulder muscles tight, she tipped her head to the left then to the right to stretch and relax the muscles. She swayed almost losing her balance.

"You're a little pale." Katherine took the cup and sat beside her on the bed. "Are you feeling okay?" She set the water on the table.

Hannah shook her head. "My head hurts. I feel kind of sick to my stomach, and I just want to lie down."

Katherine stood and headed for the door. "I'll let you get some rest."

"Please turn the lights off."

The steady rhythmic ticking of the wall clock punctuated the silence. Hannah stared out the window with the drape partially opened, watching raindrops hit the glass and roll down. Images flashed in her mind too quick to grasp. The harder she tried to grab hold of one it eluded her, like a feather caught in a breeze. It only made her head hurt more. Her stomach rolled.

Someone walked past her room, and she turned to see who it was, but they were gone. She tucked her legs under the sheet and pulled up the thin blanket. Her head sank into the pillow. Light from the hall spilled into the room. Her eyelids grew heavy, and she yawned.

Whispered voices drifted through the open door. "Is she slipping back into darkness?"

A melodic voice answered. "No, she's falling asleep."

"What about the boy?"

"He is safe."

She opened her eyes. Two small shadows stood in the doorway.

"Lucky?" She sat up.

But no one was there. She shivered. Was she hearing things?

A sharp pain sliced through the right side of her skull. She moaned and fell back against the pillow.

She rocked back and forth on her side, hugging the pillow. Tears seeped from her eyes, dampening the pillowcase. Words flitted about her head as music played. *I surrender all. . . . I need thee, every hour. . . . There is a place of quiet rest. . . .* A cacophony of tunes crammed her head. The words jumbled. The music didn't follow a pattern nor make sense.

"Jesus, please," she whispered, desperate for the chaos to cease.

My hope is built on nothing less. . . . She sighed as the words came, and the musical notes of guitar and piano blended to beauty. *Than Jesus' blood and righteousness. . . .* She grasped for the thread and softly sang, "I dare not trust the sweetest frame. . . ."

Before going back to the hospital, Luke stopped by the library to check if they had a copy of the accident article. The librarian led him to a computer where he typed in the date and scrolled till he saw the picture of a mangled vehicle upside down on the highway. Emergency vehicles were on the scene. In the dark, the lights on the fire trucks and police cars shined, creating shadows on the pavement.

It happened around nine p.m. on the highway coming into town. The temperature had dropped after a brief bout of sleet. Hannah approached the bridge crossing the Walla Walla River. The bridge deck had iced over.

Why was she out so late? Where had she gone? Where was she going? He stared at the vehicle, trying to determine what kind it was. There was little left of the car to help him say for sure. If he had to guess, he'd say it was a foreign-made, four-door sedan. Didn't she have a temperature gauge in the car to warn her it was freezing?

He left the library with more questions than answers.

As he strolled down the hospital corridor, he slipped his hand into his pocket and toyed with the ring. Plagued by uncertainty, he paused outside the room.

Should I do this?

He didn't want to lie to her, lead her to believe something that simply wasn't true. Yet he didn't want to explain the reality while she was in such a tender state of mind. He certainly didn't want to throw his own kid under the bus for spinning up such a story. He tucked the ring back in his pocket.

Someone was singing as softly as a mother singing her baby to sleep. Glancing around the hall, he was alone. The voice drifted from Hannah's room. He stepped into the dark room, the drapes partially opened, the lights off.

114

Hannah lay on her side with her back to the door. Curled in a fetal position, she hugged a pillow rocking. Not wanting to frighten her, he walked around to the other side of the bed and knelt beside her. Tears stained her cheeks, the pillow damp, her eyes closed.

He cupped his hand on her arm. "Hannah?"

A moment passed before recognition flooded her brown eyes. She released the pillow and struggled to sit.

He helped her upright. His heart beat fast. "Are you okay?"

She nodded then shook her head as if unsure. She opened her arms. "Hold me."

His breath caught. He eased down beside her and took her in his arms. Ever so gently, he cradled her.

Hannah's arms wrapped tight around his neck. "Oh, Luke," she said, her breath warm against his neck. "Take me home."

His heart slammed against his ribs, and he couldn't speak.

She loosened her grip and searched his eyes. "Please take me home. I don't want to be here anymore." She wiped the moisture from her cheeks.

"Soon. We have a meeting with your doctors in about a half hour."

"I don't need a psychologist. I'm not crazy. I may not be able to remember everything, but I'm not crazy."

"No, you're not crazy."

"I'm so tired of being here. I miss the mountains, the deer, and the expansive blue sky. I want to see the river."

Was she describing the Bitterroot? Or did she know she was in Washington? "Soon, be patient."

"This place is so noisy, and it stinks. The lights hurt my eyes. Please tell them to let me go home. I'll heal faster in the peace and fresh air."

"Do you mean the Bitterroot?" He held his breath for her answer.

"Yes, of course, I mean the valley. Where else is home? I long for it. Please take me home."

His heart expanded in his chest. "I will, I promise."

"*Tomorrow.* Ask them to let me go tomorrow."

"I'll talk it over with your doctors."

"And my family. Explain to them I can't stay. I need the peace and quiet. I need to just be with you and Lucky."

His phone vibrated in his pocket, and he removed it, seeing the fifteen-minute alert. "I have to go meet with your doctors."

"They don't want me in there?" Her eyes darkened.

"Everything will be fine. Trust me." He stood. "Will you be all right?"

She touched her head. "Yes. My headache has subsided."

Luke squeezed her hand. "I'll hurry back."

A plea softened her gaze.

Reluctant to leave, he backed out of the room then hurried down the hall to the elevator, up one floor, and down another long corridor. Outside a waiting area, he sat next to Dane, across from Paula and Joe.

"How is she?" Paula asked.

"Tired."

Dane sat forward. "Rest is the best thing for her."

Luke braced his elbows on his knees, clasped his hands, and stared at the floor. How would they react when he told them he was taking her back to Montana? Maybe he shouldn't say anything at all. After all, it was her decision.

Katherine exited her husband's office, John a step behind her. "We're going to meet in a small conference room down here." She motioned, and they all followed. Luke made sure he was last.

They sat around an oval table where another doctor joined them.

John spoke first. "Today's physical therapy went as well as to be expected. She is having some issues with balance and hand-eye coordination, but in time, we anticipate this will improve. Her injuries are healing with no sign of infection." He swallowed hard and glanced at his notes. "The other issue is not so easily remedied, and we can't predict how much time it will take for her to heal. Nor can we say if she will experience a full recovery. I'm going to have Dr. Walberg speak to her memory loss."

In a gray suit and thick glasses, the good doctor sat forward with his hands clasped on the table. "Thank you all for being here. You all obviously care about Hannah very much."

With narrowed eyes, Katherine glanced across the table at Luke. What was her problem? Of course, he cared.

"Tests reveal Hannah has a condition called

117

hyperesthesia. In laymen's terms, it is an increased sensitivity to stimuli of the senses. For Hannah, that stimulus is in the form of sight and sound. Lights are too bright; sounds are too loud. Too many sounds and she has difficulty distinguishing what and where the sound is coming from. Too much visual stimulus and her brain can't process the information."

Luke leaned forward. "Is this because of the head injury?"

"Yes."

"What about the drugs she's taking?" Dane asked. "Could they be affecting this as well?"

"She is on pain medicine and a mild seizure prescription; neither is known to cause hyperesthesia. We have seen B twelve supplements successfully treat similar conditions such as ADHD and autism. I am recommending B twelve supplements. In the meantime, Hannah is going to need to be in a place of rest and quiet."

Perfect. He has just the place. This isn't going to go over well. But he didn't care. Hannah was his priority.

"Is this temporary?" Paula asked.

"Only time will tell."

John spoke next. "We recommended Hannah be admitted to a nursing facility."

Luke's temper sparked. "Absolutely not." Of all the harebrained ideas . . . "I will not have her put in some nursing home with a bunch of old, sick people."

"Luke, I don't think that's what we specifically have in mind," Katherine asserted.

"I don't care about the specifics. Hannah wants to go home."

Joe looked at Paula and across the table at Dane. "I'm afraid things at the winery may be too noisy, with tractors, workers, and everything else going on there."

"I'll take her back to Montana." There, it was out. His tone left no room for discussion.

"You will do no such thing." Katherine bolted from the chair.

He eyed Katherine then those around the table. "She wants to go home, back to the valley."

Katherine held her fist at her side. Her eyes sparked. "Montana is not her home. This is her home."

Luke rose from his chair. "It's what she wants."

"You can't march back into her life and just take her away." She stepped behind John. "I won't let you take advantage of this situation just to get custody of your son."

Luke braced his hands on the table. "I am not taking advantage of anything. I am helping the mother of my son. The woman who should've been with me all along, and I'm raising my son. Not you." He pointed to Joe and Paula. "And not you." He pointed to Dane. "Lucky is my kid."

"You want to take Hannah out of here so you can take your kid. Is that it?" Katherine hurled the accusation.

"No, I want them both."

"Stop. The two of you just stop." Paula covered her mouth, her eyes brimming.

Joe stood. "I don't like this, Luke. I understand where

119

you're coming from. I can't keep you from taking your son. And I can't stop you from taking Hannah either."

Katherine cocked her head toward the door. "I'll go down there and tell her the whole truth right now."

"I don't recommend that," Walberg said. "Her memories are best to come back on their own. If you attempt to force them, you could cause irreparable damage."

Katherine fell into the chair and put her head in her hands. "I don't believe this." She lifted her gaze to Joe. "Daddy, please don't let this happen."

"It's not up to me."

Dane cleared his throat. "If you ask me, I don't see any harm in Hannah spending time with Luke in Montana." Katherine glared at her brother. "It could help her heal in more ways than one."

Luke caught the undercurrent of what Dane was saying. Time in Montana could help Hannah reconcile with her past. At least someone was on his side. "She asked me less than an hour ago if I'd take her back to Montana. She wants to be released tomorrow."

"She doesn't know what she's asking." Katherine slapped her hand on the table.

Luke locked eyes with John. "If there is no medical reason for her to be in the hospital, then I ask that she be released tomorrow."

John gave a reluctant nod.

"Thank you," Luke said and left the room to tell Hannah the good news.

120

Joe, Paula, and Dane followed. Katherine stayed behind. Luke entered the room to find Hannah staring out the window with a forlorn expression.

"Hey there, beautiful," he said with a smile. "We have good news."

Her eyes brightened. "They're releasing me?" Hope rang in her voice.

"Tomorrow."

"Thank you." She grabbed his hand.

"It'll be a long drive. Do you think you're up to it?"

"Yes."

"We don't want to see you leave," Paula said, tears shimmering in her eyes.

Hannah stood. "It's okay. When I'm better, I'll be back."

"Well, if there's anything you need—anything—you call me," Dane urged.

"Of course." Her forehead wrinkled. "You may need to write down your number."

Dane laughed and pulled his wallet from his pocket, removed a business card, and handed it to her.

Joe stepped forward. "We will come see you off tomorrow."

Chapter Twelve

While Luke waited in the hall for Lucky to get out of class, he called his sister. "I need a favor."

"Name it, but it will cost you." She chuckled.

In more ways than one. "I need you to go shopping for me. Buy girl stuff and decorate my house."

"What do you mean girl stuff?"

"Bathroom rugs, seat covers, fluffy towels. Lotions and bath stuff. Decorate the kitchen while you're at it."

"What's going on?" Suspicion raised her voice.

"I'm bringing Hannah and Lucky home."

"Really? Wow, that was fast. She just came out of a coma, and you already swept her off her feet?"

"Not exactly. She thinks we're married."

Silence answered.

He checked his connection to be sure the call wasn't dropped. "Sam, are you there?"

"Yeah, I'm here. Where did she get the idea you were married?"

"She has amnesia and is trying to put the pieces together. She assumed we're married." He didn't want to tell her how Lucky lied to his mother.

"And you didn't correct her?"

He loved his little sister, but sometimes she asked too many questions. "We're supposed to let her memories come back on their own, so she's not traumatized."

"So you want me to make it look like you're happily married?" Sarcasm sharpened her tone.

"Yeah, can you do that for me?"

"Oh, Luke, I don't know. What's going to happen when she realizes the truth?"

"By then, she'll be so madly in love with me, she'll want to be my wife for real."

"You still love her." It wasn't a question but a declaration.

"I think so." Lucky came out into the hall. "Can you explain all this to the family, so they're aware?"

"Yes. How much time do I have?"

Lucky hurried toward him, lugging a heavy backpack.

"We're leaving tomorrow and should be home by around six or seven."

"That's not much time to turn your house into something warm and fuzzy."

"It's not that bad."

His son studied him under a thoughtful gaze.

He took the backpack.

"No, it's just sparse and plain. If it weren't for my pictures on the walls, you'd think it was nothing more than a place to store furniture."

Luke winked at Lucky. "I gotta go."

"Wait. What colors?"

"Colors? I don't know. Her house is decorated in red and yellow."

"Got it. Drive safe. I love you."

He released a pent-up breath. "Love you, too." He could always count on his sister.

He waited till he was in the truck with Lucky before telling him the news. Best not to have his busybody teacher overhear and possibly cause trouble.

"Lucky, I'm going to take you and your mother back with me to Montana."

"You are!" Lucky bounced on his seat. "Do Grandma and Grandpa know?" he asked in a conspiratorial tone. The kid was definitely smart.

"Yes, they know."

"And Uncle Dane?" Lucky reached for the seatbelt.

Luke started the engine. "He knows, too."

"What about Aunt Katherine?"

He shifted into reverse and backed up. "She knows."

Lucky slipped the side strap behind his head. "And they're okay with us moving in with you?"

"They are." Like they had a choice.

"This is awesome!" The kid could hardly contain his excitement.

"We have a lot to do before tomorrow. You have to pack your things. I have to pack your mothers." He drove out of the parking lot.

"Okay. Are we taking the furniture, too?"

"No, that stays. Just personal belongings."

"That's good. 'Cuz Mom's been talking about redecorating."

He glanced over at his son. "What do mean?"

"She's tired of red. I think she likes purple. Purple is her favorite color."

He pressed the button on the dash and activated redial.

"You forget something?" Samantha asked.

"She likes purple, not red."

"What kind of purple?"

He turned to Lucky. "What kind of purple?"

"Kind of light like a flower."

"Did you hear that?"

"Oh, is that my nephew?" Samantha gushed. "I can't wait to meet him."

"Sam, did you get the purple?"

"Yes, of course. Okay, no worries. I got it handled. By the way, how much money do I have to make your house livable?"

"No limit."

"I'm going to have some fun," she said followed by a whoop.

He laughed and disconnected the call. "That's your Aunt Samantha. She's all about fun."

By a little after nine o'clock, he had the truck packed with their personal belongings and Lucky tucked into bed. He'd never seen so many clothes and shoes. Even Samantha wasn't that bad. Probably because Hannah grew up poor.

When his sister befriended Hannah in high school, Samantha gave her some clothes. He wasn't sure, but he wouldn't doubt it if Sam went to the thrift store in Missoula and bought clothes for Hannah.

When Dane arrived, Luke finished setting her laptop and printer in the back of the truck and closed the tailgate.

"Howdy," Dane said, holding a bottle of wine. "I was going to drink this myself, in honor of Hannah, but then I figured what the heck, I'd see if you'd like to share it with me."

"I think I'm finished here, come on inside."

Dane entered the cottage and helped himself into the kitchen, finding the corkscrew and two glasses.

As Dane poured the rich red liquid into the goblets, he said, "I made this for Hannah's twenty-fifth birthday." He handed him a glass. "She likes blends. This one," he hoisted the glass to the light and tilted it, "is fifty percent syrah, twenty-five percent cab and the rest is merlot." He took a sip. "Aw, yeah. Juicy and sweet. Just the way Hannah likes her wine."

Dane's feelings for Hannah were obviously strong. "Did you come here to talk me out of taking her back with me?" Luke took a sip before walking into the front room.

"Nope. Like I said today in the conference room, I think this is the best thing for her." Dane took the rocking chair near the fireplace.

Luke perched on the couch. "What makes you think so?"

"Because she's always loved you."

His breath caught. "How do you know?"

Dane rocked back in the chair. "Because she told me so."

It wasn't any of his business, but Luke wanted to know. "Sounds like you two are close."

"Like I said, as close as brother and sister." He raised his glass in salute.

Gently put in his place, Luke still couldn't let go of the possessive streak coursing through his blood. "Has she ever dated?"

"No." Dane shook his head. "And believe me, it's not for the lack of opportunity."

Relief flooded Luke's veins. Her letter had said as much, but he needed to make sure.

Dane propped his ankle on his knee. "It's going to be difficult, you know, living in the same house with her."

"She's always been easy to get along with, and from the looks of this place, she keeps a clean house."

"That's not what I mean." Dane grinned. "The chemistry between you two is obvious, and she thinks you're married. How do you think that's going to play out?"

Luke shrugged as if to say he hadn't given it much thought, but that wasn't true. He had given it a great deal of thought. He planned to sleep downstairs in the guest room. "You're worried I'm going to take advantage of her."

"No, I trust that you're a man of honor and that you've learned from your past."

"So, what's your concern?"

"None." Dane leaned back in the chair. "I think God is giving you both a second chance to make things right."

"I hope you're right." Luke hoped this time he'd not mess up. For everyone's sake.

Chapter Thirteen

The sun glared off the wet pavement. As she stared out the window, Hannah was thankful for the sunglasses Luke gave her. Rolling hills of brown grass rose on either side of the highway. Clouds floated overhead in a patchwork against the deep blue sky. The winding two-lane highway was familiar, and yet it felt different.

Behind her, Lucky played with an electronic toy that beeped periodically, punctuated by a low "cool" or "oops" marking his success and failure. Equipped with games, coloring book, and crayons, even a book to read with a pillow and blanket, she hoped it was enough to keep a young boy occupied for the six-hour drive home.

Yet only recently had she and Lucky made this trip to visit her parents. Thankfully, Lucky wasn't with her in the accident. Poor Luke must have been beside himself when he got the call. Tempted to ask about that day, she glanced back at her son. No, she'd talk with Luke later.

Luke drove with one hand on the wheel. The other

arm rested on the console between them. She fingered the simple, yellow-gold band on her hand and eyed the one on his finger. For the life of her, she couldn't remember their wedding day. How sad. The happiest day in a woman's life and she couldn't remember anything, not even an impression, a faint feeling—nothing.

She entwined her fingers with his.

He squeezed her hand. "Okay?"

She nodded. "No headache today. The sunglasses help."

"I loaded up the CD player with some of your favorite music if you want tunes." From behind his sunglasses, he winked in the rearview mirror at Lucky.

The two were close. He was such a good father. Love expanded her heart. God had blessed her. She leaned forward to turn on the stereo but couldn't seem to figure out how it worked.

"Press the button," Luke said doing so. "Here's the volume."

She kept the volume low.

"Hey, Dad, can we go fishing when we get home?"

"It's too cold."

Beep, beep followed by a whirl drifted from the back seat. "Can't wait to see Bear."

"Bear?" Hannah asked, alarmed. Do they have bears?

"Our dog," Lucky said.

"Oh." She didn't remember a dog named Bear. Then again, she remembered very little of her life.

"And we have a cat, too. His name is. . ."

"Toby," Luke said. "His name is Toby. And four horses—Lightning, Branson, Dakota, and Alexis."

Her husband seemed eager to help her remember things. She smiled over at him.

He lifted her hand to his lips, kissed it, and then released it as he navigated up a long hill past a slow-moving semi. "I plan to stop in Lewiston for lunch. Does that sound good?"

"Yes," she said.

"I'd like a hamburger. No—cheeseburger." Tap, tap, blip, and a descending electronic twirl. "Oops."

"What would you like?" Luke asked her.

"A salad."

"I got just the place."

They continued east on Highway 12, weaving through rolling hills. Then the road followed alongside the Snake River.

She peered past Luke at the river. "It's beautiful."

"Yes, it is."

As he drove through Clarkston, she had to close her eyes. The many stores, signs, and traffic caused her head to throb.

"Doing okay?" Luke asked.

"Yes, just closing my eyes—it helps." As she rested her head back against the seat, the earth spun and she gripped the armrest. The frequent dizzy spells a nuisance.

"The stereo okay?"

She nodded.

"Mom, does your head hurt?"

131

"A little bit."

A small hand rested upon her upper arm. She patted Lucky's hand to reassure him she was okay.

As they drove, listening to music, she periodically opened her eyes to see where they were.

"We're coming into Lewiston," Luke said.

She opened her eyes. They were on a bridge crossing the river. The sensation of falling swept over her, and she clutched at Luke's arm.

"Hannah?" Alarm raised his voice.

"Mom?"

She shook her head, unable to speak. Her heart pounded. Sharp pain shot through her head, and she broke into a cold sweat. She gasped for breath. Luke drove across the bridge, circled around, and found a place to pull over.

"Hannah, breathe." He grabbed her hand. "Breathe with me."

She took deep breaths.

"Slow and easy."

He flipped up the armrest, unbuckled his seat, and scooted toward her. "Honey, breathe slowly. That's it."

She did as he asked. But her heart raced and her head throbbed.

"Can you talk to me? Tell me what you're feeling."

"Like . . . falling."

"You're not falling. You're right here."

She nodded, knowing the reality, but her head said differently.

"You're having a panic attack. It's not reality. Do you understand?"

She nodded again and pressed her hand to her pounding heart, but she couldn't catch her breath.

He opened his door, raced around to the passenger side, and flung the door open. Unlatching the seatbelt, he eased her to him and wrapped his arms around her. His big hand rubbed up and down her back. In time, her heart rate eased to a normal rhythm.

"Stay in the truck, Lucky," Luke whispered.

Tears dampened her cheeks. "I don't know what's wrong with me."

"Nothing that time and rest won't heal." Luke's warm breath stirred her hair.

The strong, steady beat of his heart soothed her nerves. "I'm sorry."

"Nothing to be sorry about." Luke didn't release her until her breathing returned to normal.

"Lucky, trade places with your mom." He took her face in his hands and kissed her forehead.

Lucky slipped between the seats. Hannah stepped onto the dirt and climbed into the back seat.

"There's a pillow. Maybe you should lie down and close your eyes."

She propped the pillow against the window and tugged the blanket over her. As Luke navigated through Lewiston, she was aware of every turn, stop, and start. Finally, he pulled into a parking lot and cut the engine. She sat up slowly to maintain her equilibrium and blinked at the restaurant sign.

"I'll get a menu, and we'll order to go. It's a fine day for a picnic on the river. Don't you think?" He glanced back at her.

Hannah slid her sunglasses back on. "Just a cobb salad is fine for me with ranch dressing." Although she wasn't sure she could eat.

"And you want a cheeseburger?" Luke asked Lucky.

"Yes, please."

"Okay, stay here with your mom."

He strolled into the chain restaurant with its apple logo.

Lucky peered out the window at Luke. "He's the best Dad in the world."

Hannah smiled at her son's obvious hero worship.

"I'm glad he's my dad."

"Me, too." She was truly blessed.

Tears sprang to her eyes at the trouble her accident caused both her son and her husband. If she could go back in time, change whatever decisions she made that led to the accident, she would.

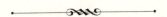

At a picnic table in a park along the Clearwater River, they ate lunch. Surprisingly she had an appetite after her meltdown, the plastic container empty. The salad gone.

Luke devoured a club sandwich and french fries. Cheese stuck to Lucky's cheek. Ketchup dripped onto his jacket. Taking a napkin, she wiped his face and dabbed at the red spot setting into the navy-blue fibers.

A cool breeze whispered through her hair and she tucked loose strands behind her ear. The warm sun caressed her face. "It's a beautiful summer day, don't you think?"

Luke and Lucky exchanged glances.

"Mom, its February."

February? "I thought it was June."

Luke reached across the table, taking her hand in his. "You're right, it's a beautiful day."

She thinly smiled an apology and squeezed Luke's hand.

He squeezed her fingers. "Let's get you home."

In a short time, they were back on the road. Hannah sat up front and turned the stereo on. The music Luke had chosen was inspiring, comforting, and enjoyable. Apparently, it was some of her favorites. She knew every word, anticipated the next song.

They crossed another bridge; she steeled herself, afraid she'd have another panic attack. Luke observed her with a sideways glance. No doubt waiting to see if she'd fall apart.

She concentrated on breathing, and once across the bridge, she relaxed. The road followed the river, and wide-open spaces gave way to rolling hills, then to rugged mountains. An hour later, they wound along the river through a narrow canyon.

Luke entertained Lucky with stories about the history of the area; the Nez Perce Indians, Lewis and Clark, and

Chief Joseph captivated their son.

Impressed by Luke's knowledge, she asked, "How do you know so much about this area's history?"

"My business is dependent on tourism, and tourists like to know the history of an area." He shrugged. "I read a lot of books."

"I'm sorry to have to ask this, but what do you do for a living?"

Lucky poked his head between the seats. "Dad takes people fishing and hunting."

"I operate a guiding business."

Of course, it made sense. Luke loved the outdoors. It came from his father, his brother—it was in his blood. Too embarrassed to ask much more, she vowed to get to know what he did and help where she could.

"I have a background in business and accounting, don't I?"

Luke's eyes brightened. "Yes. You've always been good with numbers."

"You have an MBA, Mom."

An MBA? If she was that smart, then how come she couldn't remember her life?

As she stared out the window, a deep sorrow penetrated her heart. As if she was leaving something dear to her. A loved one? Tears collected in her eyes. Gripped by a strong urge to grasp Luke's hand, she reached for him. His hand wrapped tightly around hers.

Stop. Turn around. The words pressed on her tongue.

What is it that made her so sad? She was going home;

she was getting well. She touched her fingers to the stitches on her forehead. Where did the feeling of grief stem from?

Surely leaving her parents in Walla Walla wasn't a big deal. She was a grown woman with a family of her own.

She held her hand to her chest, rubbing the ache. Out the window, the river wove in and out of view, collecting in deep green pools before spilling into white rapids. A few inches of snow lined the highway and covered the ground in the shaded areas. The warm sun melted the snow, making the road wet and shiny.

Sadness and grief dissolved, leaving behind a vague impression.

"How did I find the time to go to college?"

Lucky popped up from the back seat. "You went to night school."

Night school. Of course. No wonder they only had Lucky. She was going to school. An MBA takes time, a lot of time. The sacrifice Luke must have made to accommodate her schooling. Her heart swelled with love.

"Right, Dad?"

"Uh, yeah."

The river veered away from the highway as they climbed in elevation.

"Dad, what's the temperature?"

Luke checked the gauges. "Forty-two."

"When does water freeze?"

"Thirty-two."

"Oh, okay." Lucky sat back and picked up his

electronic game.

As they crested the pass, a blue sign welcomed them to Montana. Her heart leaped. The bright blue sky accented with fluffy white clouds seemed to expand overhead. She had the oddest sensation as if she was coming home after being away for a long time. Probably a remnant of being in a coma for over a week. It skewed her sense of time.

The canyon widened to a narrow valley till they came to an intersection of a major highway. She read the signs Highway 93—Missoula was to the left, Hamilton to the right. Luke turned south.

Captivated by the beauty and wide-open spaces of ranch land, she sat forward. Her breath caught at the sight of the rugged mountains to her right covered in snow.

"The Bitterroots," she whispered.

"You remember the mountains, Mom?"

"I sure do. They're beautiful." She stopped short of saying she missed them.

The corners of Luke's mouth turned upward. "It's good to see you smile."

Joy filled her heart. "It's good to be home."

The sensation of returning after a long journey didn't subside. Happiness bubbled up inside. She pressed her fingers to her mouth and swallowed hard. Tears swam in her eyes, and her lower lip quivered. She laughed and cried at the same time.

"Mom, are you okay? Is it your head?"

"No, honey." She reached back for Lucky. "It's my heart. I'm so happy to be home."

It didn't make sense. She couldn't have been gone for more than a couple of weeks, but it felt like years. It felt as if she'd been gone, unable to return. As if she had been held captive in a foreign land and was finally released.

She wiped tears from her cheeks. Some things were familiar, like the stores coming into Florence and then into Stevensville, yet she didn't remember the newer grocery store on the highway.

They veered down the cutoff road and drove into Stevensville. She remembered this place with its wide streets, diagonal parking, and historic brick buildings. There was a gallery and an espresso shop she didn't remember, but the drugstore, bank, and beauty shop were familiar.

"Dad?"

"Yeah."

"Are we almost there?"

"Yep, we're just south of town."

"Good, because I have to go to the bathroom."

A few miles south of town, Luke headed to the left, east, on a narrow paved road. Anticipation, apprehension, sadness, and joy all collided and swirled inside her heart.

Hannah was learning to heed her feelings and impressions more than trust her ability to remember. A row of mailboxes on the right and a large wagon wheel will mark the driveway on the left. At the wagon wheel, Luke veered off onto a gravel driveway. Yes, she remembered.

A one-story rectangular house with a two-door garage attached with a breezeway appeared before her. A covered

139

porch ran along the expansive front. Two dormers accented a green metal roof. The house was stained, the trim around the front door and windows painted dark green.

What happened to the big two-story, cracker box farmhouse?

A large dog ran up alongside the truck, barking a welcome.

"Bear!" Lucky called from the back seat. "It's Bear."

Before Luke could turn the engine off, Lucky jumped out of the truck and rushed to the dog. Bear licked his face and spun in a circle happy to the see him.

Luke got out of the truck. "Lucky, the door is unlocked." He closed the driver's side door, and Hannah didn't hear the rest of what was said. Lucky ran inside the house.

Luke opened her door and held out his hand. His smile warmed her. "Welcome home."

She followed him onto the porch and inside the house. Down the hall to her left, the toilet flushed, and Lucky sped past them back outside.

"Did you wash your hands?" She called after him.

"Yeah," he said, but she knew he didn't.

She shook her head and shrugged. "He's been cooped up inside the truck too long."

Funny, the house was not at all familiar, not even the vaguest sense stirred within her. She glanced around trying to find something to stir a memory, but nothing. Light-stained pine trimmed neutral cream walls. A woodstove radiated heat from the right corner on a slate hearth, and a large leather sofa and two recliners formed the boundary of the living room in the open space.

A bar separated the open kitchen, and a slider, draped in gray, lavender, and green checkered print, framed the round oak dining room table. A vase with dried lavender formed the centerpiece surrounded by four placemats in plaid lavender, gray, and cream.

Out back, horses grazed in a pasture, and a weathered barn dominated the back yard. Tall, sprawling oak trees flanked the big old barn.

She excused herself and slipped into the bathroom. She, too, was happy to be out of the truck. Cute wildflowers splashed the shower curtain, accentuating the pale lavender bath rug and toilet seat cover, while cream-colored towels piled soft and fluffy on a nearby shelf above a woven laundry basket.

She opened the door to see Luke in the den, powering up a laptop. "Purple is my favorite color."

He smiled. "Yes, it is."

"And yours?"

"Green."

She ventured down the hall to the next open door. Two twin beds covered in matching red and navy-blue comforters flanked the room. A photo of Bear hung framed on the wall. A small dresser and end table completed the room. Horseshoes created a unique bookshelf on the wall lined with children's books.

Lucky's room.

At the end of the hall, a room with a full-size bed resided with a small white dresser and white bedside table. The yellow comforter with lavender flowers coordinated with a valance over the window. Several photos of flowers adorned the walls.

"This is a guest room," Luke said. "Upstairs is the master."

She followed him, and he stepped aside to let her go upstairs first. Her hand slid along the log banister as she ascended steps of slabs of wood stained a light pine. In the loft, two bedside tables with tall, black, iron reading lamps flanked a king-size bed centered against the left wall.

Muted light from the skylight warmed the room. She ran her hand over the dark amethyst jacquard print comforter and picked up one of the gray suede throw pillows. At the opposite wall, she opened a door with an oval glass pane. The small balcony faced directly west. Two green plastic lawn chairs invited her to sit and enjoy the view of the rugged mountain peaks.

"Perfect for watching the sunset," she said and closed the door.

"The closet is right there," Luke said, pointing. "And the bathroom is back there."

A photo of them sat framed in silver on the long dresser. "We were so young." In the picture, she sat in front of Luke on a lawn. "High school?"

"Yeah." He took the picture and set it back on the dresser then folded her hands in his. A veiled expression cloaked his eyes. "Hannah, until you're well, you can have this room. I'll sleep downstairs."

"No, Luke. I'm not kicking you out of your bed."

"I want you to get better."

She released his hands and wrapped her arms around him, pressing her head against his chest. His arms wound tight around her. It felt right. Like she was right where she belonged—in Luke's arms.

She peered up at him. His gaze fell upon her mouth; her heart beat fast. Luke cupped her cheek in his warm hand and lowered his head, pausing as if unsure of following through. Her heart soared. She rose up on her toes, and her eyes slid shut. When his lips met hers, she sighed. He moaned and deepened the gentle caress. Her knees threatened to give out from under her.

The kiss intensified. She trembled. When the kiss ended, she stood breathless, safe in the arms of the man she   loved.

Chapter Fourteen

By the time the kiss ended, Luke could scarcely breathe. To be on this property, holding Hannah, kissing her—it was as if they picked up where they left off. His grandparents' house was long gone, but he built his house where the old one had sat.

That night when Lucky was conceived, they stayed in the abandoned farmhouse. They knew what they were doing, what they wanted. They were young and foolish, but that didn't stop them. Luke wouldn't make the same mistake twice.

She may have a ring on her hand and believe they're married. But someday, she'd remember they weren't married, and on that day, he could only hope to have won her heart so she'd *want* to be his wife.

Until then, he'd sleep downstairs, give her the time and space she needed to remember, to heal, and to choose.

Luke released her, and then headed downstairs.

Behind him, she gave a startled cry. Hannah stood frozen on the top step. Fear laced her big brown eyes.

"Hannah?"

Her hands clutched the railing. The color drained from her face.

"What is it?"

"I . . . I can't," she stumbled over her words. "I'm afraid . . . I'll fall."

"Fall?" He stood on the step below. "Is it stairs? You went up okay."

Her gaze glued on the steps.

"Okay, don't look down, look at me." He reached for her hand that gripped the railing. "Give me your hand."

She trembled, her breathing labored.

"Hannah, listen to me. I'm right here. You're not going to fall. I won't let you." He gently pried her hand from the rail. "Breathe."

Her nostrils flared with fear like a skittish horse.

"One step at a time. Come with me." He stepped down and waited for her to follow.

A tear escaped and rolled down her cheek. She glanced down and stiffened.

"Look at me."

She fixed her eyes on him, lifted her foot, and stepped down. Her hand clenched his.

"That's it. One more."

She placed her other foot on the step. One by one, he walked her down the stairs, talking to her, soothing her fears.

He waited in the entryway, holding her till her breathing returned to normal and she stopped trembling.

"I'm so sorry." She covered her face with her hands. "I don't know what's wrong with me."

"You have a head injury." *You're lucky to be alive.* "Probably better if you sleep down here."

The front door busted opened, and Lucky tromped inside carrying Toby. "Look what I found."

Good thing Toby was easygoing, because he didn't appear comfortable with his long body stretched out from Lucky's arms, exposing his underbelly and dangling his legs. Gold eyes pleaded to be saved from the situation.

"Here." Luke took the big cat from Lucky. "That's not the way to carry a cat." He petted Toby on the head then set him on the floor, granting him his freedom.

Bear trotted inside to the rug in front of the woodstove, circled twice, and plopped down. Toby brushed Hannah's legs, rubbed his cheek against her, and broke into a loud purr.

"Oh, how cute." She always was a cat person.

Luke closed the door before all the heat escaped.

She bent down and petted Toby. "Lucky, what have you been doing?"

"Exploring with Bear." Mud caked his shoes, and grass stains streaked the knees of his now-damp jeans. "Down by the stream that runs behind the barn."

"Lucky, you're not to go near the stream by yourself," Hannah scolded.

"Why?"

She blinked at her son. Did she remember her younger brother drowned in the fast-running Kootenai Creek?

She pressed her hand to head. "Just do what I ask." She went into the kitchen, and Toby followed.

Luke knelt in front of his son. "Lucky, I don't want you at the creek on your own, okay?"

"All right. Gosh." He folded his arms and pouted.

"Take your shoes off on the porch and come back inside." Luke rubbed Lucky's head. He'd deal with the kid's pouting later.

For now, he joined Hannah in the kitchen. His sister had stocked the fridge and cabinets right down to Lucky Charms for cereal. Samantha had outdone herself with the flowers on the kitchen table, new dishes in the cabinets, glasses; even new bed covers, towels, and shower curtain. But the half dozen pillows on the bed were over the top.

He wasn't sure what to think about the framed picture she extracted from her archives. He remembered when the picture was taken. They met at the park for Western Days. Sam had them sit in the grass while she took the picture. One week later, they drove her to Walla Walla.

"I don't mind cooking," he offered.

"No, I see we have the makings for spaghetti. I can manage." She removed a jar of sauce from the cabinet. "Besides I need to get to know my way around this kitchen sooner or later." She shrugged. "I'm sure it will all come back to me eventually."

He offered a nod of encouragement. Yes, he was sure her memories would come back. In the meantime, he'd win her heart all over again in hopes she'd stay.

Toby watched Hannah from the corner of the kitchen. He let out one of his cute hey-pay-attention–to-me meows.

"What does he want?"

"Food. You're near his canned food." Luke pointed to the stack of short cans in the cabinet.

"Oh, are you hungry?" She read a label. "How about savory whitefish dinner in gravy?" She held up the can for Toby to see.

Toby sat back on his hind legs and waved his paw in affirmation.

"Did you just see what he did?" Enchanted by Toby's antics, she laughed.

Luke leaned on the counter, watching his cat score points. "That's his way of saying yes."

"That's the cutest thing I've ever seen."

Toby definitely won her heart.

"Does he do other tricks?" Lucky knelt down on the floor by Toby.

"That's the extent of his talent."

His son held out his hand to the cat. "Can you shake?" But Toby heard the distinct sound of the lid peeling back from his canned food and couldn't be bothered with Lucky.

Luke squeezed Lucky's shoulder. "After he has his dinner, you can work on teaching him more tricks."

"Cool." Lucky jumped to his feet.

Luke headed from the kitchen to the truck. He

brought their suitcases in then went out to the barn to check on things. He removed his cell phone and called his sister.

"Thank you," he said when she answered.

"How is she?"

He rested against a horse stall. "She's got a ways to go. She had a panic attack in Lewiston. Then here, she couldn't go down the stairs. Something about feeling like she was going to fall."

"Poor thing. When can I come see her?"

"Give us a couple of days. I need to get her a doctor and into physical therapy."

"Will you be putting Lucky in school?"

"No, I plan to homeschool him for a bit until I can check out some schools in the area. He can't go to public school; he's two years ahead of his grade."

"There's Valley Christian."

He glanced over his shoulder at the house. "Yeah, I was going to check into that."

"How are you doing?"

Interesting question. "What do you mean?"

"How's your heart?"

He wasn't one to discuss his feelings, least of all with his little sister. "I'm okay."

"I can imagine it must be nerve wracking waiting for her memory to return and at the same time dreading it."

"You did a real nice job with the place." He changed the subject. "You think you have enough pillows on the bed?"

"That's the way girls like it."

He grabbed some hay and tossed it in the stall for Branson. "Thank you for stocking the kitchen."

"You didn't have hardly anything in those cabinets. Stale crackers, peanut butter, and protein bars."

"I'm not here much."

"You do realize your life will never be the same?"

He brushed his hands clean on his jeans. "Thanks for stating the obvious."

"Irene wants to know when you're bringing Hannah and Lucky over."

"Maybe next weekend. Right now, I'm taking one day at a time."

"When have you done differently?"

"Thanks again, Sam. Give everyone my best."

Not wanting it to be obvious that she hadn't been living at the house, he decided to leave the rest of the things in the truck. He would deal with Lucky's bike, toy box, and Hannah's stuff later. He pulled the truck into the garage and returned to the house.

That night, the Daniels family shared dinner together for the first time. He could get used to nights like this. After they loaded the dishwasher and cleaned up the kitchen, they retired to the living room and watched a television show. A popular reality program about a wealthy businessman who helps struggling entrepreneurs.

Hannah sat beside him, her stocking feet resting on the coffee table edge. "Their gross profit margin is too low. They have to cut cost or increase their prices."

He raised an eyebrow. "You really like this show, don't you?"

"It's Mom's favorite." Lucky rolled over on the floor and rested his head on Bear.

Her eyes narrowed and she shook her head. "Their profit margin is too low."

Not only was she good with numbers, but she apparently had a head for business. Wait till she gets a hold of his books. They're a mess.

When they went to bed, Luke brought Hannah her flannel nightgown, fuzzy socks, and toothbrush.

She took the items. "I'm sorry about this."

Taken back, he stuttered. "Sorry for what?"

"For having to sleep down here."

He grappled for something to set her mind at ease. "It's not forever."

She rose up on her toes and gave him a quick kiss. "Goodnight." She turned and went down the hall to the guest room.

Before going up to bed, Luke checked in on Lucky who was fast asleep.

At four in the morning, he tossed back the heavy purple comforter, almost tripped over a pillow on his way to the closet, and dressed. Then he crept downstairs and went to work emptying the truck and hauling upstairs all of Hannah's personal belongings. He set the toy trunk and bike in the back of the garage. By six, he had everything put away, right where it belonged.

Hannah woke to the dim morning light filtering through the wood blinds. She slept hard, and if she dreamed, she didn't remember. It was peaceful, quiet here. The aches and pains diminished; her cuts and bruises were healing. As she sat up, the room tilted. She braced her hands on either side until the dizziness subsided.

The alarm clock beside the bed informed her it was a little after nine. Lucky would be very late for school. She threw back the covers and stood. Her balance compromised, she steadied herself with a hand on the door until she regained her equilibrium.

She wrapped her robe around her, slipped her feet into fuzzy slippers, and padded out into the living area. The lemony scent of baked goods drifted toward her, along with the nutty scent of rich coffee. Luke and Lucky sat at the dining room table hunched over a textbook. A laptop was open, and Luke instructed his son on the finer points of simple fractions.

Hannah grasped the back of the chair. "Lucky, aren't you going to be late for school?"

Luke and Lucky exchanged glances.

"I don't go to school, Mom."

She combed her fingers through her hair. "What do you mean you don't go to school?"

"I'm homeschooled."

Luke rubbed his hand over his mouth. "Just for now. While you're healing, then he'll go back to school."

"Is the school okay with this?"

Luke stood. "It's temporary."

152

"I go to a private school."

"What's wrong with public school?"

Lucky chuckled. "I can't be in the fifth grade; I'll get beat up. And I can't go to third grade; I'll get bored."

She pressed her hand to her head, trying to follow what her son was saying. "You're not old enough to be in fifth grade."

Luke interrupted before Lucky could get in another word. "What Lucky is trying to say is he's in fifth-grade studies, but he's the age of a third grader."

"I have a high IQ," her son boasted.

Luke held up his hands. "Not from me. He's got your brains."

She frowned. "I'm sorry. I didn't remember."

"That's okay, Mom. We're making new memories."

Her throat seized shut at her son's tender words. Such a dear sweet boy. She swallowed hard to keep her tears back. "Now I know why I call you Lucky. I'm very lucky to have you in my life."

Lucky beamed and glanced at his father who smiled back.

Luke headed for the kitchen. "Would you like some coffee?"

"Dad made scones, and they're really good."

Luke shrugged. "They came from a box."

"Yes, thank you." She massaged the back of her neck. Wasn't Lucky going to school when they were visiting her parents? No, he was getting his lessons by e-mail. Her accident was keeping Lucky from going back to school.

153

Tears pricked her eyes.

If she could go back in time . . .

Luke moved through the kitchen with ease, placing a scone on a plate, pouring her a cup of coffee, and sitting her down at the table. He seemed to enjoy taking care of her.

"Can I get you anything else?"

"Can I have some cream and sugar?" she asked.

"On the way." He grabbed a carton of half-and-half from the refrigerator and a sugar container from the counter along with a spoon.

His attentiveness touching.

"Dad, when can we go fishing?"

"Once the water warms and spring runoff has subsided. Besides, you have homework to do, and I have work to get done."

Her accident no doubt caused an interruption in Luke getting his work done. Again, she was so sorry for all of this. She sipped the rich, bold coffee and bit into the moist, warm lemon poppy-seed scone.

"Next weekend is Valentine's Day," Lucky said. "Are you taking Mom to dinner?"

"Uh." Luke's mouth dropped open, and his eyes grew large. "I haven't thought about it."

She smiled at his obvious discomfort.

"I guess we could get Samantha to keep an eye on you while we. . ." His eyes brightened. "We could do something nice."

"I'm not sure I want to go out. It's just. . ." How could

she put into words her fear of getting into a situation that could embarrass them both?

Luke placed his hand on her shoulder. "We could do something here at home."

"Yeah. Mom, you can make Dad a nice dinner, and Dad can get you roses."

"All right, Lucky, I don't need your help on how to romance your mother."

Eyes a sparkle, mouth spread wide, their son was too pleased with himself.

Chapter Fifteen

Hannah patted her hair dry with a towel and ran a comb through the wet strands. Seeing movement out of the corner of her eye, she turned toward the door. But no one was there.

"Lucky?" She peeked out the door and down the hall, but she didn't see her son. Across the hall, he wasn't in his room either.

She padded down the hall and scanned the living room, but again no Lucky. Odd, she thought she saw him in the bathroom doorway.

Draped on the back of the couch, absorbing the rays of sun streaming through the south-facing windows, Toby sprang to his feet. Fully alert, he stared toward the dining room, arched his back, and hissed.

"Toby!" She hurried to the sliding door to see what the cat could possibly be hissing at. Another cat? A raccoon? But nothing was on the deck.

The cat leaped from the couch, scurried under the

dining room table, and with a menacing scowl, glared out the sliding glass door.

She rubbed the stiff hairs on her arms and shivered. "There's nothing there, silly cat."

But Toby wasn't convinced. His tail twitched as he stared out the sliding glass door.

Lucky tromped in through the front door. "Hi, Mom."

She glanced out the kitchen window. Luke stood talking with another man.

"Who's with your father?"

"Wade. He helps Dad around here with the cows and is helping build the cabins." Lucky sat at the kitchen table and opened up the laptop.

"Cabins?"

"Yeah, the cabins at the foot of the mountains."

"Why are they building cabins?"

"For the guiding business. Wade helps Dad with that, too. He was in the war."

"What war?"

"Afghan."

"Afghanistan?"

"Yeah. He was over there and got hurt with a bomb. He has PS . . . uh, PD . . . something that makes him jittery."

"Post-traumatic stress disorder?"

Lucky shrugged.

She guessed him to be in his mid-thirties and in good shape. An attractive man, he didn't seem wounded. By the interaction between the two men, she could tell they were close. She tried to recall meeting Wade, knowing him, but nothing came to mind. Not even a trusted impression. Hannah slipped into a sweater, put on her boots, and stepped out the slider to meet Wade. Toby dashed past her, bumping her leg.

Wade nodded her way. "Howdy, ma'am."

"Hello. Wade, right?"

"That's right." He tipped his black cowboy hat. A scar ran just above his left eye. Several days' growth covered his face. His green eyes appeared to hold the storms of life.

"Wade and I were just talking about this old barn. Trying to determine how much life it might have in it."

"Do you live close by?" she asked.

He pointed east. "Just up the road on the other side."

A breeze caressed her cheeks. "Can I interest you two in some coffee or hot tea?"

Wade spoke first. "No thank you. I've got work to do."

Luke placed a gloved hand on her back. "Thank you, but I won't be much longer."

"Some other time?" She wanted to know Luke's friends—their friends.

Wade patted Luke on the shoulder. "Well, my friend, you take care."

It wasn't until Wade headed toward his truck that Hannah caught the extent of his injuries. He walked with a slight limp. She stiffened—he was wearing a prosthetic on his left leg. His jeans fit loose over the device.

Embarrassed she was staring, Hannah turned back

toward the house.

After dropping Hannah off at her first physical therapy appointment, Luke and Lucky went grocery shopping. Luke had wanted to stay with Hannah, be there for her in case she needed him. But an eight-year-old's patience wasn't enough to sit in a doctor's office for over an hour with nothing to do but read "baby" books.

"I'll be fine," Hannah assured him. "Go, get your errands done."

Luke kept his cell phone in his coat pocket, the ringer on high and vibrate switched on, making sure he didn't miss a call. Pushing a cart around the grocery store, he thought about what to make for their special dinner. He didn't need meat, not with his freezer full of every kind of cut—elk, deer, even bear. A whole salmon, too. The problem was he wasn't sure what Hannah liked.

"Can I have Cocoa Berry's?" Lucky pulled down a box of the sugary cereal.

"No, I'd prefer you eat something healthier." Luke grabbed a box of almond granola and dropped it in the cart.

Down the frozen food isle, Lucky asked. "Can I have some Moose Tracks ice cream?"

Luke gave in to the ice cream but put the kibosh on the soda. The kid was too wound up as is; he didn't need all that sugar.

Wendy Holley

Determined to feed his kid and Hannah what was healthy, Luke bought apples, broccoli, potatoes, onions, and salad fixings. For a snack, he picked up two kinds of granola bars—peanut butter chocolate chip and cinnamon apple. A package of whole wheat bread, although he wasn't one for sandwiches, but he saw Samantha put peanut butter and jam in the cabinet. He'd have to make sure to instruct Sam to keep the sugar to a minimum when she took Lucky for the night.

Luke loaded everything on the conveyor belt. The young couple in front of them seemed an odd combination. The girl was very pregnant and hardly looked old enough to be expecting. She wasn't wearing a ring. She swiped the card through the credit card machine, the logo revealed they paid with a state benefits' card. The guy seemed a good ten years her senior, probably about his age. Why wasn't the guy working this time of day? In the winter months, things could get tight in the valley, but the log home manufacturers were always hiring. That's what he'd done for several years as he built his business—built log homes in the winter months.

"Dad, can I have a candy bar?"

"No, Lucky. I've got granola bars."

"Yuck, I don't like granola bars."

He really needed to put a stop to the whining.

Remembering the advice from Hannah's letter, Luke sought the best way to handle the situation. "Tell you what, you can have a candy bar." He snatched the ice cream from the conveyor and handed Lucky the carton. "If

160

you put this back."

His little mouth dropped open. "But I want ice cream."

"You can't have both. Your choice, ice cream or candy." Luke's fingers ached from the cold as he held the carton.

Lucky crossed his arms and stuck out his lower lip. "That's not fair."

Luke needed to address this pouting issue, too. "Make your choice."

Realizing he had the attention of the couple in front of them and the cashier, Lucky pushed harder to get his way. "I don't like you." His son's face squinched. "You're mean."

Like a dagger to his heart, his son's words wounded him. But he wasn't going to be manipulated by an eight-year-old. "I don't care if you like me. But you will respect me. Now, I'm your father, and I say no candy." He placed the ice cream on the conveyor, unable to feel anything in the tips of his numb fingers.

"You're not my dad. My name is Lucas Brady."

His temper sparked. "Your name is Lucas Daniels. Now, Lucas, you knock this off, or I'm putting the ice cream back."

"You wouldn't."

"Don't try my patience." His blood simmered.

"You do, and I'll go home and tell Mom everything she can't remember."

Luke's temper flared. Heat rose up his neck. He clenched his hands into a fist and was sorely tempted to swat Lucky right there in the store. He would not put up with his kid making ultimatums and endangering Hannah's well-being.

"Go outside and wait for me in the truck." He managed to say in a voice with a calm he didn't feel.

The young couple finished their transaction and grabbed their bags.

Lucky marched out of the store, arms crossed and muttering defeat. Luke drank in deep, calming breaths. "I don't want the ice cream." He removed the carton from the belt.

The cashier smiled thinly. "How old is he?"

"Eight. He's been through hell lately. His mother was in a serious car accident."

"I'm so sorry. How is she?" Sympathy resonated in her voice.

"Recovering."

"Well, if it helps any, you handled that well."

He shook his head. He had no experience in how to handle a defiant, hurting kid.

"Most parents give in, and it only gets worse when they do."

His hands trembled as he swiped his debit card and entered his pin. "Thank you." He pushed the cart outside to the truck.

Lucky leaned against the passenger door, his legs crossed at his ankles, his arms crossed and his head down. Luke was tempted to ask why he didn't follow his instructions and wasn't inside the truck rather than standing outside, but decided that was a battle not worth fighting. He opened the rear passenger door and stacked the groceries on the seat. Then he opened Lucky's door, and without a word, his son climbed up inside.

Luke slid in behind the wheel, but Lucky hadn't fastened his seatbelt. Luke fastened his seatbelt and sat with his keys in his hand.

"Aren't we going?" Lucky asked, his tone challenging.

"Not until you fasten your seatbelt."

Blue-gray eyes, filled with defiance, glared at him. He waited for his son, and eventually, Lucky complied. *How long is this battle going to last? Was he like this at eight? God help him if he was.* He remembered an episode in the grocery store, a fit on the floor and his mother simply stepping over him and going on her way. Incensed, he got up and stomped after her.

"Look at me," he demanded of his mother.

"I can't, Luke. When you're like this, it hurts my eyes," his mother responded while reaching for something on the shelf.

That night when he got home, his dad gave him a paddling to make sure he understood never to treat his mother with disrespect.

Luke started the truck. The doors auto-locked. He called the therapy office. "Is Hannah ready?"

"Not for another thirty minutes."

Enough time to race home and put the groceries away.

"I think when we get home," he glanced over at Lucky, "I'll need to give you a paddling for your behavior."

Lucky's eyes widened, and he pressed himself up against the door. "But Mom never spanks me."

"Well then, you're probably overdue." Way overdue. "Is this how you treat your mother?"

"No."

"That's good because I better never hear or see you treat her with disrespect."

They drove home in silence. Lucky helped carry the groceries inside.

"Son, thank you for helping me. While I put things away, I'd like you to go to your room and wait for me."

"But—" Lucky's voice cracked.

"Do as I say."

Lucky shuffled down the hall to his room. As Luke put the groceries away, he dreaded the thought of spanking his kid. It tore at his heart. With his temper diffused, now he was left with a deep slice in his heart.

He warred within himself.

On the one hand, he could spank his son and give him a lesson he hoped he'd never forget. On the other, maybe just the thought of a spanking was enough. But if he didn't discipline Lucky, he'd most likely act out again.

Luke leaned over the counter near the sink. "God, I don't know what to do. Help me do the right thing."

There he goes again, talking to God. Must be a sign of his desperation.

He wished he could talk this over with Hannah. Or better yet, his mother. His mother would know what to do. His heart ached, missing her.

164

Luke walked into his son's room and sat on the twin bed beside him. "Do you understand why I'm upset?"

Lucky nodded but didn't make eye contact. "Because I was a brat."

"You were disrespectful and manipulative."

His son lowered his head. "I'm sorry, Dad." The words were barely audible.

It was a start. "Excuse me? I'm not sure I heard you."

Lucky looked him in the eye, swallowed hard, and said, "I'm sorry. I won't do it again."

"That's what I needed to hear. Now, since you've apologized and you won't do this again, I won't spank you." Luke hid his relief.

The kid released a big sigh.

Luke stood. "We better go get your mother."

"Are you going to tell her what I did?" Pleading blue-gray eyes met his.

He rubbed his chin, making it appear like he was giving it some consideration. "No, not this time. This is between us men."

Lucky nodded again.

In the truck on the way to the therapist's office, Lucky asked, "Who were those people in front of us in line?"

"What people?"

"That man and a girl who had a big belly."

"I don't know."

"They talked to me outside."

"They did? What did they say?"

"They wanted to know Mom's name."

The man's face flashed in his memory. There was something familiar about the guy, but living in the valley all his life that happened a lot. But . . . there was something about him, something in his brown eyes. And a hint of recognition on his face when he glanced at Luke. Then a flash of surprise when he saw Lucky.

"Did you tell them?"

"Yes."

"What did they say?"

"'Figures, I knew it. I think they know Mom."

Luke's hands grew sweaty. His heart raced. "Did they say what their names were?"

Lucky shook his head. "No, oh wait. She called him David."

David Brady, Hannah's twin brother. Great, now they know she's back.

Chapter Sixteen

David carried the grocery bags inside and set them on the kitchen counter. Jenny, his half-sister, waddled into the living room and lowered herself onto the faded couch then turned on the television.

"Can you believe that kid back-talking like that?" Jenny called from the other room. "What kind of a mother raises a kid to behave like that?"

That was the least of his concern. Hannah had been in a car accident. A serious one. From what her son said, it left her with some memory loss. But where had she been these last nine years? Had Luke kept her hidden all this time?

Something didn't add up.

He headed for the door. "Call if you need anything."

"You're leaving?" Her voice rose above the drone of a daytime talk show host.

This wasn't his house. Soon, her no-good husband would return, and David didn't want to run into the likes of Jacob Mitchell. "You needed groceries. Now, you're stocked up for a while."

She leaned back with a heavy sigh. "Fine. Some big brother you are."

His shoulders tensed. He wasn't going to be baited into a verbal sparring match. The fact that he picked her up and took her to the grocery store proved he wasn't a heartless jerk like Jacob.

He pulled open the front door. "Next time, call on one of the Mitchell wives for help."

"They don't like me."

No big surprise. Jennifer was young and pretty but had the disposition of a cornered feral cat. The youngest of his father's daughters, she was spoiled. Jen hadn't been treated like the rest of his siblings. She learned early how to get her older siblings to do her chores. She'd pretend she didn't know how or would do such a poor job, someone would be sent in to redo what she messed up.

Still, pregnant, she needed help. He closed the door behind him.

David climbed into the truck and started the engine. Nine years his sister, his twin, was gone. No goodbye, no explanation. Later, he learned why she probably left. Still, Hannah's disappearance stung.

He needed to find out where she'd been. Why surface in the valley now after all these years? Did she know about Pa? Maybe that's it. She found out Pa isn't well and came back. Or maybe this accident of hers had something to do with it. How bad was she hurt?

If Luke had kept her hidden away and brought her back, how long had she been back?

Curling his fingers around the steering wheel, he headed toward the valley. A new mission set before him. Find out what had happened to Hannah.

Something was going on between Luke and Lucky; she could feel it ever since they picked her up from therapy. Her son was unusually quiet and her husband unusually talkative.

"Everything go well in therapy?" Luke asked as he navigated the truck onto the highway.

She shrugged. "I guess so." But she wasn't sure. "As I sat on the ball and closed my eyes, I couldn't lift my foot off the floor without losing my balance. Bending over to touch my toes is impossible without falling over."

Luke reached for her hand. "It's going to take time."

She nodded. "How about you guys? How'd your afternoon go?"

Luke glanced up in the rearview mirror. She turned to see Lucky's eyes grow wide. He lowered his head.

What was going on?

"We picked up groceries. How does salmon sound for this weekend?"

"I think I like salmon."

From the back seat, Lucky said, "You do."

Luke rattled off everything he bought at the grocery store and kept looking in the rearview mirror at Lucky.

Luke smiled at her. "I even bought a bottle of wine."

Her heart lifted at his attentiveness. "I appreciate you planning our dinner."

She squeezed his hand. The strength and warmth in his hand and the simple intimacy warmed her and gave her hope that soon she'd recover. Soon, their lives could return to normal. Whatever that might be.

Luke took on so much more since her accident. Her husband worked with Lucky on his homework, cooked for them, and did all of the shopping. All while running the ranch and working on building cabins. He needed her well again.

Once home, Luke and Lucky went outside. She entered the office and worked on redesigning the business website. As she worked, making the main page, she had the sense it was something she'd done before. After she had drawn out each page on a separate piece of paper, she taped them to the wall. They needed pictures of the outings, fishing trips, and hunting expeditions.

Opening the closet, she searched through the boxes for one containing photos, but only found bank records, receipts in envelopes, and booklets of duplicate checks. Nothing was arranged by date or in any kind of order. It made no sense—she was usually very organized. Right?

In the room at the end of the hall, the one where she slept, hopefully not for much longer, she opened the closet. No boxes, no photo albums, just her clothes, a spare blanket, and a pillow.

Hannah walked through the living room. Toby raised

his head then rolled over to his back stretching in the sun. She ascended three steps before catching herself and stopped.

Glancing up the stairs, she waited for fear to sweep over her, but it didn't come. She sighed and stepped up to the fourth and paused. No fear, no panic attack, no concern. She took two more steps and froze. The living room far below her. She clutched the railing in a damp hand. Her heart beat fast.

You can do this. She struggled to breathe and broke into a cold sweat. Her legs faltered.

She sat on the step and worked to calm her breathing, slow her heart rate. She longed for life to return to normal, and that required that *she* return to normal.

Hannah lowered her head and closed her eyes, willing the fear to subside. "Lord, please."

Outside, Lucky laughed.

"That's it. Good job." Luke's deep voice carried from the porch.

She scooted down a few steps. Through the window at the bottom of the landing, she watched them.

"Aim to set it nice and easy in the circle I drew," Luke instructed Lucky on the fine art of casting a lure. As her husband taught their son, he was so patient and encouraging. Her heart swelled.

Luke deserved a wife who was whole, not broken. She wanted to sleep beside him, not in the guestroom. Turning around, she scrutinized the steps leading to their bedroom. If she could go up and down the stairs without freaking out, she could sleep with her husband.

You have to get past this.

Hannah took a deep breath and marched up several steps before she stopped. Her legs like limp noodles, she couldn't bring herself to take another step. She sat on the ninth step and edged down one by one. Scooting, sitting, scooting and sitting until reaching the bottom. She pulled herself to her feet, disappointment weighing down her limbs. Before she could force herself to do it again, the phone rang.

She reached it before Luke could get to it. "Hello," she answered.

"Oh, Hannah, how are you?" Her fear dissolved at the sound of her mother's voice.

Luke poked his head in the door. She raised her thumb to give him the okay it was for her then turned her attention back to her mother. "I'm feeling better." But she left unsaid that stairs terrified her.

"I wanted to check and see how things are going?"

Her mother's voice brought a big smile to her face. "They're going . . . good." Aside from the fact that she can't remember much about her life and the occasional headache and sore muscles.

"You don't sound certain."

"I'm just . . . I don't know." She crossed her arms as she searched for the words to explain.

"I'm listening." The encouraging words came across the line.

Hannah touched her forehead. "I still get dizzy

sometimes, and I can't seem to go upstairs."

"Is physical therapy helping?"

"Not so much. My balance is off."

"Give yourself time, Hannah. It takes time to heal."

"I know." She couldn't hide her disappointment.

"Have you had any memories come back?"

"No, and Luke refuses to talk about our past. He says the doctors advised him to let my memory return on its own and not to force it."

"That's true. Will you be seeing a neurologist or mental health professional?"

"We haven't pursued that."

"It might help."

But did she want to? What if she and Luke were having marital problems? Maybe that's why he wouldn't discuss any aspect of their past.

"How is Lucky doing?"

"He's happy as can be. His daddy is teaching him how to cast a lure and hit the mark. He's getting quite good."

"And his studies?"

"Well, we're still homeschooling him. But we're talking about putting him in a Christian school. It's probably time he goes to school."

"He was doing good in . . . private school."

"That's what I gather. But until I can drive again, it will be hard for Luke to do so much."

Her mother sighed heavily. "Have you checked your e-mail lately?"

"Uh, no." She leaned against the kitchen counter. "I'm

embarrassed to say I didn't think about it."

"That's understandable." Her mother changed the subject. "Are you going to go to church this weekend?"

"I haven't thought about that either. I'm not sure about being around a lot of people just yet. Sunday is Valentines, and Luke and I are just going to stay home."

"That will be . . . fun."

"Yes. Samantha is coming to take Lucky for the evening. Give us some time alone."

"Oh, that's nice." Tension heightened her mother's voice. "You know, Hannah, you'll want to be careful. Now is not the time for you to have another baby."

"I know. My body needs to heal."

"We all miss you and love you."

Miss me? What an odd thing for her mother to say. As if she's there all the time.

Lucky rushed in through the side door, tracking in dirt and mud. "Dad's going to put me on Dakota." He sped toward his room.

"Wait a minute." Hannah returned to the phone conversation. "I better go."

"Tell Lucky we love him."

"I will. Love you." She placed the phone back on the wall and hurried toward Lucky's room. "Goodness, Lucky, you just tracked in dirt. You need to wipe your feet before coming inside."

"Sorry, Mom." He had pulled open a dresser drawer and tossed several T-shirts on the bed.

"What are you doing?" She grasped a T-shirt and

folded it.

He yanked a gray sweatshirt from the drawer. "I need my sweatshirt. It's getting cold." He dropped his jacket on the floor and slipped the sweatshirt over his head.

She picked up the discarded coat and helped her son slip back into it. She snatched a pair of gloves off the dresser. "Here, wear these."

He darted for the kitchen and climbed up onto the counter. "I'm hungry." He removed a box of graham crackers and peanut butter from the shelf.

"Be careful." They need to get him a step stool. She slathered peanut butter on a cracker and poured him a glass of water.

"Is Dad out there yet?"

She glanced out the window. "He's putting the saddle on now."

"I have to hurry." He shoved a cracker in his mouth.

He stood at the table eating while she grabbed a few paper towels and dampened one. She picked up pieces of mud and wiped the damp cloth over the wood. The room shifted. She swayed, and before she could catch herself, she fell over.

"Ouch." She rubbed her right arm. Feeling foolish, she sat up. The spell ended.

"You okay, Mom?" Lucky blinked down at her with a smudge of peanut butter on his cheek.

"Yes, I'm fine." Struggling to stand, she couldn't coordinate her legs and balance.

"Here, let me help." Lucky offered her his hand.

Fearing she'd pull him over, she rejected his offer with a shake of her head. "Get your dad."

Lucky took off out the same door he entered.

A moment later, Luke sprinted into the house. "Lucky said you fell."

"Not far." Heat infused her cheeks.

"Are you okay?" He bent and ran his hands over her arms and legs as if checking for a broken bone.

"I'm fine. Embarrassed is all."

He put his hands under her arms and lifted her to her feet. "Can you stand?"

"Yes. I just lost my balance." It's not like she fainted.

"Come sit down." He guided her to the couch.

"Really, I'm fine now." He's making too much of a fuss.

"What happened?" He sat beside her.

"I bent over to wipe the floor and got dizzy. I lost my balance and fell." She massaged her sore arm.

"Are you dizzy now?"

She shook her head.

He addressed Lucky. "Maybe we should save riding Dakota for later."

She cringed. "No, don't change your plans. Really, I'm fine. In fact, I'd love to see the horses."

Luke hedged.

"Let me just get my coat and scarf." She stood, tested her balance, and, when assured she was okay, walked down the hall. She opened the closet and rummaged through her clothes, searching for her red scarf, but it wasn't there.

Right. Most of her clothes were upstairs. She came back out. "I forgot." She shrugged at the irony of her words. "My things are upstairs." Why did she think her room was down the hall? Because it is—for now.

Luke jumped to his feet. "What do you need? I'll get it for you."

"My coat and red cashmere scarf."

He sprinted upstairs.

"Hey, I remembered something."

He peered over the banister. Luke and Lucky exchanged glances.

"My red scarf."

A shadow passed over Luke's eyes before he disappeared into the bedroom. It took a few minutes for him to appear at the railing. "This one?" He brandished the scarf.

Looking up, she rubbed the back of her neck. "Yes, thank you."

"You want your ski jacket?" he asked, leaning over the railing.

"Yes."

He came back down. "Here, I brought your gloves, too."

Lucky led the way to the barn with Bear right beside him. Luke clasped her hand as they crossed the back yard. The simple pleasure of feeling his big strong hand around hers was something she never wanted to forget.

He untied Dakota from the fence and lifted Lucky onto

his back.

"Wow, this is cool." Lucky sat tall in the saddle.

"Sit forward," Luke instructed, and with the fluid ease of someone used to riding, he got on Dakota behind Lucky. His arms on either side of their son, he held the reins and guided the horse out of the barn.

Why, at Lucky's age, did this appear to be his first horse-riding lesson? It made her smile, seeing the two of them together, enjoying themselves galloping around the yard.

Inside the barn, a horse snorted. Hannah approached the big black horse and ran her gloved hand along the white splash on his nose. "What's the matter, big fella? You want a ride, too?"

His big tail swooshed. In the next stall, a chestnut mare munched on hay. Her belly swollen with a colt.

"Well, look at you. You're about ready to give birth."

A memory of her belly swollen with Lucky surfaced. She held her hand to her stomach and tried to hold on to the memory, but it fled as quickly as it came. She turned around to something large covered under a blue tarp. Hannah peeled back the tarp. An old, red and white Chevy pickup sat covered in dust.

Memories of sitting in the truck beside Luke flooded her mind. Another memory of sitting between him and Samantha flashed. Samantha's shoulder-length blonde hair caught in the breeze from the open window.

A hole opened in her heart and ached with missing Samantha. She wanted to see her friend. Where was Sam?

Why hadn't she come to see her?

The truck appeared before her, its paint bright having just been washed. It was a warm summer night; Luke drove them to the farm. The house was quiet, empty except for a few pieces of random furniture, including a bed upstairs. Her heart pounded. She was afraid yet excited. Uncertain and yet confident.

"I love you." His lips brushed hers.

She rose on her toes and wrapped her arms around his neck.

"Hannah?"

She spun around. Luke stood in the bright sunshine streaming through the open barn doors.

"Is everything okay?"

She stared at him, seeing him younger until he stepped out of the bright light toward her. Doubt and fear clouded his eyes.

She let the tarp drop from her hand. "You kept the truck."

He shrugged and shoved his hands in his front jeans pockets. "It's not worth anything. Nobody is going to buy it."

"It's worth the memories."

He nodded. "You remember the truck?"

She sighed. "With fondness."

His shoulders dropped as if he'd been holding his breath, steeling himself for something. "Do you remember anything else?"

She lowered her gaze as a bout of shyness swept over

her. It was silly, of course, to be too shy to talk about their first time. "I remember the night in the old farmhouse."

Chapter Seventeen

His heart slammed against his ribs. He swallowed hard and waited for what else she remembered.

"I guess we were too young and too poor to honeymoon anywhere else."

Honeymoon? Dumbfounded, he couldn't respond.

Lucky led Dakota into the barn. "Hey, Dad, when can I ride Lightning?"

He didn't take his eyes off her. "Not until you're older."

"What are you guys doing?"

"Talking," Hannah said with a sweet smile.

"What about?"

The kid asked too many questions.

"Your father's old truck. I saw it in here, and I remembered it."

"Oh," Lucky responded and glanced up at him for reassurance.

"Come on, kid. We need to brush Dakota." He ruffled

the boy's hair and, with a protective hand on his back, led Lucky to the stall.

Lucky glanced back at Hannah then whispered, "Is it good that she remembered?"

"Yeah, it's good."

"Was it a good memory?"

"Yeah, it was a good memory." He lifted the saddle off Dakota.

"Dad?"

"Yeah, son."

"Maybe you ought to marry Mom," Lucky whispered.

Luke kept his voice low. "That's the plan. Just waiting for her to get all her memories back."

"What if she doesn't?"

"We'll cross that bridge when we get to it."

"I think you ought to sooner."

"Do what sooner?" Hannah asked.

Luke jumped. How much of the conversation had she heard?

"Get married," Lucky said.

"We are married."

"No, you're not."

Luke ribbed his son in the back.

Lucky staggered forward. "I mean you are, but you can't remember."

Hannah cocked her head, and her forehead wrinkled. She seemed to be trying to recall a memory that wasn't there. "Maybe you're right." Her eyes brightened. "We're making new memories now, right?" She smiled at Lucky.

Lucky's head bobbed up and down.

"What do you think?" she asked Luke.

He scrambled to find the right words. "If that's what you want."

She glanced at her hand, pulled off the glove, and fiddled with the pawnshop ring. A shadow of sadness swept across her face. "It would be nice to have that memory," she said almost to herself.

Luke really would prefer to do this right. To buy a beautiful ring with diamonds that sparkled, to get down on one knee, and ask for her hand in marriage, to have her get excited, jump up and down, cry, and say yes.

"Lucky put Dakota in the stall." He stepped in front of Hannah, and slipped his arm around her waist, and pulled her close. "Let's not worry about this right now."

"I wish I could remember—"

He cut off the rest of her words with a kiss. Her arms wrapped around his neck, and he deepened the kiss in hopes to wipe away the sadness. When they parted, her eyes were bright with a smile and something else that just about took him to his knees. Desire.

David walked along the back of Luke's property, staying on the other side of the swift-running stream, swollen with snow runoff. Thankfully, he knew the owners of the property bordering Luke's. For a year, he ranched for the older couple. That was when he learned Luke Daniels inherited his grandparents' property and was tearing

183

down the old house.

In all that time, though, he'd never caught a glimpse of his sister. Never even saw a clue that a woman was around. Luke must have kept her somewhere else. Missoula maybe? No, that was still too close to Pa and the Mitchells.

Maybe Hannah wasn't at Luke's. Maybe she was still hidden away somewhere. He intended to find out. But before he paid a visit to Luke, he'd best to get a feel for the situation. Besides, he wasn't sure he'd be welcomed on any Daniels property. Not after what his father had done.

Beneath his boots crunched a thin layer of crystallized snow. A voice carried on the cool breeze, and he paused, staying behind a sprawling old oak tree.

"I'm gonna catch me a big fish." A splash and a plunk followed the whiz of a reel.

The boy—Lucky—stood on the bank, casting his fishing rod. David groaned inwardly. The banks were soft this time of year, and the boy was standing way too close to the frigid water. Tempted to yell at Lucky to step back, he clenched his jaw. What if Luke was nearby and heard him? How would he explain lurking around the backside of his property?

What if the boy recognized him from the grocery store parking lot? It was Jenny who talked with him, and he had a full beard that day. He rubbed his fingers over the stubble on his chin.

Lucky reeled in the line and cast again. His feet slipped as the bank crumbled into the icy water.

David ran to the boy and caught him by the back of his jacket just before his feet hit the water. He hauled him away from the stream and dropped him in the snow. Lucky lay at his feet, blinking up at him with wide blue-gray eyes. Fear etched on his young face.

"You shouldn't be that close to the stream this time of year. You could've drowned."

Lucky sat up and dropped his rod beside him. "I didn't know."

"Yeah, well, now you do."

He struggled to his feet.

"Do your parents know you're out here?"

His eyes flashed. "Uh, yeah."

No. The kid was a lousy liar. "They let you fish this stream by yourself?"

The boy's lips thinned. "I can do what I want."

Defiant little pistol. David bit back a retort. This was an opportunity to find out more about Hannah. He shifted gears. "You're pretty good with that rod and reel."

"Thanks."

"You fish often?"

Lucky picked up his rod. "Used to."

"Who taught you how to fish?"

"My grandpa and Dane."

Grandpa? But Mr. Daniels died years ago. If he remembered correctly, it was just a couple years after Hannah disappeared. "Who's Dane?"

"My uncle . . . sort of."

"Where do you fish at?"

185

Lucky reeled in the line. "The pond mostly. It's on our property."

"I didn't know your dad had a pond."

"No, my grandpa's property. The vineyard in Walla Walla."

"Walla Walla, huh? Is that where you live?"

"Used to. We live here now with my dad."

"Been here long?"

"No, we just moved here. I found my dad on the Internet." Pride laced the kid's voice.

What did that mean? "You must be good with computers."

"I am. My mom taught me."

"What's your name?"

"Lucky, Lucky Br . . . Daniels."

David held out his hand. "Nice to meet you. I'm . . ." Best not to let Luke know he was spying on him and Hannah. "Jesse." He opted for his middle name. He wanted to ask about Hannah but couldn't risk making the kid suspicious. "Well, Lucky, your name fits you. It was a good thing I was patrolling the property here and happened to see you when I did."

The kid looked up at him, squinting at the sun. "You're not gonna tell my dad, are you?"

"No, I'll let you do that. Just do me a favor and stay away from the banks of this stream until about July."

"Why July?"

"Then the water is warmer and not moving so fast. Do you know how to swim?"

"Yeah."

"Good. You know the fish aren't biting this time of year?"

"They're not?"

"No, best to wait until June."

"Oh." Disappointment wrinkled his forehead. Man, he was the perfect combination of Hannah and Luke. Amazing.

"How did you get across the stream?"

"There's a tree that fell up there." Lucky pointed.

"I'll walk up there with you and make sure you get back across safely."

They ambled along the stream, staying back from the soft bank. Sure enough, a good-sized tree had given way and fallen across the stream. He wasn't entirely comfortable watching his nephew crawl across the tree, but plenty of limbs sprouted out in all directions providing handholds. He waited till Lucky landed safely on the other side.

"Hey, Lucky. Do me a favor and from now on, stay on that side of the stream."

"Yes, sir. Is that your property?"

"No, I'm just a hired hand." He turned back. "You take care of yourself," he said over his shoulder.

"I will."

As he walked back to his truck, David tried to put the pieces together. From what Lucky said, they recently moved here from Walla Walla. What did he mean by he found Luke on the Internet?

Wendy Holley

He stopped dead in his tracks. Luke didn't know about Lucky. Hannah must have left on her own, had Lucky, and never told Luke. That can't be. Pa was sure the Daniels family had helped Hannah run away. Could he have been wrong?

Chapter Eighteen

An older Subaru wagon proceeded up the driveway, crunching over the few inches of fresh snow that fell overnight. Hannah watched through the window as a blonde stepped out of the car and walked toward the door. Her heart jumped, recognizing her friend and sister-in-law.

She rushed to the door and pulled it open. "Samantha!"

A big, bright smile swept across her face. "Look at you. You look great."

They embraced on the porch. Powerful emotions of joy and deep affection seized Hannah as tears blurred her eyes. "I'm so happy to see you."

"I'm happy to see you." Tears shimmered in Samantha's eyes. "Now, don't be doing that. You're making me cry. I swore I wasn't going to cry."

"Come in." Hannah led her friend inside the warm house. A fire crackled in the woodstove. "It feels like years."

Samantha's smile faltered.

"I know it's silly. The coma messed up my sense of time."

Luke entered through the back door. "Hey, Sam."

Lucky followed. "Hello, Aunt Samantha." Lucky ran up to Samantha and hugged her.

Samantha stumbled back before catching her balance and wrapped her arms around him. She knelt and considered his face. "Well, aren't you the spittin' image of your daddy?"

"Every day I look more like him, don't I?"

"I don't doubt that." Samantha reached for Hannah. "It's so good to see you. How are you doing?"

"Better. Can I get you some coffee or tea? I don't know what you prefer."

Samantha brushed her hair from her shoulder. "Coffee, are you kidding me. I drink tons of the stuff."

Luke and Lucky took off their coats and boots, apparently residing to visit with the ladies.

Luke leaned against the counter. "Sam, did you hear back from that producer yet?"

"I did. He wants me to send him a demo along with a video."

Hannah scooped grounds into the paper filter. "What is this about?"

"I sent this producer in Nashville a song I wrote and recorded on CD. He liked it and wants to hear more. I'm hoping he'll fly me out for a visit and offer me a contract."

"You produce music?" The moment the words left her mouth, she knew it was true. "Of course, you do. Oh my gosh, that's exciting."

Samantha nodded.

"And how are things with you and Jared?" Sam wasn't wearing a ring.

Samantha's blue eyes dulled. "We're just friends."

"Jared's head is up his. . ." Luke caught himself and looked at Lucky.

But Lucky, being too smart for his own good, knew what his father was going to say. "His butt!" he blurted and broke into a fit of laughter.

"All right, Lucky, it's not that funny," Luke cautioned. "You got your overnight bag packed?"

"No."

"Well then, I think you ought to get that done."

Lucky tromped to his room.

Samantha frowned at Luke.

What happened between Samantha and Jared? Since they were kids, Jared had a crush on Samantha. They were sweethearts in high school.

Hannah wanted to ask what Jared was up to these days, but the hurt in her friend's eyes made her think twice. Something must have happened, wounding her friend terribly. Only if she could remember. She should know what happened. After all, Samantha was her best friend. Guilt mingled with frustration.

Hannah set cream and sugar on the table. "Thank you for taking Lucky and giving us some time together."

"Of course, I'm happy to do it. We're going to have fun."

"Don't let him wear you out."

"And," Luke added, "don't feed him a ton of sugar either."

Sam raised her right hand. "Scout's honor, I'll take good care of him."

Luke stood and walked down the hall toward Lucky's room.

Samantha's gaze roamed over Hannah. "Looks like quite the bump on your head."

Self-conscious, she touched her fingertips to her forehead. "Stitches come out next week. Bruises are almost gone. I wish my memory and balance would cooperate."

Sympathy softened Sam's eyes.

"So, if I ask a stupid question or say something silly, I hope you'll forgive me."

"Don't be so hard on yourself. You've been through a horrible ordeal."

Hannah went to check on the coffee brewing and removed cups from the cabinet.

Samantha propped her elbow on the counter and rested her chin in her hand. "You know, sometimes I think it might be nice to start parts of my life over, forgetting some of my past mistakes and be given a second chance."

Hannah poured two cups of coffee and set one in front of Sam. "Yes, but I haven't been able to remember things I'd like to."

"Such as?"

She glanced down the hall to hear Luke talking with Lucky. "The birth of my son."

Samantha's eyebrows drew together. "I'm sorry." She stirred a teaspoon of sugar and cream into her coffee and brought the cup to her lips.

"And my wedding day."

Sam spewed coffee and choked. "Sorry," she said hoarsely, grabbed a napkin, and dabbed her mouth. "Sorry, hot." Coughing, she covered her mouth.

"You all right?"

"Yeah," she croaked.

"We're talking about renewing our vows."

Sam's blue eyes widened. Her smile thinned. "That would be . . . nice."

Why was her tone so stiff? "I suppose you were my bridesmaid."

She gulped. "Will you excuse me just a moment?" Samantha hurried down the hall. The thick heals of her boots clicking on the wood floor.

Whispered voices drifted from Lucky's bedroom. What's all the fuss about? Hannah strolled down the hall.

"You can't," Lucky said in earnest.

"Can't what?" Hannah stood at the door.

The three of them exchanged glances.

Her friend appeared flushed.

"Take you shopping," Lucky blurted. "For a dress. Not until you're better."

Luke placed a hand on his son's shoulder. Lucky

winced.

"Thank you. That's sweet to offer. But until I have my balance back and, well. . ." She ran her fingers through her hair. Too embarrassed to admit that she was afraid to go out in public, feared stairs, crowds, and heaven knew what else might cause her to panic. She wasn't ready for a shopping trip.

The waitress set a steaming hot plate of hash browns and two eggs over easy in front of David. He smiled his appreciation then said a quick prayer. His stomach grumbled as the scent of greasy potatoes, grilled onions, and buttered sourdough toast filled his senses. The popular diner hummed with activity, mostly hunters and ranchers. In a few hours, it would be packed with those getting out of church. He wished he could attend Sunday service, but working the graveyard shift in Missoula didn't leave space in his schedule. On his day off, Wednesday nights, he attended church in Lolo.

Working graveyard messed with his schedule and his sleeping habits, but it afforded him time to tend to his father during the days. Today, he'd slip in, see how his old man was doing, and then head home for some much-needed rest.

He took a bite of potatoes and reached for the catsup bottle, but stopped. Owen Mitchell zeroed in on him, pushing past the patrons, around a waitress, with his son, Gene, in tow. David swallowed hard, his face freezing in a non-expression and steeled himself for what may come next.

"What's a nice young man such as yourself eating alone on the most romantic day of the year?" Owen's upper lip curled in a wry smile.

David sipped his coffee as if having his Sunday-morning meal interrupted by the likes of the Mitchells didn't matter. "Morning, Owen." He cocked his head to get a view of Gene hiding behind his father. "Gene." He set the coffee down and proceeded to slice through a spicy sausage link, stabbed it with his fork, and brought it to his mouth. "What brings you two out so early?"

Gene batted at a red heart hanging from the ceiling. "Saw your truck. Thought we'd pay you a visit."

David chewed slowly, waiting for their point to be made. The Mitchells had big mouths. If he gave them a little time, they'd use it—mostly to dig themselves a hole. He dipped a piece of toast in the egg yolk and took a bite. His appetite all but gone.

"Heard your twin is back in town, with a kid no less." Owen leaned against the booth.

"Where'd you hear that?" David already knew the answer, but having it confirmed might come in handy.

"Jen done told Jacob," Gene piped in.

David expected nothing less of his half-sister.

Owen slid into the booth across from David, leaving Gene to stand in the aisle, blocking traffic. "We had a deal with your father," Owen sneered.

He'd heard it all before. Right before he put his little

sister on a Greyhound bus to Hood River.

"Your father hasn't lived up to his end of the bargain. So, it's up to you to deliver."

Since he didn't have any daughters to turn over to the two of them, that would be near impossible. But since he was never officially part of the negotiation, it was best to pretend he didn't know about the deal. He set his fork down.

Owen leaned across the table. "Now, since your daddy hasn't lived up to his side of the bargain, we want the mine back."

"I don't know what you're talking about."

"Don't play me a fool boy."

David held up his hands. "I don't know of any deal, and I sure don't know about any mine."

Owen stood and towered over him. "We'll see about that."

Gene scurried behind his father as they stormed out of the restaurant. David's pulse raced. He'd have to be extra careful the next time he went to the mine.

Chapter Nineteen

If he'd actually been married for eight or nine years, Luke supposed he'd have this Valentine's Day thing down to a science. But cast into the deep end of being a husband, it was sink or swim.

Not since he was nineteen had he paid much attention to the holiday. He had no need to learn the finer art of romance. Thankfully, the many radio and television commercials provided some guidance. Wanting to keep some of his pride intact, he sure wasn't going to call his big brother for advice.

The light in Hannah's eyes when he presented her a box of locally made chocolates and a dozen red roses assured him he hit the mark.

She stuck her nose in the tender red buds and breathed then captured his eyes with a sweet smile. "They're lovely." She set the vase of flowers on the dining room table.

His heart expanded in his chest. Thankful that she

liked the roses.

"I can smell the chocolate." She moistened her lips with the tip of her tongue, unraveling his self-control.

Luke slipped his arms around her waist, drew her to him, and planted a kiss on those lips. She wound her arms around his neck, her body fitting to him like a missing puzzle piece.

When the kiss ended, he held her head to his shoulder, wound his fingers through her hair as he grappled with the emotions ricocheting inside him.

"Silly, I know, but this feels like our first valentine," she whispered into his neck.

No, not their first. Their first was spent sneaking away after school, sitting in his truck, drinking hot chocolate and eating cream-filled doughnuts in the park, under the cover of darkness. He gave her a bracelet, silver with two charms—two halves of a heart interlocking. Wonder if she still has it.

Hannah pulled back. "I guess it's the first one I'll remember."

Luke leaned his forehead against hers. "We'll have many more."

She ran her fingers along his jaw before kissing him.

Before he lost all good sense, he ended the kiss. "I better get dinner going."

On the back deck, he lit the barbecue grill. After seasoning the salmon fillet with lemon juice, salt and pepper and a little garlic powder, he set the foil-wrapped fillet on the hot grill and closed the lid.

Yes, there will be more first, more memories to make, to cherish for years to come. He hoped.

Through the sliding glass door, he watched Hannah chop asparagus and slather garlic butter over a loaf of sourdough bread. It was crazy, but he enjoyed the simple things with her, like cooking a meal, sitting across the table from her as they ate. He stepped inside, closing the door behind him, and fought the temptation to wrap his arms around her waist and draw her close, move her hair aside, and sprinkle kisses down her neck. She was beautiful, as beautiful as the first day he laid eyes on her.

His chest tightened with regret, wishing he never took her to Walla Walla. Wishing he found a way to keep her here, keep her safe. But as a minor, she was still subject to Vince Brady's control. When he saw the welt on her face, it was clear to his father that old man Brady would stop at nothing in forcing Hannah to do his will.

His father knew enough to make the difficult decisions they needed to. His mother agreed. Their only option was for Hannah to leave until they could get married.

She smiled at him. "What?"

He shrugged. "Nothing. Just came inside to be with you."

Her cheeks rosy from the oven, she set a pan of chocolate chip cookies on the counter. She pulled off the oven mitts and braced her hands on her hips. "You're staring at me."

"I can't help it. You're beautiful."

Being with her celebrating Valentine's Day coupled

with the heavenly scent of fresh baked chocolate chip cookies, it felt like a weird spell was cast on him, blurring his senses.

She tucked a stray strand of hair behind her ear. "Is this where you say as beautiful as the day you married me?"

He rubbed his hand over his mouth and shook his head. If only it were true. "As the day we first met." That was true.

Luke set the bottle of red wine on the table, but Hannah grabbed it, placing it in the refrigerator.

"It's red not white." He knew a little about wine being around Trent and Irene.

"I know. You're supposed to chill red for a few minutes then take it out, open it, and let it breathe."

"Guess you learned that from Dane."

"David?" she asked.

"Dane," he said.

"Dane? Oh, yes, Dane." She pressed her hand to her head. "Silly me."

Luke swallowed hard, fighting the temptation to assure her she was right, David was her brother. Not Dane. But he feared what might happen if he did. Would telling her about David, seeing him at the store with a pregnant woman, open up memories she'd rather not have?

Or worse, trigger a total recall of her past and send her running back to Walla Walla?

Samantha wasn't happy with him. She wanted to tell

Hannah the truth, that they weren't married. Lucky, fearing for his mother's mental health, was adamant that she not be told the truth. Luke tried to explain that the doctor advised them to let her memories come back on their own. Just as her cuts, scrapes, and bruises were healing with time, so would her memories. Forcing them back could be like peeling off a scab and could leave a permanent scar. He assured his sister he was following the doctor's advice.

Upon leaving the hospital, she had stopped taking the seizure medicine. The pills sat on the counter in the downstairs bathroom untouched. But she hadn't had a seizure, so he was okay with her not taking the pills. Besides, they made her sleepy. Hannah was convinced the pills were keeping her from remembering.

Her headaches seemed to have gone, or at least if she had any, they weren't bad enough for her to say anything. Earlier in the day, he received an e-mail from Joe. Hannah's business partner and friend, Tanya was asking about her. Joe ran interference, saying that Hannah was still recovering and unable to tend to the business.

How much longer could they keep her life from catching up with her?

He lit two tall candles on the dining room table. Hannah lifted the chocolate cookies from the cookie sheet and placed them on a plate. One broke, and she snagged a piece, sampling the sweet dessert.

"Um." She licked chocolate from her fingers.

Luke reached around her for two wine goblets in the

cabinet.

"Here, try." She offered him a broken edge of the gooey chocolate cookie. He lowered his mouth to her fingers, and she fed him the warm morsel.

"Um, very good." He set the glasses on the counter.

Hannah wrapped her arms around his neck, rose up on her toes, and pressed her lips to his. His arms encircled her waist, and he stumbled back, catching himself on the counter. Her fingers sifted through his hair as the kiss deepened.

Luke trembled with the effort it took to break off the interchange. His hand lingered, holding hers as he gathered the control he needed to step away.

"I've got to check on the fillet." Needing to put distance between them, he stepped onto the deck. The cold air did little to quench the fire building inside him.

If what just happened was a preview of the evening, he was up to his chin in swift water. His worst fear was to act on the passion and undeniable chemistry between them, only to have her regain her memories and hate him later.

As he stood outside shivering from the cold and the wind from the storm crossing the rugged mountains, he chastised himself a coward. Part of him wished she'd remember everything while another part of him feared what would happen if she did.

After testing the salmon with the pronged fork to be sure it was done, he set it on a plate and ventured back inside. Was it his imagination or were her eyes especially bright tonight? Her lips ruby red and full; her hair soft and silky.

God, give me strength.

She smiled at him in a playful, flirtatious way as she set a bowl of mashed potatoes on the table. His heart lurched.

Hannah handed him the wine bottle. "Would you like to do the honors?" Her voice spilled over him like warm honey.

He wasn't quite sure how to finesse the opening of a wine bottle. He had watched Dane open the bottle they shared in the celebration of her coming out of the coma. If he was cultured like his brother, he'd have the bottle open in no time. But he was a beer kind of a guy, so if it didn't have a screw top or a tab, he was at a loss.

"I'll let you."

Hannah took the small tool, sliced the foil, and peeled it back. Inserted the corkscrew, twisted it down, and popped the cork in nothing flat. She set the bottle on the table near the asparagus and potatoes.

Luke pulled out her chair, and she sat, tossing her long hair over her shoulder.

He sat across from her and poured her a healthy glass of wine, figuring the only way to get through this night was to get her tipsy enough to fall asleep.

She lifted her glass. "A toast."

He hoisted his.

Her smile flashed soft and seductive. "To new memories."

"And new beginnings."

Their glasses clinked, and he took a long drink before digging into the feast before them. Conversation flowed easily as they discussed the ranch, Lucky, and the building of the cabins.

As dinner neared the end, the conversation turned to the future.

"Have we ever been to Hawaii?" she asked.

He didn't know if she had, but he'd never been. "No."

"We should go. Maybe for our tenth anniversary."

The sip of wine went down the wrong way, and he coughed. Covering his mouth, he hurried to the sink for a glass of water.

"Okay?" she asked over her shoulder.

He pressed a napkin to his mouth. "Wrong canal," he rasped.

Hannah stood and cleared their plates then sat on the couch with expectancy in her gaze. Luke sat beside her and poured them both more wine. Even though she'd only drank half a glass.

"Do you like the wine?" he asked.

"Yes." She nodded. "I noticed it's from Yakima Valley. I love Washington wines."

"I know." He handed her back her glass. "Where else might you like to travel?"

"Alaska would be nice."

"I've been to Alaska . . ." He winced. He could kick himself.

"You have? When?"

"It was a while ago. I went with Trent to visit Gabe. Do

204

you remember Gabe?"

"Gabe?"

"He was Trent's friend, so you probably don't. But he was in Alaska for a bit, and we went for a week to fish."

"Gabe?" Her forehead wrinkled with her trying to recall.

"He's back here now as the fire chief."

"I don't recall."

"That's all right," he quickly added to set her mind at ease. There was no reason for her to remember Gabe.

Hannah set her glass on the table and tucked her feet beneath her. Resting her elbow on the back of the couch, she threaded her fingers through her hair and met his eyes. "I want to ask you a question, and I want you to answer honestly."

"Of course." He set his glass on the table and faced her.

"Have you been happy these last several years?"

The question caught him off guard. The immediate answer that came to mind was no. But if he answered honestly and said no he'd have to say why.

It's true, he'd built a business from the ground up, rebuilt this ranch with long days and a lot of hard work. But if he was honest with himself and with Hannah, he hadn't been happy. He'd been angry that life didn't turn out the way he wanted and the one woman he loved had walked out of his life. Everyone kept saying he was young, he'd find someone else, but no other woman captured his heart like Hannah.

The hurt that her rejection left behind tainted every aspect of his life, from his relationship with his family to his tendency to work until he dropped from exhaustion. He took his hurt out on his father. Being angry at him for taking Hannah to Washington and then convincing him it was best to leave her be and not chase after her when the letters stopped.

If he could only go back in time and do what his heart told him to. Drive to Washington and see her, convince her he loved her, would protect her, and do anything for her.

Luke vaulted off the couch and stood at the window, staring off into the darkness with only the yard light illuminating a small portion of the gravel drive. Snowflakes drifted in the air, swirling in the wind.

"Luke." Her touch was gentle on his shoulder, yet it seared him to the core. "I didn't mean to upset you."

He stared at the yellow light. "It's all right."

"Were . . . were things between us bad?"

Bad? It couldn't have been bad when they were nonexistent. He shook his head.

"Then what is it?"

He stared down at his ring. The fake ring taunted him with what could've been and what wasn't. "Just thinking about my father."

His father meant well. Rhett didn't know what they'd done and that he had a grandchild in Washington. If he'd known, his father would have made a different decision and the outcome would've been different.

Rhett Daniels was a man of honor, and family was the most important thing next to his faith in Jesus Christ. Luke was raised with those values. That's what gnawed at him now. His responsibility to Hannah and Lucky came before anything else.

She wrapped her arms around his waist and pressed her head against his back. "I'd like to see your parents soon."

He tensed. She wasn't aware of his parents passing. He struggled to find the words to tell her. Loosening her embrace, he turned around. "Hannah, my parents are gone."

His words were slow to penetrate, but when they finally caught, the light left her eyes. "Gone? You mean . . ."

"They passed away."

She cupped her hand over her mouth. "How could I not remember?"

The truth clogged the back of his throat.

Tears pooled in her eyes. "I'm sorry."

Not as sorry as he was. If he could turn back time and do it all over again, he'd do things differently.

He missed his father and mother. He had distanced himself from his family, staying busy, visiting on Christmas and Thanksgiving. Making excuses the rest of the year until Trent tracked him down and told him their father was dying.

He made amends with his father that last month he was alive, but he couldn't help but wonder how things might have been different. Now as a father, he could only imagine the pain he caused his dad with his anger and getting into trouble.

Thankfully, he had more time with his mother, but he almost messed that up, too.

Taking Hannah to Washington had set the path for years to come. Now all he wanted was a second chance.

Chapter Twenty

The torment in Luke's eyes sent daggers through her heart. How could she have forgotten the death of her in-laws? Fleeting memories of spending time with Eloise, canning, cooking, and learning to play the piano danced on the edge of her recollection.

And Rhett, he was so strong, confident, and a godly man. She respected him, admired him. Luke was so much like them both. But for the life of her, she couldn't remember their passing. It was as if a veil hung between today and her memories.

Sadness hammered on her heart. "I'm sorry I don't remember."

Luke shook his head. "There's nothing to be sorry for."

She fit her hand to his cheek. Whiskers pricked her palm. "If you had it to do over again, would you marry me?" The loss of her memory had to take a toll on him.

"Oh, Hannah." He cradled her hand and brushed his lips to her fingers. "It's all I've ever wanted. The rest means nothing without you and Lucky."

His words salved her regret.

"The question is what do you want?" Her husband's gaze bore deep into her soul.

"To be your wife, to live here with you and raise a family."

"Are you sure?"

The insistence in his voice confused her. Where is this question coming from?

"Of course, I am." How could he doubt her heart, her love for him? There was only one answer, and it nagged her off and on since coming back. "Were we okay, I mean before the accident?"

"Why do you ask?"

"You asked me what I want. Like maybe you think I don't want to be here."

He wiped his hand across his chin. "I only meant that you can't remember things so you may not remember what you want."

Did he doubt her love, since she couldn't remember their life together? She wanted, *needed*, to prove to Luke how she loved him. Given the opportunity to start over, she'd make the same decision—she'd marry Luke Daniels.

Then the thought took root. "Maybe Lucky is right."

Luke's brow wrinkled. "About what?"

"We should get married again." She kissed him to show him even though her memories were missing, her love for him would never fade.

Tonight, she wanted to be his wife in every sense of

the word. Threading her fingers through his hair, she drew him closer and could feel the heat of his body against hers. She moaned with the delightful sensations his kisses awakened in her.

He groaned from deep within his chest.

Luke broke off the kiss and moved out of her arms. "More wine?" He grabbed the bottle and poured more into her glass. The rich red liquid sloshed in the goblet.

She took her glass, sipped, and then set it down. The last thing she wanted tonight was to get tipsy. Luke took a big gulp and wiped his mouth with the back of his hand. She stepped toward him. He stepped back. His smile was shy, fleeting. How endearing—her big strong cowboy was nervous. Her stomach fluttered.

Hannah took his glass and set it on the table next to hers. She spread her hands over his chest, ran them up to his shoulders, delighting in the feel of his hard muscles beneath her fingers. His hands rested on her hips, and she rose on her toes and kissed him. Her fingers worked at his shirt buttons.

"Hannah." Her name escaped as a groan. "Hannah."

"It's okay."

"Hannah, I don't think this is such a good idea." He backed against the couch.

"I won't break." She pulled his shirt from his jeans.

"It's not . . . we can't." He pushed her hands away.

"Yes, we can." Again, her fingers fumbled with the buttons on his shirt.

"Hannah, please." He stilled her hands, holding them

in a firm grip.

Indecision danced in his eyes.

His rejection stung. "Why? What's wrong?"

"Nothing." He rested his forehead against hers. His breath stirred her bangs. He trembled.

"Don't you love me?" She sought for answers in his eyes as dark as a thundercloud.

"Oh, Hannah. With all my heart."

"Then why don't you want me?"

He squeezed his eyes shut and tilted his head back. "I do want you. It's just—" The phone rang, and Luke stared at it hanging on the wall.

Fear threaded through her heart. There was something he wasn't telling her. Something he was hiding.

"I should probably get that." He caught it just before it went to the answering machine. "Hey, Wade. Cows? . . . Mine? Are you sure? . . . I'll be right there." He slammed the phone back in its cradle. "That was Wade. The cows are loose on the road."

"How could that happen?"

"I don't know." He buttoned his shirt.

"Can I help?"

"Yeah." He tossed her the truck keys. "Block the road." He bolted out the back door toward the barn.

Hannah caught the keys in the air. She hurried to get her coat on, shoved her feet inside a pair of boots, grabbed her scarf and gloves, and ran out the door.

Bear scrambled up from his place on the rug and followed her. When she dropped the tailgate, he leaped into the truck.

With the seat back, she couldn't reach the pedals. She fumbled for the button to bring the seat forward. Once she could reach the pedals, she started the engine. She backed out of the garage and sped toward the road turning left to the east pasture. Up ahead in the bright headlights, cattle ambled toward her. Hannah parked the truck, blocking the road.

She clasped her gloved hands under her chin. "Lord, help them."

Bear jumped from the truck and rushed the cattle, barking to move the beasts back. Behind her in a black streak beneath white flurries, Luke rode Lightning. She waited in the warm vehicle as Wade, Luke, and Bear rounded up the strays. Snow swirled in the beam of the headlights.

When the cattle were off the road and back in the pasture, she drove the truck to where Luke and Wade were examining the fence. Wade's truck lights shone on the fence. Hannah wrapped the scarf around her head and stepped out of the truck.

"Somebody cut your fence," Wade said as Hannah approached.

She gasped. "Who would do such a thing?"

Luke spun around and stared at her then turned away. "I'll have to fix this tomorrow. In the meantime, I'll round them up and put them in the north pasture."

As Luke rode into the pasture with Bear, Hannah crossed her arms to ward off the chill. But the shiver crawling up her spine had little to do with the cold night air. Someone had purposefully tried to cause her husband harm.

Hannah drove the truck back to the house. She put the wine and glasses away, washed the dishes, and sealed the leftovers in plastic. Not wanting the wine to go to waste, she drank the rest in her glass.

Worry weighed heavy on her heart. The night didn't go as planned. Dinner was wonderful, the conversation intimate, but it hadn't ended the way she wanted—in her husband's arms.

She needed to convince Luke she wasn't fragile, he could touch her, make love to her. Fearing something between them made Luke keep his distance, she grasped for a memory, a feeling, anything to help her understand.

"Please, God. Give me my memories back."

She put another log inside the woodstove. Bear scratched at the door, and she let him inside. Snow clung to his fur. She dried him off with an old towel.

Wrapped in a blanket, she sat on the couch. Her eyes grew heavy, but she fought falling asleep, wanting to be awake when Luke came home. She yawned, and her breathing slowed. The fire popped and crackled. So sleepy.

She tensed as the front door slammed. The thud of boots on the floor told her he was coming down the hall. Hannah turned her back to the bedroom door and pretended to be asleep. The door squeaked open, and light from the hall spilled into her room. She held her breath.

Did he know? *Please*, she prayed silently.

"Hannah." Her father's deep voice echoed in the room. Her sister stirred. Was Katy really sleeping or just pretending?

"Hannah, get up. I want a word with you."

Was her secret out? Did her father find out about Luke? She'd tried to keep Luke a secret, hide her feelings for him. They were so careful. But she knew someday her father would find out the truth. She loved Luke.

"Hannah!" He grasped her arms. "Wake up."

Don't show fear.

"Hannah!"

Her eyes flew open. She stared into deep blue-gray eyes. "Luke?"

"You were dreaming."

She wound her arms around his neck and held on to him for dear life. "Oh, Luke." Her heart pounded.

It was a dream. But it felt so real.

Chapter Twenty-one

Luke dragged a spool of wire fencing from the back of the truck and set it on the gravel as Wade rode his ATV across the road, meeting him at the fence.

"Do you remember seeing anything last night?" Luke asked. Thankfully, Wade had called.

"No, just the occasional headlights. I spent most of the night in the back of the house."

A light snow fell from the gray sky as they rolled out the wire.

"It wasn't till I went out to get a few more logs for the fire that I heard them. They sounded too close, so I went to the end of my drive, and that's when I saw them." Wade held the wire to a post. "Any idea who'd want to cut your fence and set your cows loose?"

"Yeah, I have an idea." Luke stood and looked around before continuing. "I think Hannah's family knows she's back and they're sending me a message."

"What makes you think that?"

"At the grocery store, I saw David Brady with one of his wives. He recognized me and saw Lucky. He put the pieces together. Lucky said that David talked with him and asked about his mother."

"Are you going to tell Hannah about this?"

He shook his head. "How can I? She doesn't remember them. She thinks Joe and Paula are her parents and Dane is her brother."

"Is she in danger?"

"No, Brady wants to mess with me. Let me know he knows she's back with my kid." He tightened the wire to the post. "If I ignore this, then maybe he'll let it be."

"And if he doesn't?"

"Then I guess I'll have to deal with it." He slipped the pliers in his back pocket and pulled the wire taut. "My main concern right now is Hannah's well-being. She had a nightmare last night."

Wade grunted a response.

"She couldn't remember what the dream was when she woke. But she was scared. I think her memories are trying to come back."

"Dreams are the mind's way of dealing with pain that can't consciously be dealt with."

Luke knew his friend was speaking from experience. Wade never talked about his time as a Navy Seal or what left him in the shape he was. Luke respected his privacy and never asked.

By the time he returned to the house, Samantha had brought Lucky home.

Lucky held an imaginary guitar. "And she gave me guitar lessons, Mom."

"That's wonderful."

"I played the piano too; Sam taught me a new song."

His sister's smile shone bright. Apparently, she'd had as much fun last night as Lucky. "I should be heading back," Sam said, rising from the recliner.

"I'll see you out." Luke followed her to her car. "Things go okay last night?"

She shoved her hands in the pockets of her fake fur coat. "Yes, he's a very bright boy. Quite the storyteller, too."

"Oh?"

"Yes, told me how you kissed Hannah and woke her up just like Sleeping Beauty." His sister raised an eyebrow.

He chuckled. "That's not what happened."

"No?" His sister braced her hands on her hips. "That little boy wants his parents together."

"I want us together."

"Luke, I know you think you're doing what is best for Hannah. But starting a relationship built on lies." She shook her head.

His chest burned. "I'm not lying to her."

Samantha dropped her voice to a whisper. "You two aren't married. It's not proper you're living together."

He crossed his arms. "We're not sleeping together."

She leaned toward him. "We are to avoid all appearance of wrongdoing."

His temper sparked. "Sam, don't give me your

righteous religious lecture right now. I know what I'm doing."

Sam held up her hands in surrender. "Okay, I'm just saying."

"Please don't. I haven't asked for your opinion."

"Aren't we testy?" She smiled as if to say she knew he was crawling the walls with pent-up desire.

He plowed his fingers through his hair. "I want her to remember. Once she does, she'll have a choice to make. Until then, my hands are tied. Doctor's orders."

"Yeah, well, tie them behind your back until she is your wife." Samantha opened the car door with a loud squeak and a clunk. The old car protested.

He watched Samantha drive away. And not for the first time, he thought about taking Hannah to the Justice of the Peace and making her legally his. But she deserved better. She deserved a real wedding, in a church with bridesmaids, flowers, a big cake, and a real ring.

Chapter Twenty-two

In his stocking feet, Lucky skidded out of his bedroom and answered the phone on the third ring. "Hello, I mean Bitterroot Outdoor Adventures."

"Lucky?"

"Grandma!"

"How are you doing?"

"Doing good. I've learned how to ride a horse."

"How wonderful. I bet you enjoy it."

"Yeah, it's a lot of fun. And I'm learning how to care for the cows, and we ride ATVs, too." He opened the fridge and rummaged for something to snack on.

"How is your mother?"

"A lot better. Her headaches are gone. She seems happy." String cheese? Nah.

"That's good to hear. Is she getting her memories back?"

"I don't think so." He grabbed a jar of strawberry jam.

"I'm sorry to hear that."

But he wasn't so sure that was a bad thing. It might even be a good thing because his parents are together and they're happy.

"Is your mother there? May I speak with her?"

Something in his grandmother's voice caused his insides to tighten. He glanced out the back door. His mother raked pine needles and leaves from where she wanted to create a flowerbed. "Uh, she's unavailable." He slammed the refrigerator door.

"I can wait, and we can talk more until she's finished."

"Uh, no, she's not here." He removed a butter knife from the drawer.

"I see. How are you doing?"

"Fine." He set a jar of peanut butter on the counter. Out the window, his mother set the rake against the deck and stretched. Was she coming inside? "I'll tell her you called."

"Please do. Lucky, it's important I talk with her."

He swallowed around the lump in his throat. "Okay. I'll tell her. I got to go. Love you, Grandma. Bye." He didn't give her a chance to say anything more and hung up.

What's so important Grandma Paula wanted to speak with Mom? They've been gone for almost two months. Maybe it's to tell her people are looking for her, like her customers or her friends.

If she knew about Tanya, Ms. Peters, or any of her customers, would his mom want to go back to Walla Walla?

He put the knife away, no longer hungry.

Hannah rubbed her hands across Luke's broad shoulders. "What's the matter?"

He shook his head. "There's a lot to get done and not enough time to do it."

She rested her chin on his shoulder and peered at the notes he'd written on a pad of paper. "Like what? Maybe I can help?"

He exhaled. "I've got to get Cabin 3 built. They all need to be furnished and decorated before Memorial weekend."

"I can help. Let me handle the inside. I'll buy the furniture and everything else."

He glanced over his shoulder with a smile. "You got a deal. I hate shopping."

"I can do most of it online."

"Even better." He reached into his wallet and set a credit card on the counter. "Go easy on me."

She laughed. "What else can I help with?"

"Nah, I got to run into town and get a few fence posts and some more wire."

"I can handle that."

"The farm and feed doesn't have an Internet store."

"I can take the truck."

He grimaced. "I'm not comfortable with you driving and being out on your own."

She placed her hands on her hips. "Why not? It's not

like I'm going to get lost."

"No, I'll take care of it." He rose from the table and strolled toward the door. "Shoot, I forgot." He checked the time on the wall clock. "Jared is delivering more logs today."

She sauntered to him and slipped her arms around his shoulders. "Please don't treat me like I'm a piece of porcelain. Let me help. I'm supposed to be your helpmate."

"My what?"

"Helpmate. It's in the Bible." She cocked her head to the side and held out her hand. "Keys please."

He hesitated. "I can see if Wade is free."

"Don't bother Wade. Besides, you need his help when Jared arrives. Luke, please. I'm doing better. No headaches. My balance is better."

"No."

"I'm going stir crazy, Luke. Please, don't keep me locked away in this house."

"I'm not. You go to therapy. You go to the store."

"With you." She huffed. "I just want a little independence."

His hesitation hinted he was giving in. Good, because she needed a little time to herself.

He dug into his pocket and removed the truck key.

She curled her fingers around the key, gave him a quick kiss then tugged the keys free, and spun around. "I won't be long." She grabbed her purse. At the door, she offered him an encouraging smile.

Uncertainty drew Luke's brows together.

On the way into town, Hannah followed the sign to the library and parked the truck outside a new building. The library used to be on Main Street. Curious, she went inside and strolled through the shelves of reference books, then through history, around the corner to fiction before heading to the back wall where the children's books resided.

She found several books she'd like to check out for Lucky. She dug into her purse for her wallet, but she didn't find a library card. Her breath caught—she didn't have her driver's license with her. Hannah put the books back in their respective place. Perhaps another day.

What happened to her driver's license? Was it lost in the accident?

Must have been because she had to dig this old purse out of the closet along with the wallet. She never liked this purse.

She sucked in a quick breath as a fleeting memory danced on the outer edge of her thoughts. Katherine had talked her into buying the blue leather bag. No wonder the thing looked like new, she preferred brown or black purses with lots of compartments.

She fished around the bottom of the bag for the truck key and headed outside.

Clouds parted and sent a warm ray of sunshine on her head. She lifted her face to the sun and breathed in the cool, clean air scented with pine and fresh-cut grass.

Yes, freedom felt wonderful.

Chapter Twenty-three

Outside the feed and farm, David heaved a bale of hay into the back of his truck. He paused as Luke's truck swung into a parking place. Maybe now was a good time to ask Luke about his sister.

He jumped down onto the pavement. A door slammed. Instead of Luke, his sister strode toward the store. His heart crashed against his rib cage.

Hannah grew up to be a beauty that's for sure. She hadn't appeared to change much, same long brown hair, but styled a little different. The youthfulness he remembered replaced by maturity—a confidence in her walk and her clothes fit better.

She pulled open the door and disappeared into the store.

As his heart pounded, he struggled to catch his breath. Torn between the desire to run inside and demand to know where she'd been, tempered by the knowledge she'd been in a major accident. Yet she seemed to be walking just fine.

Maybe it was best to just walk up, calm like and say, "Hi. Long time no see." If he could keep his voice from betraying the swirling emotions inside.

He yanked off his work gloves and tossed them on the tailgate. What was he a chicken about? It was his sister. His sister who hadn't bothered to call or attempt to reach out to him. Then again, why would she? She ran off a long time ago, only to surface under mysterious circumstances. Could he blame her for leaving? It wasn't like she was leaving him. After all, he had sent Katy away someplace safe.

He'd entertained thoughts of getting away from Pinegrove, away from his controlling father. Someplace where no one knew him, and he could start over. But obligation and sense of responsibility shackled him here.

He rubbed his hand over his bearded jaw. Would she even recognize him? Sure, they're twins, with similar eyes and hair, but he'd filled out, grown in the last nine years. He was no longer a skinny runt with knobby knees, self-conscious to a fault.

Just walk inside, see what happens.

He took a deep breath and swung the door wide, his boots making a hollow thud on the wide wood plank floors. The scent of sweet hay mingled with cedar and the salty aroma of feed.

"Get it all loaded?" Darcy asked from behind the register.

He shook his head. "Forgot something."

226

"I'm sorry John's not here to help."

He waved her off as he scanned the store for Hannah. The top of a woman's head moved down an aisle. Brown hair had to be Hannah. He cut down the next aisle to beat her to the back of the store. When he turned, he almost collided with a woman, knocking a box of mouse killer from her hand.

Not Hannah. "Sorry, excuse me, ma'am." He spun around and peered over the top of the aisles. From the mirror hanging in the corner of the double bay doors leading out to the yard, he caught sight of Hannah strolling along rolls of fence wire.

With his heart beating like a reggae drum, he hurried toward the fencing supplies. He paused outside the door and gawked at her. She hadn't grown none, topping out at just a little over five feet tall. He wanted to see her face, but his feet felt anchored in cement.

Did she want to see him?

Would she be happy, sad . . . angry?

His throat tightened. Regret mingled with sadness— what a mess of a family they had. A dead mother, a tyrannical father, a baby sister off in Oregon, a twin disappearing and now showing up again. Maybe this wasn't the place or the time to get reacquainted with his twin.

Hannah pulled on a fence post, tugging it free from the stack leaning against the wall. She got it out enough to wrap her arms around the large wooden post and attempt to lift it. Good grief, she's going to hurt herself.

227

David rushed to her side. "Here, let me help you with that."

"Thank you." She stepped back, holding the post steady. On her left hand, a gold band glinted in the sun. "I should've asked for help. I thought I could lift it."

She's married to Luke? "No problem." He wrestled the beam free and set it on the ground.

"Thank you, I really appreciate this. I'm going to need two."

The sound of her voice washed over him, and he trembled. He kept his back to her and his head down. Everything in him ached to take her in his arms and hug her. *It's me, David.* He swallowed hard to find his voice.

"That one there looks straight." She pointed to a post.

He nodded and removed it from the stack, setting it next to the other. "I'll carry these up front for you." He hoisted the beams onto his shoulder and strode toward the register. Once up front, he'd slip out the door.

No need to make a scene in the feed and farm. Now that he knew she was well, he'd stop by Luke's place some afternoon. That way they could have some privacy, get reacquainted on their terms.

But he still needed another bale of hay. No matter, he'd go for a walk around the block and come back later.

From behind him, Hannah said, "Maybe you could help me with a bag of dog food."

Dog food? That's right, Luke had that bear of a dog.

Darcy smiled at him and Hannah. "Sure good to see you two."

He stumbled the last two feet toward the counter and almost took out a display of garden gloves. He set the fence post up against the wall near the register.

Before Darcy took a hankering to yapping, he darted down the pet food aisle. Hannah followed and gestured to a fifty-pound bag. "That's the brand he likes."

David heaved the bag onto his shoulder, making sure to keep his face hidden. "I'll just take this outside, put it in your truck." He made it to the door.

"Wait, David." Darcy stopped him in his tracks. "I need to scan the barcode."

He cringed and reversed his steps to the register and set the sack on the floor, looking for the barcode.

"There it is." Darcy aimed the scanner gun at the bag.

With a beep, he was good to make his escape.

"David?" Hannah's voice drifted to him.

A hand lightly settled on his arm. He stiffened and pinched his eyes shut. She knows. Guess *now* was the time to get reacquainted with his twin. Slowly, he faced his sister.

Her brown eyes searched his face, her forehead wrinkled, and she pressed a hand to the side of her head.

"Hello, Hannah." His voice strained on the words.

She paled, held both hands to her head, and groaned.

"Hannah, are you all right?" He grasped her upper arm just as her legs buckled.

He caught her before she hit the floor.

"What's wrong with her?" Darcy shot around the counter.

"She fainted." He lowered her to the floor, cradling her head in his palm. "Call 911."

Voices sifted through the heavy fog. She opened her eyes and peered up at a man, with vivid blue eyes.

"Hannah, can you hear me?" His words penetrated the ringing in her ears.

"Yes." Her mouth dry.

"You're going to be fine." He wore a dark blue uniform with a patch that informed he was a fireman.

She glanced toward her feet. Darcy stood with her hand over her mouth, her face puckered with worry.

"What happened?"

"You fainted," the fireman said. "But it sounds like you were lucky. You didn't hit your head."

Aware she was lying on the hard floor, Hannah struggled to sit up. "I have to get up."

He pressed her back down with a hand clad in a blue rubber glove. "Before you do that, let's make sure you don't feel pain anywhere. How's your head?"

"Fine." A dull ache, but nothing like what she'd experienced before.

"Does your back or neck hurt?"

She took a mental inventory. "No."

He ran his gloved hands over her arms. "Legs and arms okay?"

"Yes."

He slipped a hand behind her back. "Take my hand."

She grasped his hand as he helped her sit up.

Darcy released a huge sigh. "Thank God."

"Dizzy?" the fireman asked.

"No, just thirsty."

"We can deal with that. Darcy, can you get us a cup of water."

"I can do better and get you a brand-new bottle."

"We're going to take this in stages, nice and slow." He accepted the bottle of water, twisted off the cap, and handed it to her.

Hannah took a few sips and swished the cold water around her mouth. She looked into those blue eyes once more. "Do I know you?"

"I'm a good friend of Luke's."

That would explain it. Of course, she knew the man, and yet she couldn't remember him. "Forgive me, but what is your name?"

"Gabe. Want to take a few more sips?"

She did and handed him back the bottle.

"Sometimes dehydration can sneak up on you." He passed the bottle to Darcy. "Let's see about standing you up."

She clutched his hand as he pulled her to her feet and held her arm to steady her.

Gabe kept his hand on her back. "How are you doing?"

"Fine."

"Luke is on his way. We can't have you driving right now."

She inwardly groaned. "But I have his truck."

"Someone went to fetch him. How about we have you take a seat over here." He guided her toward a chair beside the counter.

Overcome with embarrassment, she buried her face in her hands.

"She going to be okay?" someone asked behind her.

"Looks like it. You did the right thing," Gabe said.

"Then I'll be on my way."

This is going to be the talk of the town—Luke's wife faints in the feed and farm. Her cheeks grew hot. She peeked up and behind her, needing to thank the man who did the "right thing". But he was gone.

Luke busted in through the door. "Hannah!" He dropped to his knees in front of her. "Are you all right?"

She nodded.

"She's all right, Luke. She fainted is all, but she didn't hit her head."

Luke's eyes grew wide. "That's the last thing you need. Are you sure you're okay?"

She swallowed hard. "I'm sorry. I don't know what came over me."

"She's a little dehydrated," Gabe said.

"We better get you home." Luke assisted her out to the truck. Once the door closed, she propped her arm on the armrest and placed her head in her hand. How embarrassing.

She was trying to help. Trying to inject some semblance of normal into her life, into their lives. She failed. He'll probably never let her drive again, let alone go shopping by herself. So much for freedom.

Luke fired up the engine. "This is exactly what I was worried about."

"I fainted is all. You heard the fireman. It's from dehydration." She took another swig of water.

He shook his head. "You could have hit your head again. Or worse." He pulled onto Main Street.

"Luke, please, don't treat me like a child."

"I'm treating you like my wife!" His voice rose with each word.

"No, you're not!" Tears pooled in her eyes. "You won't even make love to me."

He slammed on the brakes. "Not until you get your memory back." The muscle in his jaw clenched.

"And   if   I   don't?"

Chapter Twenty-four

Sitting atop Dakota and riding alongside his father was right where Lucky wanted to be. While he missed Grandpa Joe, Grandma, and Uncle Dane, he never wanted to be without his dad ever again.

His dad was cool. He knew how to build things. He taught him how to cast a lure and land it right where he wanted. Now he was letting him ride a horse on his own.

"Hey, Dad." He glanced over at his dad sitting atop Lightning.

"Yeah?"

"Do you think Mom will ever get all her memories back?"

Luke stared off into the distance like he was searching for the answer written in the puffy clouds against the blue sky. "Not sure, son. I hope so."

The uncertainty of what would happen if his mom remembered she never married his dad kept him awake at night. He shouldn't have told her she was married to

Luke. He'd gotten in trouble before for lying. If she remembers she never married Luke, maybe she won't love him anymore, and she'll want to leave.

"Hey, Dad?"

"Yeah, son."

"How come Mom didn't tell you about me?"

Luke stopped his horse. "Because she was afraid."

Dakota naturally halted alongside Lightning. "Of what?"

Luke shifted in the saddle and faced him. "Of her dad, mostly."

"Is he mean?"

"You could say so."

"Does he live here in the valley?"

"Afraid so." Luke urged the horse to continue.

Lucky's horse followed. "What about Mom's mom. Does she live here, too?"

"No." Luke shook his head. "Your Grandma Brady died when your mom was young."

"You wrote Mom a lot of letters. Didn't she ever write you?"

"She did for a while, but then she stopped."

"How come?"

"She was afraid."

"Of her dad?"

Luke nodded.

"If she had told you about me, would you have come?"

His dad slowed the horse. "Nothing could have kept me away." Luke's eyes grew dark. "You know, Lucky, I made mistakes."

"Like what?"

"I shouldn't have given up so easy. I let my pride fool me into thinking your mother didn't want me around, that she had moved on. I should have driven out there and talked with her. Then I would have seen for myself, and I would've known about you sooner." His father's voice grew deep, and he cleared his throat.

Lucky hadn't meant to upset him. "That's okay, Dad."

Luke's smile spread wide across his face. "I'm really happy you had the smarts to call me."

"Me, too."

They continued across the pasture.

"What were Grandma and Grandpa Daniels like?"

Luke tipped his hat back. "Your grandfather was a hardworking, honorable man. He loved his family very much. Your grandmother liked to paint, and she managed the library."

"Oh, yeah. That's where you met Mom." Lucky remembered the story that first night with his father.

His father grinned. "She made the best oatmeal chocolate chip cookies."

"Were they old? Is that why they died?"

"No, son. They both got sick."

"Was it cancer?" He had heard about cancer. Grandma lost her sister to the disease.

"For my father, it was lung cancer, and your grandmother had problems with her lungs, too."

"Did they live in the city? I hear pollution makes

people sick."

"No. My father managed a mine, and that made him sick. The bad chemicals also made my mom sick."

"So the only grandparents I have are Grandpa Joe and Grandma Paula?"

"You have your Uncle Trent, Aunt Irene, and Aunt Samantha."

"I like Aunt Samantha. She's fun."

It wasn't natural to be this nervous about going to visit her brother-in-law and his wife. Hannah anticipated each turn Luke took as he drove to Trent and Irene's.

"Trent had moved back in with Mom when she got sick. Samantha lives in his house in Missoula. I don't see that changing." Luke drove up a hill.

The moment the simple ranch house on the rise came into view, Hannah remembered afternoons with Samantha and Eloise. At the thought of Eloise gone, remorse gripped her heart.

She glanced at Luke as he steered the truck into the gravel driveway. "I remember the house."

Lucky stuck his head over the seat. "That's good, Mom. Right, Dad?"

"Yes, that's good."

"Can I play the piano?" Lucky asked.

"We'll see." Luke glanced up at Lucky through the rearview mirror. "We need to be respectful of Irene's condition."

"Is Irene not well?" Maybe they shouldn't have come.

"She's pregnant."

"Trent has children?"

"This is their first."

She glanced back at Lucky. "Samantha and I would ride horses along this road and sit on the deck, eating Eloise's amazing oatmeal chocolate chip cookies." Her heart lifted.

Lucky poked his head between the seats. "Do you think they'll have cookies?"

"We'll see. Sam and I would sit on the deck, making up songs and sing." She placed her hand on Luke's arm. "Do you remember that?"

Luke smiled. "I used to sit in my room with the window open and listen."

They parked out front, and Hannah took in the familiar barn, horses, and valley views.

She followed Luke to the door. He ruffled Lucky's hair and winked. Her husband and son shared a secret way of communicating that often made her wonder if they were keeping things from her. Silly, of course.

Trent answered the door. "Well look at you."

Hannah's heart took flight.

Her brother-in-law held the door open. "Come in, come in." He leaned over and extended his hand. "Howdy, Lucky."

"Hi," Lucky said somewhat shy.

Trent wasn't as she remembered him. A faint image of him—tall, clean shaven, and in a uniform—came to mind.

This man who stood before her was tall, but he sported a beard and mustache, wore faded wranglers and a flannel shirt. His eyes were the same—kind, wise, and warm. He had always been a little taller than Luke.

The house smelled of freshly baked cookies and brought back memories of all the times she visited Samantha after school. It felt like a lifetime had passed since the last time she'd seen the house. But that didn't make sense.

A woman with brunette hair and soft brown eyes came to stand beside Trent.

"This is my wife, Irene."

Irene held out her hands, and Hannah took them, staring at the woman. She was beautiful, radiant.

"Hello, so nice to meet you." As soon as she said the words, she wanted to take them back. This was her sister-in-law; of course, they knew each other. "I mean. . ."

Irene graciously smiled as if to say not to worry about it. Her maternity clothes were designer, her nails manicured, her makeup perfectly executed. Hannah struggled to reconcile her memory of Trent as a rugged outdoorsman married to a woman of such refinement.

"When are you due?"

"First week in August." Irene pressed her hand to a slight baby bump. "May I get any of you something to drink, tea or coffee? I made cookies. The Daniels family recipe."

Lucky jumped on the offer. "Cookies? Do you have hot chocolate?"

"I certainly do. Luke, Hannah, what can I get you?"

"Coffee for me," Luke said.

"Tea," Hannah answered.

Trent waved them toward the living room. "Make yourself comfortable while I assist in the kitchen."

Hannah glanced around the room, her eyes resting upon a painting above the fireplace. "Eloise's paintings?"

Luke nodded. "Irene owns the gallery in town. She had several of Mom's paintings made into limited-edition prints. These are the originals."

A memory of sitting beside Eloise, learning how to paint with watercolors, rose up from the recesses of her mind. Her throat tightened. The woman who cared for her like a daughter was no longer here.

Did they do mother-daughter things together, like shopping? Were there Thanksgiving dinners, Christmas gatherings? Birthday parties? She wished she could remember.

Trent handed his brother a cup of coffee.

Lucky carefully took the mug of hot cocoa from Irene. "Thank you," her son said, exercising good manners.

"You're welcome." Irene turned back toward the kitchen.

Trent caught his wife by the hand. "I'll get the rest."

Irene sat in a padded rocking chair near the fireplace. "Hannah, you look like you're recovering well."

"Yes, slowly." She touched the patch of hair growing back on her forehead, thankful to have had the stitches removed.

"No more headaches?" Irene accepted the cup her husband offered.

Hannah took the teacup Trent handed her. "They come and go but aren't as strong."

"We are incredibly grateful you're here." Irene smiled, her eyes alight as she glanced at Luke.

The interchange between Irene and Luke was a curious one of tenderness and alluded to a secret shared only between them. She'd ask him about it later.

Irene sipped her tea. "You know, I hear there's a new chiropractor in town who specializes in cranial sacral therapy. You might consider giving her a call."

"What's that?" Lucky asked, sitting beside his father.

"It's therapy that works on the skull and spine. I don't know much more about it except that a lady came into the gallery a month or so ago handing out business cards."

"She's in town?" Hannah asked.

"Sure is. Next door to the beauty salon on the same side of the street as the drugstore."

Luke placed his hand on her knee. "It's worth a try."

She nodded, willing to try anything to get her memories back. Get her life on track and be the wife and mother she desperately wanted to be.

"Yeah, Mom, you can get your head worked on then go next door and get your head worked on." Lucky snorted at his joke.

Hannah smiled thinly, hoping to excuse her son's poor attempt at humor.

Luke shook his head at Lucky, not pleased with the

joke.

Her son lowered his head and slurped on his hot drink.

Trent sat back in a recliner. "Are you almost ready for fishing season?"

"Yep, I just need to get the boat out of storage."

She didn't realize they had a boat.

"Remember when you took Dad's aluminum drift boat on the river and got it stuck on a rocky sandbar?"

Luke winced. "Yeah, I scraped the bottom up pretty bad."

"I had to help you get it loose."

"Then there was that time you took Dad's brand-new fly rod out and snapped the tip off."

Trent grimaced. "Man, I felt so bad. I tried to glue it back together."

"With superglue and got your fingers stuck together."

Trent chuckled and held up his hand pressing his index finger to his thumb. "I took the money I was saving for a new rifle and replaced the rod."

Her son chuckled at his father and uncle's antics. It made Hannah want to give Lucky a brother or sister.

Vague impressions of her pregnancy drifted on the edge of her memory.

Luke slipped his hand over hers. "Hannah has been reviewing the business website," Luke added. "I'm hoping she won't mind taking over the bookkeeping."

That explains the mess she found in the office closet. Why hasn't she been doing the bookkeeping? Probably her schedule with college and everything else, she didn't have the time. She'd ask Luke about it later.

Trent laughed. "That would be a good thing."

"Hey, I make sure the bills are paid." Luke smiled good-naturedly at his brother's ribbing.

"Yeah, but when you get busy you can't keep up."

"That's why I've asked you to join me."

"And leave my cushy, high-paying job with the state?" Trent teased.

Irene's restrained smile and raised eyebrow made Hannah wonder if Trent was considering working for Luke.

"What kind of work do you do?"

"I'm a game warden."

"What's that?" Lucky asked.

"I make sure people follow the rules when hunting and fishing."

Hannah tried to keep up with the banter, but confusion swirled in her head. How did she fit into the picture? They spoke as if this was all new to her. Even how Trent introduced her to Irene as if they'd never met.

She sensed she'd been doing accounting for some time. They must have had the guide business for several years. Surely, she worked alongside Luke, supporting him, encouraging him, and helping him build the business. What did she need an MBA for?

Luke squeezed her hand, bringing Hannah back to the conversation. "She is." The warmth in his eyes comforting. "She's doing a great job with the cabins, too. You should see them."

"It's been fun." She couldn't think of anything more to say. Thoughts and questions dizzied her. She forced herself to focus on the conversation.

Irene clasped her hands in her lap. "We ought to go shopping sometime. I'm sure Sam would enjoy it, too. The three of us, it would be fun."

"I'd like that. I've been doing most everything over the Internet. And this time of year is the best time to buy linens." There, that sounded intelligent. But the throbbing in her head persisted.

"There's a few stores in Missoula that have cute, locally-made crafts you could decorate the cabins with."

Hannah took a sip of tea. "I'd like to do each cabin in its own theme."

Irene swept her hair behind her ears. "And of course, there's all the big department stores—Dillard's, Sears, Ross, Costco."

Trent chuckled. "Yeah, Irene makes at least three trips a week to Missoula. I think it helps her not miss the big city so much."

"Don't miss it all." Irene warmly gazed at Trent.

The way Irene talked, it was almost as if they'd never done anything together. But that can't be right. Surely, she'd gone shopping with Samantha and Irene before. At least with Samantha, her best friend. Tempted to ask when the last time she got together with her sisters-in-law, she opened her mouth to speak, then closed it. No, best not to ask and make everyone feel awkward, reminding them of her condition.

The longer they stayed, the more Hannah felt things weren't quite right. As if she had been gone for a while and came back. But that doesn't make sense. The muscles in her neck tightened.

It was in the little things they said, the expressions on the faces of those she loved. The disconnect she couldn't shake as she mentally tried to sort through the discussion. Her head ached and keeping up with the conversation tired her. She covered her mouth as she yawned and pressed her hand to her head.

"Mom, does your head hurt?"

She nodded.

Concern filled Luke's eyes. "Maybe we should head home."

"I'm sorry," she addressed Trent and Irene.

"Don't be." Irene set her cup aside. "You can come back when you're feeling better."

"I'd like to take you up on your offer to go shopping."

"That would be wonderful." Irene smiled reassuringly. "When you're in town, be sure to visit me at the gallery. It's at the north end of Main Street."

On the way home, Hannah said, "I don't remember Irene."

Luke said nothing, and Lucky remained silent in the back seat.

"I don't remember your mother being sick or passing away."

Luke reached across the seat and wrapped his hand

around hers. "Hannah, there's a lot you don't have memories of."

"Yes, but some things I do. Stuff that happened in the past with us, even with Samantha and your mom, I have those memories. It's more recent things I can't recall."

"Maybe that's the part of your brain that was damaged," Lucky suggested from the back seat.

She desperately wanted to make sense of it all. The more she tried to remember, the more her head hurt.

They turned into the driveway. Wade's truck was parked by the barn. "I don't remember Wade either."

Bear barked a greeting and ran beside the truck. The noise and commotion increased the throbbing in her skull.

Upon hearing the truck, Wade stepped out from the barn and waved for Luke to come.

"I'll only be a few minutes." Luke parked then jogged to the barn.

When Hannah's feet touched the ground, her balance was off, and she caught herself, bracing her hand against the door.

Lucky hurried to her side. "Mom, are you okay?"

"I'm okay." Steadying herself against the truck, she made her way toward the door. Gripping the railing, she stepped onto the porch. Toby dashed past her, eager to come inside. She stumbled.

Lucky wrapped his arm around her waist, offering his support.

"Thank you," she said.

"I'll get Dad."

"No, I just need to sit down."

She didn't want to worry Luke or let on how bad this headache was. It would only make him hover, and he'd not let her leave the house by herself.

Her son helped her to the couch.

"Can you get me a glass of water and the blue pills in the bathroom?"

Lucky dashed into the kitchen, filled her glass, and brought it to her. Then he ran down the hall and brought her the white bottle with its blue lid. She struggled to open the childproof cap.

"Here, let me." Lucky opened the bottle for her.

"Thank you." She poured two capsules in her hand.

She swallowed two painkillers and leaned her head against the back of the couch. Toby jumped up on the couch and lay beside her. She ran her hand along his thick fur, and in return, he broke into a loud purr.

Vaguely aware of the back door opening and closing, she sat with her eyes closed, waiting for the headache to subside.

Chapter Twenty-five

Lucky slipped out the back door to let his dad know Mom wasn't feeling well. Luke stood beside Wade, looking inside a stall. Their gaze intent, but when Wade turned toward him, the man was smiling. He rarely saw Wade smile.

"Hey, Lucky, come over here." His dad motioned for him to come near.

"What is it?"

Luke lifted him up to stand on the stall boards and peer inside. Branson stood nudging a small horse on wobbly legs.

His heart jumped. "Branson had her baby."

"Not so loud."

"Sorry," he whispered. "Is it a boy or a girl?"

"It's a boy," Wade said.

Bear pushed between them to stare through the slats and find out what all the activity was. His tail beating against the backs of their legs.

"This is really awesome," Lucky said, keeping his voice down.

His father nodded. "That it is."

Wade propped one foot on the stall door's lower rung and rested his chin on his hand atop the rail. "Mighty handsome fella."

"Got a name for him yet?" Luke asked.

Wade shook his head.

"Can I name him, Dad?"

"No, Lucky. He belongs to Wade."

Disappointment stung. "He's not mine?"

"No, son."

Wade set a big hand on Lucky's shoulder. "I'd be grateful to have you help me train him once he's old enough."

His chest tightened. Lucky lowered his head, accepting the fact he didn't get a horse today.

"I'll go get your mother," Luke said.

"She's got one of her headaches." Lucky jumped down from the stall.

His father's smile faded. He rushed out of the barn to the back of the house.

"Is she all right?" Wade asked.

Lucky shrugged. "I think her memories are trying to come back."

Wade took his hat off and ran his fingers through his short hair. "Memories can be painful."

Luke hurried into the house to find Hannah on the couch, her head back and her eyes closed. Careful to close the door quietly, he slipped off his coat and draped it over the dining room chair.

Her fingers sifted through Toby's fur. The cat seemed to be doing what he could to provide her comfort, maybe even a distraction from the pain.

Luke knelt on the floor beside her and slid her hand into his. She moved her head and looked at him, then rested her head back and closed her bloodshot eyes.

"What can I do?" He kept his voice low.

She slowly shook her head. "Nothing, it's going away."

God, please, he prayed. *Help Hannah. Take away the pain. Bring her memories back, Lord. Please.* "I love you," he whispered and pressed his lips to the back of her hand.

"I love you." She raised her head and weakly smiled. "I'm sorry."

He sat beside her. "What are you sorry about?"

"For the accident." She laid her head on his shoulder and wrapped her arm around him. "For whatever decisions I made that landed us here."

He held her tight and kissed the top of her head. The irony of her words struck him. For the accident had brought her back to him. All those years ago, their decisions took her away.

"I get so confused. I can't make sense of everything."

"Don't try so hard. It will come back to you in time." He threaded his fingers through the silky strands of her hair.

Her soft brown eyes captured his heart. "Can't you just tell me everything? Start at the beginning and tell me our story."

He stiffened. "I can't. The doctor said to let your memories come back on their own."

"But I want to know."

"I know you do, and you will. Just be patient."

She laid her head against him. "Aren't you tired of only having half a wife?"

He closed his eyes. It was better than having no wife at all. "You're doing your best." He kissed the top of her head. "Don't be so hard on yourself."

After a moment of silence, she asked, "Have I always been hard on myself?"

"You're driven, and you've always been a perfectionist."

She lifted her head. "I hope I'm not too demanding."

"You're harder on yourself than others."

"Is that why Lucky is the way he is?"

"What do you mean?"

"He's smarter than most kids his age, isn't he?"

He nodded. "He's got your brains."

She rested her hand on his chest. "And your good looks."

He squeezed her close and set his chin atop her head. "I guess our son got the best of us both." His tone playful.

Before the sun rose above the Sapphire Mountains, David packed his gear in the truck and headed into the Bitterroots. Living in Missoula provided him anonymity he didn't have in Pinegrove. In Pinegrove, everyone knew everyone's business, or at least, they sniffed and snooped to be in the know.

He turned off the highway onto the dirt road leading into the mountains. The truck headlights cutting through the early-morning darkness.

The Mitchells were always watching him, and Jenny was the worst. Always asking questions, prying into his business. What really got under his skin was she hounded him about needing a wife. He didn't need nor did he want a wife. He couldn't trust the women of Pinegrove. No way would he follow his father's example and have three wives and a whole passel of kids he couldn't properly provide for.

He walked away from his father's lifestyle and religion shortly after Hannah left. When he discovered the deal his father made. As if women could be bought and sold like property.

Besides, he wanted nothing to do with its rules and regulations. What kind of a God would take the life of a young mother, leaving her three kids to be raised by a mean old cuss like his father and indifferent stepmothers?

Thankfully, he got Katy out of Pinegrove. How was she doing? He really should try to reach out to her. But the more time passed, the harder it became to pick up the phone and call his little sister. Besides, she's in a better place, with a new life. Probably graduated from high school and entered college. That'd stick it to their old man.

When he overheard his father saying he was going to take Katy out of school and that he had pledged her to wed Jacob, he knew he had to do something. That afternoon he went to take Katy away, he caught Jacob taking what wasn't his.

David gripped the steering wheel, his knuckles turning white, like the white-hot anger that rose up in him that afternoon he found Jacob on top of his sister. He heard her screams and ran to the back of their property. He wanted to kill Jacob that day.

The road narrowed, and the engine whined as he climbed higher in altitude, twisting and turning on the switchbacks leading up to the mine.

By now, Jenny most likely spouted off to her father-in-law that Hannah was back, but he doubted his sister was in any danger. He had what the Mitchells wanted, and while they'd stop at nothing to get it, Hannah was of no use to them. That had to give old man Mitchell an ulcer. They tried parading a few of their daughters under his nose as if he'd be tempted. He scoffed. They weren't even pretty. Homely girls, without a brain of their own.

No way he'd be interested in a girl from Pinegrove. Get involved with one of the Mitchell daughters and he'd likely end up dead within a year. Then the mine would once again belong to the Mitchells. Not a cold chance in—.

He slammed on the breaks, and the truck shuddered

to a stop. Two trucks, parked off the side in the brush, sat empty. A little steam rose from their hoods, engines still warm. David scanned the tree-lined road for signs of an ambush. No sign of anyone.

Reaching across the seat, he popped open the glove compartment and removed the 9-mm Smith and Wesson. He flipped off the safety, pulled back the hammer, and heard the click of a bullet slide into the chamber.

His blood thundered in his ears, and his heart pounded. The trucks didn't look familiar, but he could never be too cautious. He rolled down the window. A blast of ice-cold air hit his bearded jaw. He listened intently. A gentle cool breeze whispered through the trees.

In the distance, barking erupted, and a gun blast echoed. Hunters. Mountain lion, no doubt. It was early in the season for hound hunts. He rolled up the window and inched past the parked trucks. His tires crunched over snow as he continued toward the mine.

Chapter Twenty-six

On this mid-March afternoon, the sun shined bright and warm. Spring was coming. Hannah made soup and sandwiches then packed it in a cooler and set it on the back of the ATV. Bundled in her coat, scarf, and gloves, she sat atop the four-wheeler and headed for the road then up to the cabins.

She steered into the driveway and slowed, accessing which cabin the men were working on today. Lucky stepped out of Cabin 3, the one farthest from the road, and waved. She pulled up to the small porch and turned off the engine. Inside, a saw's high-pitched screech and a hammer's steady rhythm gave testimony of the men working hard to get the cabins ready.

Even Lucky had his own tool belt, helping his father and Wade build the cabins. Three cabins were all they had plans to build, for now. Rather than have their customers stay in a hotel in Hamilton or Missoula, they'd stay on the property—a great marketing strategy. Some might want to come and stay for a week on a real working ranch while others would book to hunt or fish, and Luke wouldn't have to drive a long way to pick up their guests.

Hannah looked forward to making lunch and breakfast for their guests. She lifted the cooler off the back of the rig and carried it inside the cabin. The sweet smell of fresh sawdust tickled her nose.

At seeing her, Luke smiled and patted Wade on the back after he finished cutting a piece of molding.

"Lunch is here." She lowered the cooler to the bare floor.

She set out plastic bowls and thermoses of chicken noodle soup. Luke grabbed another thermos of hot coffee and poured some into his empty to-go cup. Wade tossed what little there was of cold coffee in his cup out the back door then held it while she filled it.

She scanned the small kitchen. "You guys are making great progress." The cabinets were hung, the molding around the doors and windows almost finished.

"Almost ready for a woman's touch." Luke winked before biting into his ham and cheese sandwich.

Identical in size and structure, the cabins boasted one bedroom and full bathroom downstairs and a loft bedroom upstairs.

She'd decorated the first cabin in a moose theme with colors of green and blue. The second cabin would be an elk theme. This cabin would be decorated with bears in red and navy blue.

After sharing lunch with the men, she drove down to

Cabin 1—the closest to the street and driveway. Several boxes had been delivered over the last week, and she went to work decorating.

Bending over a box, she sliced it open with Luke's pocketknife when the room shifted, and her head felt light. She caught her balance with her free hand, narrowly missing the knife's sharp tip.

Hannah let go of the pearl handle. The knife rocked atop the cardboard box. She sat on the wood floor. These dizzy spells were a nuisance. Sometimes they happened when she bent her head forward. Other times, they happened when she looked up. She rubbed the back of her neck where the muscles were drawn tight and took deep slow breaths, willing the spell to pass.

As she rubbed the muscles, she worked up to the base of her skull where it was tender. Maybe the dizzy spells weren't related to the concussion she sustained in the accident, but possibly due to something wrong with her neck. A reminder, she really needed to call the chiropractor Irene told her about.

The spell passed, and she stood, testing her balance. Once assured she was okay, Hannah went back to unpacking the curtains. Wade had hung the metal curtain rods. She moved the small stepladder to the window and took the rod down, slipping the moose from one end to thread the curtains on.

A memory surfaced of hanging red and yellow curtains. She paused. Where had she hung red and yellow curtains? Their house was decorated in purple. The odd sensation of déjà vu hung like a heavy veil. Another woman was with her, helping her. They were close. Was it Irene? No. Samantha? Katherine! She closed her eyes and grasped for the memory, fighting to keep it from slipping away, but it vanished. Leaving behind the residue of the thought she'd hung curtains before with Katherine.

She sighed.

After hanging the curtains, she unpacked the dishes she had washed and set them neatly in the pine-stained cabinets. She saw a much younger self, holding a baby carrier. Lucas was fast asleep as she stood in the entry of a cottage.

"Think you'll be right comfortable here," a man's voice echoed in her mind.

"Thank you." Gratitude welled up inside. The kindness he showed her was more than she deserved.

Hannah paused, setting the bowls on the counter. The memory flitted away as quickly as it came. She grasped for it, replaying the pieces in her mind, willing for more to be revealed.

But the memory was gone.

Starved, Lucky heaped mac-n-cheese on his plate next to a pork chop. His stomach grumbled, reminding him he hadn't eaten since lunch.

"Easy there, son. You can always have seconds."

"But I'm hungry."

"I know. But you eat what you got on your plate." His

father took the serving spoon and set it back in the bowl on the table.

Lucky sat back and swallowed noodles drenched in yummy cheddar cheese.

His mother placed her hand on his arm. "Okay, Hoover, you need to chew your food thoroughly."

Gosh, what was with his parents tonight?

"You did really good today helping me measure and pounding nails."

"It was fun." Lucky beamed under his father's praise.

Luke shook pepper over his mac-n-cheese. "Glad you think so."

"How far did you get today?" his mother asked.

"Bathroom fixtures are in. We wire the lights next," his dad answered in between bites. "How is Cabin 1 coming along?"

His mother raised her wine glass. "Curtains are hung; the kitchen is stocked. I didn't get to the beds."

Luke cut into his pork chop. "I think we're on track for opening the end of May."

She forked a piece of broccoli. "Our first clients arrive the weekend before Memorial Day."

Luke sipped his wine, smacked his lips, and held the glass up to the light. "That's good. What is it, Syrah?"

"Malbec," his mother answered.

Luke raised an eyebrow.

Lucky laughed at the perplexed expression on his dad's face. "Mom is going to turn you into a wine sommer . . . simily. . . ." He knew the word; he just couldn't say it.

"Sommelier," his mother offered.

"Yeah, that," he said around a piece of pork.

"Don't talk with your mouth full."

He snapped his mouth shut.

"I think I figured something out today with regards to my headaches and dizzy spells."

Setting his fork down, Dad gave Mom his undivided attention. "What's that?"

"I think there's something wrong with my neck."

Lucky smashed broccoli on his plate, hoping to make it look like he'd eaten some.

"The muscles in my neck are tight and . . ." She rubbed the back of her neck. "At the base of my skull is very tender."

"Maybe you should see that chiropractor."

She nodded. "I called today, and I have an appointment tomorrow afternoon."

"What time?" Luke took a bite of meat.

"Two."

Luke shook his head. "The vet is coming then to check on the colt and Branson."

"I forgot about that." His mother's forehead wrinkled. "I can drive myself."

"Not with dizzy spells, you're not."

She set her fork down. "They don't happen all the time."

His father lifted a scoop of mac-n-cheese. "I'll have Wade take you."

"I don't want to bother Wade." Her lips pressed tight.

Luke swallowed. "I'm sure he won't mind."

She rested her arms on the table. "Luke, really."

Lucky watched the exchange. This could be his parents' first fight, and he had a front row seat. He stabbed a piece of pork.

Bracing his elbows on the table, his dad leaned forward. "I'm not risking it, Hannah."

"You're overprotective." She smoothed her napkin on her lap.

"Yep." His father took a drink of wine.

Mom's chest rose with a deep breath. When she glanced at him, Lucky shrugged.

"Luke," she said in a sweet voice. "It's not that far."

"I know. That's why Wade can take you."

Dad dug in, showing no signs of budging.

Mom lowered her hands calmly to her lap. But he'd seen that fire in her eyes before, and Dad didn't know what was coming.

"I don't want him to waste time waiting for me."

Luke reached across the table and turned his hand up in an offering. His eyes went all soft and mushy as he gazed across the table. "Because I care, I can't let you drive alone. I couldn't take it if something happened to you."

Diffused, his mother slid her hand in Dad's and smiled lovingly. "Okay, I understand."

Well, that was over much quicker than he thought. His father knew how to get his way with his mother. In order to get his way, Lucky had to pitch a fit, but that didn't always work in his favor. From now on, he'd take cues from his father.

Hannah lay face up on the narrow vinyl table as Dr. Foster sat on a small stool. Her fingers probed firmly around Hannah's skull and neck.

"You say you had a car accident?" Dr. Foster inquired.

"Yes. I was in a coma for about a week."

"Do you remember the accident?"

"No. I don't remember the last eight or nine years of my life."

"That must be an odd feeling." Dr. Foster positioned her fingers against her skull and pressed. "Okay, do as I taught you. Breathe in and bring your toes up, breathe out and point your toes toward the door. Count to ten."

Hannah breathed in rhythm, pumping her toes, feeling the doctor's fingers pressed to her head. They repeated the routine several times as the doctor repositioned her fingers and applied pressure.

"I'll have you sit up."

She sat at the edge of the table.

"How do you feel?"

"A little lightheaded."

"That's expected. We're shifting things. In time, your memories will release. Your head took a good banging."

"Will the headaches eventually go away?"

"That's the first thing you'll notice." The doctor grabbed a plastic skull from a shelf. "The skull is not one piece. It has plates and a thin lining between it and your brain." She adjusted the skull. "Your frontal is pushed to the side." She pointed to the skull's forehead. "While the occipital," she tapped the back and underneath the model, "is pushed up. We align the skull and neck, and everything else can fall into its proper place."

For the first time since she woke up in the hospital, hope infused Hannah that she'd soon return to normal. Tears pooled in her eyes, and she bit her lower lip, battling for control of the rushing relief.

The doctor placed a hand on her arm. "That too will happen as the healing begins."

"Thank you, doctor."

"Call me Melanie."

Outside, Wade sat in the truck. She opened the door and climbed inside the big Ford. "Thank you, Wade. I'm sorry I was longer than I thought."

"No worries." With a slow grin, he lifted a to-go cup. "Gave me a chance to get a good cup of coffee."

"I hope to be able to drive myself soon."

He started the engine. "I'm sure you will. Healing takes time."

She swiveled on the black leather seat to face him. "I get the sense you're speaking from experience."

He backed the truck up. "Yeah. It's been three years now. Some days it feels like it's a long way behind me. Other days it feels like it happened last month."

"Do you remember what happened?"

Wade's eyes turned stormy. "Afraid so."

She braced her elbow against the door and propped her head on her hand. "I wish I could."

"I   wish   I   could   forget."

Chapter Twenty-seven

By the end of April, Hannah's physical therapy sessions were down to once a week. Her balance was returning. The stitches were gone from her leg, leaving behind a thin jagged scar. Her hair had grown to cover the scar on her forehead. She hadn't had a headache since seeing Melanie.

Before her physical therapy session, Hannah wanted to test her comfort level with going up and down the stairs. She stood at the foot of the stairs, staring up with a resolve to conquer her fear. With determination, she climbed the steps, not pausing halfway but climbing all the way to the top. Turned around and peered down at the living room and kitchen.

Her stomach fluttered, and she took a deep cleansing breath. *I'm not going to fall. There's a railing.* She set her hand on the smooth wood, taking deep breaths until the anxiety subsided.

Turning around, she stared at the bed with its plush amethyst comforter heaped and tousled on the bed. Silver pillows lay crumpled against the dresser. Obviously, they'd been there awhile. She wedged her hands on her hips. Her husband wasn't one for making the bed.

Hannah straightened the covers and arranged the pillows. In the bathroom, a towel hung crooked on the towel rack. Still damp, she folded it and hung it straight so it would dry. Double sinks resided in a gray granite countertop, one dulled by dust, the other marked with toothpaste and shaving cream.

A boxed window cast dim light over the large tub beneath it, also dull with dust. A dead fly lay near the drain, while water droplets from Luke's shower dotted the frosted-glass shower door. A hot bath would be wonderful. She didn't remember the big tub being up here. Then again, she remembered very little about this house.

She meandered into the walk-in closet, where her clothes hung on one side and half of the other alongside Luke's—suits, dresses, blouses, skirts, pants, and coats. Shoeboxes stacked three and four high on the shelf above. Good grief, she had a lot of clothes. A memory flashed in her mind.

"Here try this." Samantha held up a yellow sundress with flower eyelets across an A-line skirt.

Hannah hesitated to reach for it. "Oh, I don't know. That looks too nice."

"I've had it for years. Besides, yellow washes me out. It's a much better color for you."

Hand-me-downs. All her clothes had been hand-me-downs or came from the thrift store.

"I was poor."

"What are you doing up here?" Luke asked.

Hannah jumped. Her breath lodged in her throat.

"Are you all right?" He placed a hand on her arm. "I didn't mean to startle you. I was looking for you everywhere. Didn't you hear me calling you?"

"I . . . I have a lot of clothes."

He shrugged. "Yeah, that you do. Do you feel okay?"

"I grew up poor."

His eyes grew dark.

"Joe and Paula aren't my parents."

He shook his head, his eyes dark as thunderclouds.

"Was I adopted?"

"No."

His image blurred. She lost her balance and fell backward. Swallowed by an encroaching blackness, she grasped for something to stop her fall.

"Hannah!"

In vain, she struggled to stop falling. Darkness smothered her.

"Don't play me for a fool, girl. I know about you and that Daniels boy."

"No, Papa, I'm friends with his sister."

"I catch that boy anywhere near you, I'll shoot him."

Searing fear sliced through her. How did he find out?

"You're to marry Owen Mitchell. You hear me."

Her stomach dropped. *No, please, God.* "I don't want to marry Owen Mitchell." She battled a rising tide of fear.

"Don't be a fool. Mitchell is respected in this

community. He's one of our elders. You'll do as I say."

Her jaw clenched, and she held her fist at her sides. Desperation rose in her throat. "You can't make me."

His big hand swung toward her head.

Hannah's eyes rolled back and she collapsed in Luke's arms. He carried her to the bed.

"Hannah?" He smoothed her hair from her face. "Hannah, honey, can you hear me?"

"Dad, where are you?" Lucky yelled from downstairs.

"Upstairs," he hollered. His heart raced. "Get a glass of water and a washcloth."

Lucky trotted up the steps and stood beside him, gawking at his mother. "What's wrong with her?"

"She fainted." He took the glass and set it on the table. "Go get that damp in the bathroom." He pointed at the washcloth.

Lucky just stood there, tears collecting in his eyes. "She's going to wake up, isn't she?"

Luke bent over Hannah and kissed her forehead. He put his mouth next to her ear. "Please wake up."

Lucky handed him the dripping wet cloth. Not caring about the floor, Luke wrung it out then dabbed her cheeks, chin, and head.

"Is she breathing?"

"Yes."

"Mom, please don't do this." Lucky's voice cracked with unshed tears.

"She's going to be all right."

Her eyelids moved. "No, Pa."

Luke brushed his fingers over her cheek. "Hannah."

Her eyes fluttered open.

"Hey there."

Her eyes cleared, and her gaze swept from Luke to Lucky. "What happened?"

"You fainted."

She closed her eyes and sighed.

"How's your head?"

"Fine. Why? Did I hit my head?"

Luke cupped his hand beneath her head. "No." He held the glass of water for her. "Here, take a sip."

She leaned forward to meet the cup with her lips.

"I don't think you're going to physical therapy today."

She shook her head. "I'm so tired."

"Then rest."

He took his cell phone from his coat pocket, searched through his contacts, and called the therapist. After informing them that Hannah was going to miss her appointment, he peeled off his denim jacket and draped it over the foot of the bed.

Luke walked downstairs, making sure Lucky came with him. "Son, your mother needs her rest."

"Okay." Lucky's eyes filled with the same uncertainty plaguing him.

"I'm going to ask Wade to come take you for a few hours."

"No," Lucky whined. "I want to stay here with Mom in

269

case she needs me."

"I'm not going anywhere. I need to tend to your mother, so I need to make sure you're fed and taken care of."

"I can feed myself. I'm not a baby."

"No, you're right. But I think it would be good for you to spend a little time with Wade."

"Can't I go to Samantha's instead?"

"It's just for a few hours." Luke knelt in front of his son. "Please, Lucky. I need your cooperation."

Lucky nodded his consent, and Luke called his friend, asking for a huge favor. Wade was more than happy to help and came on his ATV to take Lucky back to his place.

In the bedroom, Hannah lay on her side, her eyes closed, her breathing even. He took off his boots and belt then lay beside her, carefully wrapping his arms around her.

"I haven't been sleeping very well lately," she confessed.

"How come?"

"I keep having weird dreams. But when I wake up, I can't remember them."

He squeezed her a little tighter and rolled to his back.

"I'm so tired of not being able to remember." She laid her head on his shoulder and draped her arm over his torso. "I can remember one dream."

"What is it?"

"I'm in the woods and all these animals are around, talking with me. There's a rabbit, a lion, a bear, even a wolf. They're friendly, and I can tell they care about me. Then the ground shakes, and the animals get frightened and run. At first, I think it's an earthquake, but then I realize it's a giant." She sighed. "I start to run, but he runs after me. I try to hide, and just when I think I'm safe, his big hand reaches down to grab me." Her hand gripped his shirt. "I wake up just before he grabs me." She lifted her head. "But that's the only dream I can remember."

"Are the others bad?"

She thought for a moment. "No. It's like I'm living my life in my dreams. Going about day-to-day stuff. I just can't remember what when I wake up."

He laid her head against his shoulder. "What were you doing up here?"

"Testing to see if I could handle the stairs." She rose up on her elbow and pressed her hand against his chest. "I just want my life back."

He threaded his fingers through her hair, lifting the silky strands from her shoulder. "Give it time."

"Don't you want your life back?"

No, he didn't want his former life back. He liked his life with Hannah and Lucky. Never before had he felt complete, felt a sense of purpose.

She tilted her head to the side. "I'm sure you want your wife back."

He closed his eyes, not wanting her to see the truth in them. Hannah rested her head on his shoulder once more. The feel of her in his arms, the rise and fall of her body with each breath, it felt right. The way it should be.

She drifted off to sleep, and at some point, he did, too.

Awakened by the high-pitched twitter of his phone, Luke seized it from the bedside table and hit the button to answer the call. "Daniels."

The house was dark. They had been sleeping for hours.

"One of the cabins is on fire." Wade's words took a moment to penetrate. "I've called emergency."

Luke's heart plummeted, and his stomach rolled. He bolted upright. "Where's Lucky?"

"With me."

Hannah sat up. "What is it?"

He launched out of bed and grabbed his boots. "A cabin is on fire."

She gasped.

"I'm on my way." He shoved his feet into his boots.

Hannah climbed out of bed and ran downstairs following Luke. "Where is Lucky?"

"With Wade."

She snatched her coat and hopped into the passenger side of the truck. Bear charged after them up the driveway but gave up at the road.

Sirens echoed in the distance, drawing closer. The orange glow against the hillside lit the sky. Flames stretched out the broken kitchen window. The blaze clawed at the outer walls. The logs popped and hissed under the intense heat. A plume of thick, black smoke billowed out of the loft.

Using a garden hose, Wade sprayed the side of the

nearest cabin to keep it from catching fire.

Luke rushed to Lucky sitting atop the ATV. "Are you all right?"

His son nodded, chin quivering.

"Oh, thank God." Hannah was right behind him.

Luke gathered Hannah and Lucky into his arms.

Fire trucks swung into the driveway, and men in yellow suits scrambled to put out the blaze.

They stayed back and out of the way. Wade limped across the yard to where they stood. Sweat beaded his face, the heat powerful even from this distance.

"I'm sorry, Luke. By the time I got here, there wasn't much I could do." Wade struggled to catch his breath.

Luke hugged his friend. "You did what you could."

Hannah touched his shoulder. "Are you all right, Wade?"

"I'm fine." He wiped his face on his jacket sleeve. "I don't know what could have happened. The heaters aren't hooked up. I don't even think the breakers are on."

But as Wade tried to find a cause of the fire, Luke feared it was no accident.

Chapter Twenty-eight

The acrid stench of smoke hung heavy in the early-morning air. A charred, smoldering skeleton of the cabin remained.

Luke rubbed his hand across his tired eyes as he stood beside Gabe. "Can you tell me what happened?"

"I'm really sorry to say this, Luke. But this was not an accident."

He clenched his fist at his sides. "I figured."

"Then you know who might have done this?"

"Yeah, I do. Hannah's brother, David Brady."

Gabe led him to the fire truck and removed a bottle within a plastic bag. "This here was thrown through a window."

The label was burned off the bottle, but it wasn't hard to discern what it was.

"My guess is its whiskey. With a rag shoved down the neck, it served as a wick. We'll see if we can get some prints off it."

Anger boiled inside Luke. "He's going to pay for this."

Wade put a hand on his shoulder. "Don't even think about it."

"No, Luke," Gabe said. "Let us handle this."

Luke clenched his back teeth, seething.

"Why do you think this was David Brady?" Gabe asked.

"Because he knows Hannah is back in town."

"If David knows then others know, too," Wade reasoned. "Why would David want to torch your property?"

"Revenge for taking Hannah away."

Gabe handed the evidence to an officer. "We'll do a full investigation."

Wade cleared his throat. "I heard hooting and hollering right before I saw the fire. And a truck with a bad muffler tore down the road."

"It could've been kids getting out of hand." Gabe reasoned.

No, Luke knew better. "If it wasn't David then it was Vince."

As darkness gave way to dawn, Luke walked down the gravel road to his home. He passed the portion of the fence he'd repaired. All the while, his thoughts churned on the night's events, the past month, and the past nine years.

What had his father always warned? "Son, don't

borrow trouble. It'll find you soon enough."

Had he borrowed trouble by falling for a girl from Pinegrove?

In his stubborn pride, he'd tried to be the hero, not once but twice. He loved his son and wanted to be a good provider, a good father. All he wanted was to be the honorable man his father was to his family. The Bradys didn't know a thing about honor. They manipulated the laws for their own sick and perverted gain. Who in their right mind thinks having four wives is reasonable or even logical?

Mom had a saying, "Evil begets evil."

Yeah, that's what Old Man Brady was—evil, and his son, David, carried the same seed.

"We fight not against flesh and blood, but against the principalities of this world." His mother's words interrupted his thoughts.

How come evil always seems to win?

A fire truck passed him as he turned up the driveway. The porchlight shined, and the front window glowed a soft yellow.

He stood outside on the gravel, chilled to his bones, shock probably setting in.

Was he happy?

He loved Hannah; he'd always loved her. She complemented him in more ways than he dared count. From her five-foot frame, to the way her eyes danced when she laughed. From her business background and her way with numbers. Now, as she built a new website and worked to increase SEO, whatever that was, she filled in the missing pieces to his life.

Hannah brought him the most happiness he'd ever known—Lucky. Even with her missing memories, his life had never been so complete.

He wasn't going to let Brady get away with this. He'd give Gabe and his team two weeks, that's all. Then he was taking matters into his own hands. No one threatens his family or his livelihood and gets away with it.

No one.

Luke turned the doorknob and pushed the door open. Hannah sat on the couch, holding Lucky on her lap as he slept. Her brown eyes were red from smoke. A pile of tissues littered the coffee table.

He closed the door and removed his boots in the entryway. Slipping his coat from his back, he draped it over a dining room chair. Her eyes tracked his every move, but she said nothing. Finally, he dropped onto the recliner, braced his elbows on his knees, and ventured to meet her eyes.

But he didn't know what to say.

"I'm so afraid," she rasped, her voice barely above a whisper and hoarse from smoke. A tear escaped and rolled unchecked down her cheek.

"What are you afraid of?"

She shook her head and rocked Lucky in her arms. "That this is my fault."

He combed his fingers through his hair. "It's not your fault." His voice fell dull, void of emotion.

277

"I was the last one in the cabin."

He put his head in his hands and struggled with the thought of telling her arson caused the fire. He sure didn't want to lie. She was going to find out sooner or later.

"The fire . . ." He took a deep breath. "Was deliberately set."

Her eyes grew wide, and she pressed her hand to her mouth, stifling an anguished cry. Lucky stirred with his head on her shoulder.

"First the cows getting loose and now a fire," she whispered. "Who would do this?"

"Gabe is going to investigate."

She continued as if not hearing him. "It's like my dream. Like there's someone out there coming after us." She wiped her cheeks with her fingers. "I don't know who it is. I can't see him. But I know he's there."

Could her dream be prophetic?

David sat in a booth near the window, eating his usual breakfast of bacon, eggs, hash browns, and sourdough toast. The *Ravalli* newspaper spread out on the table. He was a newshound. Every day he read the *Ravalli*, the *Missoulian*, and the *Wall Street Journal*.

Inside, a picture of a burned-out cabin and an interview with Luke Daniels and the fire chief gave a detailed account of the fire. Arson was suspected. Who would burn down a cabin? And why?

Luke was well liked by most people. Then again, how

well did he really know the guy? They didn't hang out in the same circles. The only common denominator was Hannah. Actually, there was Jared Anderson. David worked at the log home manufacturer off and on over the years. Luke was probably getting his logs from Jared.

Did Luke have a competitor guiding outfit trying to sabotage him? Maybe a neighbor was upset about three cabins being built on the adjacent property. Could've been some kids partying and things got out of control. No, Luke would've been aware of something like that. Had to be someone who got in and got out fast, intentionally setting the fire.

Who would do such a thing? He brought his coffee cup to his mouth, and a cold shudder went through him. Mitchell. He set the cup down without taking a drink.

Revenge?

No, that didn't sound right. It was a long time ago. Besides, it wasn't Hannah they wanted; it was the mine.

Hannah had mastered the stairs after the night of the fire. Every night for a week, Luke came home exhausted from clearing away the debris of the burned cabin. They were still waiting for the insurance company to process the claim. But the insurance company was waiting for the official report once the investigation was complete.

Someone didn't like her husband. Probably the same person who had let the cows out. She feared to ask him who it could be. What had he done to make an enemy?

Across the kitchen table, Luke wrote out checks and paid bills. He ripped a check from the checkbook and slapped it on the table. With mechanical movements, he swiped another bill from the stack. His steely blue-gray eyes narrowed, he huffed and wrote out another check.

She trembled. The anger radiating off Luke scared her. She gave him space, and he hardly spoke a word to her. The chasm between them left her emotionally off balance.

If she could just remember.

She closed her eyes and lowered her head to say a silent prayer. *Please, God, help me to remember.*

The tension in the house with Luke threatened to suffocate her. She needed to get out.

Get away.

Sitting at the table, she swallowed hard before speaking. "Luke, I have a chiropractor appointment." She braced herself for his response.

"You'll have to cancel." He stood. The chair scraped against the wood floor.

"Could I just take the truck for a few hours? I'll pick up groceries while I'm at it."

He hesitated before digging into his jeans pocket and handed her the truck key. She didn't expect him to concede so quickly. He probably wanted to get rid of her.

She left Lucky behind with his father.

After her appointment with Melanie, she proceeded along the sidewalk toward the other end of Main Street. She paused outside the espresso shop and breathed in the delightful nutty aroma of fresh coffee. Outside an empty building, she peered inside through the oval window in the door. Too bad the building was for sale, it would make a great restaurant.

Hannah continued past the antique store, a bar, and finally came to the gallery. Before opening the door, she stood back and took in the wide front windows that displayed a painting of the river. A framed photograph of a mountain adorned the other window. Glass vases, wooden bowls, and a few select pieces of handmade pottery were artfully displayed.

Her breath caught and she assessed the front of the building. *This is the old library.*

A memory of Luke stepping through the door surfaced. They slipped behind a shelf of mysteries, and he stole a kiss. Her heart jumped just like that day when Luke came to see her. The library their safe place to meet and spend time together.

A fleeting impression of needing to be cautious skittered across her thoughts. Cautious of what? She grasped for a memory adjacent to the feeling, but it was gone.

The bell clanked against the door as she entered.

"I'm in the back," Irene called.

Irene leaned against a wooden stool sketching a scene on canvas, a charcoal pencil poised in her hand. "Hannah." She set her tools down and rushed over to her. "How are you holding up?"

She shrugged. "I don't know." Tears pressed at the back of her eyes.

"I've been praying for you and Luke."

"Thank you." Hannah's throat tightened. "I don't know what to do. He's so angry."

Sympathy filled Irene's eyes. "Sometimes, when a man is hurting, the only emotion he allows himself to feel is anger."

"But it feels like he's angry with me."

"No. I doubt that. He loves you. He's always loved you."

Hannah swallowed hard. "I don't know how we're going to get past this."

Irene placed a warm hand on her arm. "Gabe and the sheriff are doing everything they can to find who did this."

"Do you know who would hate Luke this much to want to hurt him?" Hannah's heart sat heavy in her chest.

"No. Luke's kept to himself, working and building the ranch."

"He's a hard worker. I see the time and effort he's put into the business and our home." Tears blurred her vision. "I don't think he owes anyone money."

"No. If he needed money, he'd go to Trent."

"I wish I could remember." She put her head in her hands and allowed her tears to fall.

Irene wrapped an arm around her shoulders. "I'm so sorry."

"Only if I could remember."

Irene guided her to a table in the back. "Here, sit. I'll make some tea."

While Irene disappeared into the back, Hannah

glanced around at the artwork on the walls. She recognized several prints and upon closer inspection saw Eloise's signature painted in the lower right on the canvas.

"I see you found my favorite of Eloise's." Irene entered the room, setting a tray with a teapot and two cups on the table.

"She tried to teach me how to paint. But was more successful at teaching me how to play the piano."

"Do you play?" Irene asked.

Hannah lowered her head. "I think so. I must. Do I?" Wouldn't her friend know if she played the piano?

Irene thinly smiled. "Tea?"

Hannah sat at the table. "Did Luke tell you not to share my past with me?"

"He said the doctors believed it best to let your memories come back on their own."

"What if they don't?"

"They will. When you're ready." Irene poured a cup of tea and set it on a delicate blue saucer and handed it to her. The sweet scent of cinnamon tantalizing.

"Sometimes, I feel my memories are right there," Hannah said, holding her hand a few inches from her face. "So close I can touch them. Other times, they're like trying to catch a feather in the wind."

Irene graciously listened as Hannah shared her frustrations. When the teapot and her heart were drained, she headed home.

As she put away the groceries, Irene's words played in her head like a skipping album. *Luke kept to himself. . . .*

He's always loved you . . . working and building the ranch . . . the only emotion he allows himself to feel is anger.

If she could find pictures that would fill in her missing memories. There must be photo albums somewhere. Like of their wedding. The birth of Lucas. Christmas, Easter, Thanksgiving. . . Hannah went into the office and slid back the closet door. She stared at the boxes up high on the shelf and reached up to retrieve one when her foot hit a black case wedged against the wall. She bent down and picked up the heavy, narrow case.

A computer?

She carried the case into the dining room and set it on the table, unzipped the pouch and removed a laptop. Sitting on a chair, she opened the computer and turned it on. The cursor blinked at the login, Hannah Brady.

Brady? Must be an old laptop.

Her fingers tapped out the password—JClovesme!—as if by habit and hit return.

Moving her finger over the mousepad, she opened the e-mail application. An error popped on the screen, unable to connect. No Internet connection. She set the password to the wireless router and waited for it to connect. E-mail connected, and her inbox filled with messages.

Hundreds of messages.

Her breath caught.

She covered her mouth as she read a recent message.

Hannah, I know you've moved back to Montana. I'm worried about you. Please call or e-mail me and let me know you're okay. I love you, Amy. The signature stamp one week ago, from Amy Peters.

Lucky's teacher.

Her best friend.

A tidal wave of memories rushed her. Her heart slammed against her ribs.

She vaulted off the chair, sending it toppling back and crashing against the wall.

Luke brought her back to the valley.

Her legs weakened, and she braced her hands on the table.

I catch that Daniels boy anywhere near you, I'll kill him.

Her father!

Her stomach rolled. "We're not safe."

She grabbed her purse and rushed out the door.

Hannah's jaw clenched. Her fingers held a death grip on the steering wheel as she barreled down the narrow road. How could he bring her back here?

He lied to me.

We're not married!

Turning into the dirt drive, the truck slid around the corner and then skidded to a stop out front of the third cabin.

The charred remains of Cabin 1 a bitter reminder of the danger. She swung her head back and gawked at the mangled black skeleton of logs and broken windows. The fire wasn't an accident. It wasn't retribution against Luke. The fire was set as a warning—a warning to her.

Owen Mitchell! She escaped him once before. Or was it her father? David? Could her brother be that angry with her for leaving? Katy! She needed to see her sister. Take Katy away from here. Was it too late for Katy?

Luke stood on the porch in a blue flannel shirt and faded jeans. He slid a hammer into the tool belt, his hands clad in leather work gloves. Her heart leaped.

She shoved open the door and jumped out of the truck.

His broad grin slid from his face. Her hands fisted at her sides as she stormed toward him.

Chapter Twenty-nine

Like a kick to the gut, Luke knew. Hannah's memory had returned. How much did she remember? Her eyes flared as she marched toward him. He swallowed hard.

"How could you?" She hurled the opened-ended accusation.

Luke held up his hands in surrender. "Let me explain."

"Hi, Mom. Did you bring something to eat? I'm hungry."

Luke didn't take his eyes off Hannah. "Not now, Lucky. Go back inside the cabin." Using the bulk of his body as a shield, he walked her backward toward the truck. "What do you remember?"

Her eyes bore a clarity that wasn't there before. "Everything." Her fist squeezed at her sides. "You shouldn't have brought us back here."

He placed his hands on her shoulders. "I brought you home to heal."

She broke from his grasp. "Home! This isn't my

home."

He closed his eyes and shook his head.

"What were you thinking?"

The day of reckoning had arrived. "We thought if we got you someplace quiet where you could rest, you'd heal."

Her brown eyes smoldered. "It's not safe here."

"I won't let anything happen to you or Lucky."

"You took me away from my home, my business. The people who love me."

He raised his voice. "I brought you home to the people who love you."

"I've been gone for nine years, Luke. You don't know me."

Her words cut deep into an old wound. "Not true."

"You don't know the first thing about me."

"I do too." He took a deep breath, battling the rising tide of emotions.

"You lied to me."

His jaw clenched. "I never lied to you."

Her voice rose several octaves. "You deceived me."

"Oh, and keeping my son from me is not lying and deceiving? When were you going to tell me I have a son? When? When you're dead, and I get a kid with a letter on my doorstep?" He wiped his hand down his face, struggling to contain his temper.

She blinked and pressed her back against the truck door. "Lucky," she called.

Lucky ran toward them. "Why are you guys yelling?"

Hannah lowered her voice. "Get in the truck."

"Why? Where are we going?"

She planted her hands on her hips. "Home where we belong."

His son looked at him for confirmation. "She remembers everything, Lucky."

"To Washington?" Lucky's voice wavered.

"Yes." Hannah pulled open the door. "Now get in the truck."

"No, Mom, I don't wanna go back."

"Lucky. Get in. The truck." She emphasized each word.

"No, you can't make me." Lucky's face puckered.

"You're not taking my son." Luke stepped between her and Lucky.

"Don't go, Mom."

Her eyes sparked. "I put all of this behind me. I started my life over. I never wanted to come back here."

"No, I'm staying here," Lucky declared with a will of steel. "I don't want to be like other boys without a dad." He hugged Luke around his waist.

It was all Luke could do not to lose his composure. He wrapped his arm around his son, protecting him, loving him. His anger dissolving.

Hannah stared at them, appearing unaware of the tears dampening her cheeks. "It's not safe here. You don't understand. My father is dangerous."

"Hannah, I haven't seen your father in years."

She stumbled back. "Is he dead?"

"I don't know."

"Who do you think did this?" She pointed to the

torched cabin.

Luke turned away, not wanting to say who was responsible, not wanting to cause her more pain.

"Who?" she demanded.

"I'm not sure." He kept his arm around Lucky.

"But you suspect someone."

Luke shook his head not willing to say.

Their son whimpered.

Hannah flipped her hair from her shoulder and stared at the cabin's remains. A flash of clarity ignited her eyes. "My brother. He did this. It's David, isn't it?"

Luke rubbed his hand over his eyes and across his mouth, fearing what the truth might do to her.

"It is!" She gripped her hair in both hands. "You don't understand the evil of that place." Her gaze swung toward Pinegrove.

"Maybe not, but you can't keep running and hiding from your past."

She reached for her son. "Lucky, we can't stay here."

"I'm not leaving," Lucky yelled and ran toward the back cabin.

Hannah took two steps after him, intent on getting her son.

Luke grabbed her arm. "Leave him."

She wrenched free of him. "Let go of me."

"Hannah, please. We need to talk about this." A sharp pain penetrated his heart. "Please, be reasonable."

She tugged the gold band from her hand. "Here." She held the ring out to him. "Take it. It's a farce."

"No." His throat seized shut.

Her jaw clenched, and her eyes sparked. She heaved the ring into the tall grass.

Hannah climbed behind the wheel of the truck. The engine roared to life. The tires sprayed gravel as she sped away, leaving Luke in a cloud of dust.

Tears rolled from Lucky's chin, dampening the front of his shirt. At the screech of tires, he stood up in the loft and watched his mother drive away. His father dropped to his knees and covered his face with his hands.

Was she going back to Walla Walla without him? His legs gave way, and he sat on the floor. "Please, God, make Mom stay. I don't want to leave."

His chest ached like somebody punched him. He drew his knees to his chin, hugging his legs, and rocked back and forth. "Please, God. I want both my parents. I want to be a real family."

He wiped his nose on his coat sleeve.

"Lucky, are you in here?" His father's voice echoed.

"Up here." He sniffled.

Luke climbed the stairs and sat beside him. Without a word, his father wrapped his arms around him and held him tight.

"I don't want to leave." Lucky clung to his dad and breathed in the scent of sawdust and sweet hay on his father's coat.

"You're not." His father's voice strained.

"Can you make her stay?"

"I'll try."

"I'm afraid to go home. What if she makes me go with her?"

"You can stay with Wade while I talk with her."

"I never saw her so mad."

"She's afraid."

"Of her dad?"

"And her brother."

He sat up. "Who's her brother?"

"David. You saw him at the grocery store parking lot."

He wiped his eyes. "I saw him again."

"Where?"

He looked away, unsure what to say that wouldn't get him in trouble. "Uh, at the back of the property."

It wasn't until he went to bed that night that he remembered seeing the man before.

Luke's eyes grew wide. "When?"

"Shortly after we moved here. He said he worked for the people behind us. But he said his name was Jesse."

Luke jumped to his feet and offered him a hand up. "I want you to stay with Wade."

"Is Mom's brother mean like her dad?" He didn't seem mean when he caught him from falling into the stream and saw him across the tree.

"You let me worry about that. Right now, let's take care of your mom."

292

No way was she staying. He couldn't keep her against her will. And no way would she allow Lucky to stay. The cows, the fire—didn't Luke see what they were dealing with?

Her son was in danger. She was in danger. By her being here, Luke was in danger. The sooner she got out of this place, the better. Rhett understood that nine years ago when he drove her to Walla Walla. Why couldn't his son?

David picked up where Vincent Brady left off. He'd carry on the Brady line, carry out his heritage, his duty. Men had it good in the community. They believed that they were superior, taking to an extreme the teachings that a woman was to submit to their so-called leadership and abuse. Going as far as to teach that a woman could not receive salvation unless married. She knew better.

Vincent had loved to quote the Scripture "and the truth shall set you free." Only he meant his truth. The twisted, self-serving heresy he peddled as God's word. Well, Hannah knew the real truth now.

She didn't need a man to save her.

After pulling down a suitcase from the closet shelf, she tossed it on the bed. She yanked blouses from the hangers and shoved them in the suitcase.

The only man she needed was Jesus. Yes, she had sinned, but she knew without a doubt she was forgiven. Her sins were cast as far away as the east is from the west. She slammed closed the suitcase and set it on the floor. No man was going to keep her bound and enslaved in a relationship she didn't want. She set a duffel bag on the bed and pulled open a dresser drawer, scooping out socks, and dropped them in the bag.

It didn't matter how much she loved Luke. She simply could not stay.

She yanked a drawer from the bedside table too far, and it fell from her hand, crashing on the floor. Envelopes scattered across her boots and the rug. Bending down, she bundled them up then paused, recognizing Luke's handwriting. She removed a folded piece of paper from an envelope and read Luke's words.

My Love,

I started clearing out the junk from the barn. I met a new neighbor. His name is Wade. We're using his tractor to clear the weeds from around the house. Next spring I'll buy a couple head of cattle. Good news, I booked my first hunting trip for this fall.

I think about the day that we'll be back together again. I relive every moment with you. Meeting you at the library, sitting with you in the park. Getting caught in a thunderstorm and how you laughed.

Stay strong. Know that I love you.

We'll be together again soon. I promise.

With love,

Luke

Her heart tore. Her legs week, she sat on the floor with her back against the bed. How she loved Luke. Even after all these years, she still loved him.

She opened another letter. The faded postmark revealed Lucky was only seven days old. He hadn't come home yet. Born premature, her baby was still in the hospital.

> *Dear Hannah,*
>
> *I know you must be going through a great deal of difficulty, adjusting to your new life. But I can't understand why you haven't written. Why you won't take my calls or call me back. Please, Hannah, just talk to me. I can't fix what I don't know is broke. Give me a chance. That's all I ask.*
>
> *Yours truly,*
>
> *Luke*

As steel bands of regret squeezed her heart, she sobbed. If things could only have been different.

She'd been so afraid. Once she discovered she was pregnant, she cut off all ties to Luke to protect him.

If her father had discovered she was carrying Luke's baby, he would've come after Luke. Three days before she fled, her father threatened to shoot Luke if he came anywhere near her. He forbade her to be friends with Samantha. Demanded she marry Owen Mitchell.

Terrified, she refused her father's demands. He

295

slapped her, punishment for back talk. Hannah brushed her fingers over her cheek, recalling the sting and pain of her father's hand.

Two days later, a Monday, she took the bus to school. Not sure who could be watching, who told her father about Luke, she slipped a note to Samantha. That afternoon, in the chaos of buses coming and going, she met Luke behind the library, and they went to the old farmhouse. She told him everything her father said. Seeing the red mark on her face, Luke left her at the farmhouse and went home. Later that night, he came back with dinner and a plan.

The next morning, she was on her way to Washington.

Fearful that Luke would make her come back, terrified her father would hurt the man she loved, she had no choice but to let Luke go.

She trembled as a wave of fear washed over her, threatening to pull her under.

"Please," she cried. "God, I'm so tired of being afraid."

The more time passed, her fears grew. Paula tried to convince her to call Luke and tell him about their baby. But no amount of reasoning penetrated the wall of fear that continued to expand in her head—in her heart.

As the years ticked by, she had thought about calling Luke, telling him he had a son, but she dreaded his reaction. Afraid that he would hate her for not telling him sooner, she never made the call. Tortured by what her father might do to Luke, she kept her secret. Eventually, she convinced herself that Luke had moved on, married someone else, started a family of his own. The fear of finding out he loved another, kept her from calling.

The door downstairs opened and closed. Rooted where she sat, she held her breath, waiting for Luke to find her. At the heavy thump of his boots on the steps, she stiffened. He appeared at the top of the stairs. His blue-gray eyes like lasers, seeing right into her soul.

He sat beside her and took the letter from her. Scanned it. "It's the last letter I wrote."

She nodded. Her heart lay in a thousand shattered pieces.

He checked the postmark. "Lucky was born."

Hannah stared at the floor and whispered, "He was still in the hospital."

"You didn't have to do that all alone. I would've been there for you."

She closed her eyes and lowered her head. Shame seared her heart.

"I can't let you take my son from me." His deep voice penetrated her agony.

Hot tears trickled down her cheeks.

Luke tossed the letter aside. "I won't let you hurt him."

She swallowed hard. No, she couldn't hurt Lucky. She didn't want to hurt Luke. But she had—she hurt them both. "I didn't mean to." The words stuck in her throat, her voice barely above a whisper.

"I know you didn't."

She ventured a glance at him. His red-rimmed eyes

glistened. Luke looked away.

"We did what we had to do." He exhaled long and slow. "I remember the terror in your eyes, the welt on your cheek."

Steel bands of regret gripped her heart. "He threatened to shoot you."

"That's why my father made the decision to help you. To help us."

"Now that I'm back—"

"We've got a second chance."

She covered her face. "But my father."

"We'll deal with your father. We're adults. He can't hurt us."

"He already has." She wiped the moisture from her cheeks. Her father's unreasonable demands and vindictiveness had run her off. Fearing he'd follow through on his threats, she did the only thing she could do—run away.

Glancing at the letters scattered on the floor, she ran her fingers over the envelopes.

"It's time we stop letting your father run our lives."

As the truth of Luke's words set in, she trembled knowing he was right. It was time to face her father.

Chapter Thirty

The next morning, she called Dane. Her eyes sore from crying. "My memory is back."

"That's great, but you don't sound too happy about it."

"I am," she said, her voice flat. "I mean, of course, I want my memories. It's just that. . ." She struggled to find the words to explain her heart's turmoil. "Everything is so complicated."

"Then simplify it," Dane said in his good-natured way.

She rested her head in her hands. "It's not that easy. Luke didn't tell me the truth."

"What, that you weren't married and haven't seen each other since before Lucky was born?"

Leave it to Dane to cut to the heart of the matter. "Yes."

"He was instructed by the doctors not to. We were all told to let your memories come back on their own. There was some concern that forcing you to remember could cause more trauma."

Hannah released a heavy sigh. "But he said we were married."

"No, that wasn't Luke. Lucky was the one who said you were married."

The memory of being in the hospital and Lucky's declaration came back to her.

"It put Luke in a real uncomfortable spot," Dane added.

Then she had to go and ask about a ring. Luke showed up with the simple gold band and placed it on her finger. Hannah rubbed her finger where the wedding band had once been. "Lucky doesn't want to go back home."

"Of course not. Your kid is smart. He knows a good thing when he's got it. You should've seen the first time he set eyes on Luke—instant hero worship."

She winced. "He follows Luke everywhere. Even mimics how he walks, talks, and stands."

"That little boy needed his father." Dane's serious tone pierced the armor she erected around her heart.

Hannah closed her eyes. "What am I going to do?"

"That's not the question right now. The question is how do you feel about Luke?"

Her heart skipped. "I . . . I'm not sure."

"Come on, Hannah. Be honest with yourself. You love him. You've always loved him."

"It's not that simple."

"I know, it's complicated." He chuckled. "He loves you."

She swallowed hard around the lump in her throat.

"Well, doesn't he?" Her friend compelled her to face the truth.

"Yes."

"So, what's so complicated?"

Tears stung her eyes. "My family."

"What about them?"

"They know I'm back. Someone is trying to send us a message by burning down one of the cabins."

"Whoa, burning down a cabin? Who do you think it is?"

"Probably my father and brother. I doubt my sister, Katy, would do something so vicious."

"You really think it's your father?"

"Yes. Luke says the authorities are working on the case because it's arson. But. . ."

"But what?" Dane prompted when she couldn't finish.

"What if they do more damage before they can prove it's them?"

"You're afraid for your safety?"

"Mine, Lucky's, and Luke's. The evil, Dane . . . it's hard to explain unless you've lived in it." She shuddered.

"You're right, I may not understand, but I know this world is full of evil. It's everywhere. Just watch the nightly news. I also know you are loved and protected."

"What if Luke can't keep us safe?"

"I'm not talking about Luke. I'm talking about God. So, the question is will you place your trust in God to protect you?"

Her laugh was short. "Sometimes, I wonder why I

bother talking with you."

Dane chuckled. "Because you know I'll tell it to you straight. Now what do you say, little sister?" he finished in a John Wayne imitation. "You going to run or face adversity like a man?"

Despite her aching heart, Hannah laughed, and tears of amusement mixed with frustration rolled down her cheeks. Dane always had a way of making her laugh even in times of difficulty.

"You know, Hannah, when good people don't take a stand, evil prevails."

He was right. Running solved nothing. Her past had caught up with her. Now she had to face it.

Knowing David had been lurking around the back of his property didn't sit well with Luke. Not hunting him down took every ounce of control he had. Wade, Trent, and Gabe urged him not to confront David.

When he received the call from Gabe that he and Sheriff Traeger wanted to meet with him, he drew a deep sigh. He met Gabe and the sheriff at the fire station. Across the metal desk, Gabe sat with a folder open.

Sheriff Traeger spoke first. "Luke, we want you to know we've spent a great deal of time on this. We want to catch whoever did this."

Luke faced the sheriff sitting beside him. His words raising alarm bells.

Gabe flipped through the pages on his desk. "We have

the lab results back, and while we know the accelerant was, in fact, a bottle of whiskey, we weren't able to lift any prints."

"So, if I hear you correctly, you don't have a clue as to who did this?"

Gabe shook his head.

"Did you talk to Vince and David Brady?"

The sheriff cleared his throat. "We did. Vince Brady couldn't have done this."

A fire spread through Luke's chest. "What about David?"

"David has an alibi," Sheriff Traeger offered.

Luke scoffed. "One of his wives vouch for him?" His voice dripped with sarcasm.

The sheriff tipped his hat back. "No, he was working."

"That late at night?"

Gabe sat back. "It's true, Luke. David Brady works nights in Missoula."

"Where?" He'd check into this himself.

Sheriff Traeger flipped through his notebook. "He's a security guard at the college."

Luke rested back in the folding metal chair. He didn't see that coming.

"He's not married," the sheriff added.

But he saw David with a pregnant woman.

Gabe closed the folder. "And Vince Brady is in no condition to have started the fire."

Luke cocked his head. What does that mean? Never mind, he'd take care of this. He should never have trusted the authorities. He stood. "Thanks, Gabe." He nodded at the sheriff.

"Luke." The sheriff rose. "Leave it be."

Gabe stood. "I'm sorry I don't have more to go on."

Luke left the fire department and climbed into his truck. His jaw clenched as his anger simmered. They weren't going to get away with this. He let the authorities do their job, and they let him down. Time to take matters into his own hands.

As he drove up the road to Pinegrove, Luke ran through his head what he'd say to old man Brady. Tell David he comes near his family or his property again, they'd answer to him. Forget the law. Maybe he should've asked Trent to come along, but this wasn't his brother's battle. It was his.

Sure, he could've asked Wade to come as a witness, but he really didn't want to involve his friend. No, this was his fight and his alone.

Outside the two-story farmhouse, Luke parked his truck and left the keys in the ignition. Kid's toys littered the front lawn, and paint peeled off the siding. A piece of screen on a front window whipped in the gentle breeze.

Before he got to the front door, it opened, and a man stepped outside, his hands buried in the front pockets of his well-worn jeans and his flannel shirt untucked. "What can I do you for, Luke?"

The resemblance to his sister shone in David's eyes and hair. But those brown eyes held a cold edge, his jaw set.

"I came to speak with your father."

"And what?" David snorted. "*Ask* for my sister's hand?"

"What I have to say is between your old man and me."

David crossed his arms. "I can't let you talk to my father."

Luke wiped his hand over his mouth. "Guess you know she's back."

"With your kid."

He held back a retort. "I can't have you or your father endangering my family."

David squinted. "I had nothing to do with the fire."

Luke narrowed his gaze. "But you know all about it."

"It was in the papers."

"What were you doing on my property?"

David blinked. "I wasn't on your property."

"My son says differently."

"I occasionally help your neighbors with repairs. I was on their property."

By David's steady gaze, Luke had no reason not to believe him.

"I happened to come along in time to save your boy from falling into the stream."

Luke took a half step back. Lucky hadn't said anything about falling into the stream. He should've chopped that fallen tree up into firewood a long time ago.

"Your son was on the other side of the stream, trespassing."

Fair enough. "I'd like to speak to your father."

David braced his hands on his hips and squared his shoulders. "It wasn't my father."

Luke struggled to keep his temper in check. It'd do him no good to lose it now. "I'd like to speak to him if you don't mind."

David's shoulders dropped, and he proceeded toward the door. He glanced over his shoulder and motioned for Luke to follow. "Come on."

Not convinced that Vince Brady was innocent, Luke plotted what to say to make Hannah's father realize, without a doubt, he wouldn't tolerate his mean vindictiveness.

But when he entered the house, he stopped short. His thoughts purged from his mind. Vince Brady hunched over in a worn recliner, wearing a tattered blue terrycloth robe; his hair was matted and long, his pale skin hung on his thin face and bony hands. The old man looked at him with tired eyes. His mouth drooped on one side, and drool clung to the corner of his dry and cracked lips.

"Pa, we got a visitor."

Brady grunted and slurred, "Who arrrre you?"

Luke struggled to find his voice. It never occurred to him that old man Brady was sick. Once strong, virile, and mean as a cuss, now he was old, broken, and not even half the man he'd been.

"This is an old friend of mine. He wanted to stop in say hi."

Vacant eyes stared off into the distance.

"As you can see, he's not up for visitors." David moved

toward the door.

Luke followed him outside. "What's wrong with him?"

"A stroke and Alzheimer's. Doctors say he hasn't much time left, but they've been saying that for a year."

Deflated and confused, he stared at the house. Ready for a fight, to set old man Brady straight, the fight knocked right out of him. Brady couldn't have set fire to the cabin. The old man couldn't have even had the wherewithal to hire it done. Not in his condition. Yet he believed David didn't do it either.

"Do you have any idea who'd want to torch my property?"

"No." Hannah's brother shook his head. "But I'll see what I can do to get answers."

"Hannah has been through a great deal. She's doing better now, but vandalism and the fire have her scared."

"Do you think I might be able to see her?" David's eyes softened.

Luke stared off at the mountains, giving the request some thought. "Let me talk with her. You should know she was in a serious accident. It's taken time for her to heal."

"What happened?"

"A car accident. She was in a coma and . . ."

"Your son said something about a brain injury."

He wasn't sure how much to tell David. "It's been difficult for her."

"When I saw you with your son in the store, there was no mistake he was yours. When he said his name was Brady, it was obvious Hannah was his mother. Your boy said they just moved here."

"I brought her here to heal."

"Why wait so long?"

Luke wiped his hand down his mouth. "I didn't know about him until the accident."

David's brow wrinkled. "You didn't know she had your kid?"

"Not until he called me."

David shuffled on his feet. "I'd like to see my sister."

"I'll   see   what   I   can   arrange."

Chapter Thirty-one

Hannah lay on the narrow exam table, staring up at the white ceiling tiles.

"No headaches?" Melanie asked.

"None." Hannah sat up.

Melanie glanced at her file. "You had mentioned having panic attacks."

Hannah swung her feet to the floor. "Haven't had one."

The doctor made notes. "Good. The swelling at the base of your neck is gone."

"I've been icing like you said."

Melanie tapped her pen to her lips. "And your memories?"

"I remember everything."

All the good times and the bad. Her childhood had been fraught with fear, uncertainty, and the pain of losing her mother. But she'd been close to David and protective of Katy.

"No blank spaces in time or aspects of life?"

"Not that I can tell."

"You grew up here in the valley?"

Hannah swept her hair behind her ears. "Yes."

"Here in Stevensville?"

She swallowed hard. "Pinegrove." She waited for the usual judgment to enter her doctor's eyes, but none came.

"Where's that?"

Right, Melanie wasn't from the valley. The certificates on the wall said she was from Oregon. "A little south of here."

"Is your family in the area?"

"I believe so."

Melanie tipped her head to one side. "You haven't visited them since your memory returned?"

"No." She shrugged. "Relations are a bit strained."

"Sorry to hear that."

"I suppose at some point I'll run into my brother or my father, maybe my sister. I'd like to see my little sister." Regret wound tight around her heart.

"Often facing our pasts, while difficult, can be healing."

Hannah nodded. "Thank you for helping me."

"I think you're doing well. I'll have you monitor how you're feeling and come in when you feel it necessary."

She stepped outside and strolled to the gallery. The sun warmed her cheeks, and flower baskets bursting with color hung on the streetlights.

She needed to talk to someone about all the feelings

swirling inside her. Someone impartial or as impartial as can be. Irene didn't know about her past, or at least she wasn't a part of it. The last time she had a heart to heart with Irene, she experienced a breakthrough. If nothing else, just having someone to talk to made her feel better.

She slipped inside the gallery, the bell announcing her arrival.

"Be right with you," Irene called.

A painting sat on an easel with oils and brushes. Hannah could barely make out a boat with men fishing, clouds etched in the sky.

"Hey, you." Irene walked toward her with a bright smile. "How are you?"

"I'm okay."

She wasn't sure if Luke had called his brother and told them the news, that her memory had returned. Or if he talked with Trent about her wanting to leave. Now that she stood in front of Irene, she wondered if this was such a great idea after all.

"Can I get you some tea?"

"Yes. Thank you."

Her eyes roamed the gallery, falling on photos of animals, mountain landscapes, and paintings of the river, an old barn, and a grove of aspens. Upon closer inspection, she discovered Samantha's signature on several of the framed photographs and Irene's on the paintings.

Her heart swelled, happy to see Samantha found an outlet for her photographs.

Irene held out a cup of tea. "Here you go."

"Thank you." Hannah folded her hands around the cup. "How are you doing?" She gestured to Irene's baby bump.

"I'm doing good. Morning sickness is gone."

"I remember that."

"How did you do it all by yourself?"

Clearly, Irene knew she regained her memory. Luke must have said something to his family. "I wasn't alone. Paula and Joe were terrific."

Thankfully, Irene didn't make a big deal out of her memory loss or gain.

Hannah sipped her tea. "Even Dane was supportive."

"Dane?"

"Paula and Joe's son. He was just a freshman in high school. He's like a little brother and an uncle to Lucky."

"Sounds as if the Lord provided you with a family."

"He did."

"Let's go in the back and sit down."

Hannah followed Irene to the back of the gallery.

"How long have you and Trent been married?" Hannah asked, deflecting the conversation off her.

"We were married in November."

"Oh, not that long."

"I got pregnant right away."

A blush warmed her cheeks. She, too, conceived right away, the first and only time. "Are you from the valley?"

"No, I moved here and met Trent or actually, I met Trent the same time I moved here." Irene shrugged. "It's a long story."

"Did you meet Eloise?"

"Oh yes. She was my dearest friend." Her voice wavered, and she blinked as if fighting tears.

Hannah's throat tightened. "She was an amazing person. I wish she was still here."

"I know she'd be thrilled to see you."

Hannah sipped her tea.

"And she would've been overjoyed to meet Lucky."

An arrow of regret pierced her heart. Because of her choices, neither Eloise nor Rhett got to meet their grandson. Her throat tightened. "I realize you probably don't know much about what happened and why I left."

"Trent told me about your father and the difficult circumstances you were faced with."

"I wanted to tell Luke about Lucky, but I was afraid for Luke's safety, for Lucky's, and for mine."

Irene stared, waiting for her continue.

"My father had threatened to shoot Luke if he ever found me with him."

Irene gasped. "And you believed he would?"

"I don't know for sure what he would've done. But he would've done something. But maybe if I'd come back sooner. . ."

"We can't change our past, but we can change the direction of our future."

She had the sense Irene was speaking from experience.

"Sometimes, for us to break the chains of our past, we

have to find the courage to face it."

"Does it make a difference?"

"It did for me." Irene sipped her tea.

"I keep telling myself now that I'm an adult, he can't hurt me, he can't make me do something I don't want to do."

"Standing up to those who've done us the most harm can be quite liberating." An edge of sorrow dulled Irene's eyes. "Often, if we don't confront our past, it eventually finds us anyway."

"That's what I'm afraid of."

"If you find the courage to face it head on, then you have more control over the outcome."

"If I hear you correctly, I should just face my fears and get it over with."

"Only when you're ready and feel strong enough to do so."

Hannah glanced back toward the front of the gallery, her gaze landed on a painting that made her breath to catch. Slowly, she crossed the room and stood in front of Jesus. A turbulent sea foamed around him, leaving Jesus' robe wet as the storm plastered his hair to his head. Water droplets clung to his dark beard. His warm brown eyes offered assurance as he extended his hand.

The picture was so lifelike, Hannah was tempted to reach for the hand offered. "It's beautiful."

"Thank you. Sometimes, our greatest achievements come as a result of intense trials."

She glanced around the gallery.

"Hannah, Luke never forgot you. He's never stopped loving you."

Embarrassed by the tears springing to her eyes, Hannah walked over to a framed photo of a mountain landscape and colorful wildflowers. The photo was of Angels Rest, a favorite place for Samantha, the place where Jared had first kissed her. She and Luke never did make it up there. Someday, maybe they could take Lucky and pack a picnic.

Irene placed a hand on her arm. "Hannah, give Luke a chance."

Her breath caught. A strange sense of déjà vu swept over her.

When Hannah left the gallery, she headed south on the highway. At the sign for the turnoff to Pinegrove, she slowed and turned up the road, toward the little town nestled at the base of the Bitterroot Mountains.

It's time to face her past. Time to stand up to her father.

"Lord, give me strength."

Her heart hammered against her ribs. She pulled to a stop outside the house she grew up in. Weather and lack of upkeep had taken its toll. Very unlike her father to let the house fall into such poor condition, with peeling paint and broken window screens. Discarded children's toys were swallowed in the unkempt lawn. He must have mellowed over the years to allow such a deplorable condition.

Her breathing shallowed as her conversation with Irene played in her head. She wanted to be free of her past, move beyond the fear and worry. If she confronted her father now, then she wouldn't have to look over her shoulder, wondering when she might run into him. She struggled with the idea that David could be involved with or even responsible for the fire and the vandalism to the fence. Her twin had a good heart. Or maybe that's what she wanted to believe.

But the community's teachings could've tainted him. How many wives might her brother have? She took a deep breath and released it, struggling to gather even a shred of courage to get out of the truck and go to the door.

I'm an adult, a grown woman with a child of my own. I can do this. But the little girl inside the woman's body clamored to run. Memories of being yelled out, falsely accused of "sinful" acts, slapped, grabbed, and pushed rose as bitter reminders of her childhood.

Will her father slam the door in her face or welcome her inside? Her hands grew damp. She leaned her forehead on the steering wheel. "God, give me the strength to face them. Am I doing the right thing?"

When she raised her head, she caught movement out the driver's side window, and her heart jumped. Her brother stared at her. No turning back, she couldn't leave now. Reaching for the handle, she opened the door and stepped out.

David's eyes held no anger or malice. His mouth

curved slightly upward in a tentative smile. "I wondered when you might come."

"I would've come sooner, but . . ."

"Your accident, I know."

"How do you know?"

"Luke came by."

Her mouth dropped open. "He didn't mention it to me."

"He came to find out information about who might have set the fire."

Her heart sank. She hoped Luke hadn't made a scene or threatened her father. Threatening Father was never a good idea.

"When I saw the truck, I thought it was Luke with information about the fire that might help us figure out who did it."

"Then it wasn't you?" Her voice strained with the effort to contain her relief and the emotions welling inside.

He tucked his hands into his denim jacket pockets. "No, Hannah. It wasn't me."

"What about Pa?"

Sadness clouded his eyes. "Come inside."

Hannah followed her brother along the cracked and chipped cement steps, then in through the faded and weathered front door. In the corner, near the fireplace, a man slumped in a tattered old recliner. Draped in a blanket, he wore a flannel shirt. His slippers poked out from the folds of the fleece.

317

Her breath lodged in her chest.

It can't be. She sought David for confirmation that the crumpled old man sitting in front of her was her father.

David's lips thinned.

Her father's once-dark hair now gray, his shoulders boney. He glanced up at her through red-rimmed eyes bordered in dark circles.

"Pa?" Her voice sounded small as she hesitated to kneel in front of him.

His eyes sparked, and his mouth twitched. "Lydia," he slurred.

Why would her father think she was her mother?

David stepped forward. "Pa, it's Hannah. She's come for a visit."

"Lydia," her father insisted.

She stood and faced David. "What's happened to him?"

"He has Alzheimer's, and a year ago, he had a stroke."

Tears pooled in her eyes. "I'm so sorry." Sorry for leaving, sorry David had to deal with this, sorry her father wasn't the strong, vibrant man he once was.

She blinked back her tears. "Where's Katy?"

"She's not here."

Desperate to see her little sister and apologize, make amends, she crossed her arms and shivered. "Do you know when she'll be back?"

"She left Pinegrove a few years ago." David guided her outside. The screen door banged shut behind them.

Her heart sank. "Where did she go?"

"Oregon. She's in a better place."

"She ran away, too?"

"I sent her there. She's with our Uncle and Aunt Williams."

Williams? A vague recollection surfaced. "Mom's brother?"

"Yes."

She stared at the house. The years hadn't been kind to the old place, nor her father. "What about his wives?"

"Georgia and Elizabeth still live here. They take care of him, but they work during the day."

"Our siblings?"

"Michael is in college. Leah married and moved to Utah. Diane is in Idaho. Jeremy is finishing high school. Rebekah lives here and is with Thomas Khmer."

Hannah cringed. "Jenny?"

"She's married to Jacob Mitchell."

Her stomach clenched. "I should've come back sooner."

"You did what you had to do. I'm glad you got away. That's why I helped Katy get out of here. Or you both would've been shackled to the Mitchells." He reached to touch her arm but quickly withdrew. "How's your head? Any more dizzy spells?"

"Did Luke tell you about my accident?"

He shrugged then shuffled on his feet. "The feed store . . . you fainted."

"How do you know about that?"

"I was there."

The realization sucked the breath from her lungs. "It was you."

He nodded. "I caught you." He kicked at the gravel with the toe of his boot. "It didn't seem like a good time for a reunion, so I left." A deep sadness cast a shadow over his eyes.

Her throat constricted as her vision blurred with unshed tears.

She threw her arms around her brother's neck and wept. When she finally found her voice, she said, "I'm so sorry."

"For what?" His voice strained.

"For leaving."

"You had to."

She brushed her tears away. "You don't hate me?"

"No, Hannah." His eyes glistened. "I'm just really glad you're   back."

Chapter Thirty-two

From the pain on Hannah's face, it was obvious she went to Pinegrove. Shock and disbelief dulled her brown eyes.

"Why didn't you tell me?"

Luke held out his hands. "I just found out."

"But you were there."

"Yesterday." He shoved his hands into the front jeans pockets. "I was going to tell you when the time was right."

"If we're going to make this relationship work, then you need to stop keeping things from me."

"It wasn't on purpose." He was trying to protect her. "I was waiting for a good time."

She brushed her bangs from her eyes and leaned against the back of the couch. "I'm going back to help David care for him."

After everything her father had done, she was willing to care for him? "If you can extend that level of forgiveness to your father, then can you forgive me?"

She jerked as if he'd thrown a cold glass of water in

her face. "Forgive you? For what?"

"For bringing you back here and letting you believe we were married."

She crossed her arms. "Dane said you couldn't tell me the truth. That you were following doctor's orders."

"We were."

She stared at the floor as tears ran unchecked. Her arms remained crossed as if protecting her heart. He wanted to pull her into his arms, tell her everything will be okay, but he wasn't sure that was the right thing to do.

"This is my fault," she whispered. "I should've come back sooner."

Yes, he wished she had come back sooner. He wished she would've called him, told him about Lucky. So much would be different if she trusted him.

"You can't change the past, Hannah."

She swiped away her tears. "I want to make this work."

"Me, too."

"Do you forgive me?"

"Of course, I forgive you." He drew her into his arms.

Hannah wrapped her arms around him and pressed her head against his chest. He exhaled. A thin thread of hope wound around his heart.

The front door swung open. "Hey, Dad." Lucky stopped in the entryway, his nose curled up. "Are you guys getting all mushy again?"

Luke chuckled.

Hannah released him and glanced at Lucky over her

shoulder with a smile.

There is so much riding on tonight. A real date with Luke. No Lucky, just her and Luke. Hannah stood in the closet, assessing her options. Silly, it was Luke, the father of her child. The man she's been living with, much of that time thinking they were married.

Afraid he was going to pop the question and afraid he wasn't, she was torn. She caught the direction of her thoughts. There was that word again—afraid.

"Lord, help me overcome this fear."

She had nothing for dating. Why would she? She didn't date.

Business suits, dress slacks, and jeans were her attire. A red dress she'd worn once for a Christmas party at the Chamber of Commerce hung in front of her. Amy had talked her into the dress. She held it up and examined the sleeveless red lace sheath, simple yet elegant.

"Mom, Aunt Samantha is here," Lucky yelled from downstairs.

"Okay."

For the Chamber party, she had wrapped a black shawl around her shoulders to feel less sexy and more covered. She hung the dress on the closet door as she searched for the shawl.

"Hi." Samantha stood at the top of the stairs.

"Hi." Hannah rummaged through the drawer.

"What are you looking for?"

"My black shawl I wore with that dress." She pointed toward the closet.

"Ooh, I like. You in this dress will knock my brother right off his feet."

Her fingers touched upon the shawl, and she pulled it out of the drawer. "Found it."

"What do want to wear that for? You'll take away the sexy of that dress."

Sexy made her feel vulnerable. "That's the point."

"Seriously? What are you so nervous about?"

"Everything." Hannah shrugged. "What if he proposes?"

Sam sucked in a quick breath. "Do you think he will?"

"Why would he be taking me to a fancy dinner?"

"How exciting!" Sam shrieked. When Hannah dropped onto the bed, shawl dangling in her hand, Samantha sat next to her. "You're not excited?"

"I don't know what to think."

"Don't you love Luke?"

"Of course, I do."

"Then what's wrong?"

"Someone is trying to hurt Luke . . . because of me."

"You can't blame yourself for others' actions. You're not responsible for the fire."

"But it's because I'm here."

"You don't know that."

"I do. My past is coming back to punish me."

Luke's nerves were pulled as tight as a bowstring. Sitting beside Hannah as they drove to Lolo, his insides knotted, like all those years ago when he asked her to the dance. Sam had covered for them as Hannah's alibi for the night. No way on earth would Vince Brady have let his daughter attend a dance with a boy. Especially, a boy outside the religious community.

Thankfully, Samantha's charm and quick thinking provided Hannah the opportunity to attend the Homecoming game and dance. But tonight, he didn't have his sister to cover the awkward silence hanging heavy between them. Not one for idle chitchat, he couldn't imagine how to break the tension.

He wrapped his hands tight around the steering wheel in an effort to hide their shaking. A lot was riding on the night. He needed it to be perfect, special, a night to make her want to stay and never leave.

He fidgeted in the looming silence. He had to do something to break the awkwardness. "Remember—"

"I was thinking. . ." Hannah said at the same time.

"You first." He grinned.

"No. Go ahead with what you were going to say."

He glanced over at her, all pretty in a red dress and black heels. Her hair cascaded from silver barrettes, snugged back from her face, and shimmering over her shoulders. She appeared younger—like she had the night at the dance. Then she wore a yellow dress that had been his sister's. She appeared through the gym door like a ray of sunshine.

He cleared his throat. "I was remembering the Homecoming dance."

In the truck's dim light, her cheeks stained pink, and she looked down at her hands clasped in her lap. "That's what I was thinking about."

His shoulders relaxed. "We had fun."

"Yes, I didn't know you could dance so well. Who taught you the two-step?"

Warm laughter loosened the tightness in his shoulders. "Barn dances with the McDermit clan."

"I stepped on your toes." She chuckled.

"Thankfully, I was wearing boots and not sneakers." He smiled over at her.

Her laugh was like spring rain washing away the tension. "I remember Jared and Samantha's ragtag band set up at the back of the gym."

"And the DJ the school hired kept turning up the volume until he finally gave up."

She tossed her head back and laughed. "He packed up and left. But Jared and Sam were a hit."

"Yeah, they were great."

"What happened to them?"

He shrugged. "I know Jared works a lot for his dad."

"Big Sky Log Homes?"

"Yeah. But I think that's an excuse. He left the band, and from what I hear, he's no longer on the worship team at Gabe's church."

"Samantha still loves him."

He nodded. "I think Jared still cares for Samantha."

At the steakhouse, he let her off at the entry, so she didn't have to walk over gravel in heels. Minutes later, Luke bounded up the steps as Hannah waited for him. He swung open the heavy door.

The scent of succulent, juicy steak held promise. While an amber wheat beer would've been more to his liking, he let Hannah pick out a bottle of red wine. Good thing Trent wasn't around to see him drinking from a long-stemmed goblet and talking about the fruit-forward, well-balanced wine with a hint of spice on the back of his tongue. He'd be razzed for sure.

Hannah's eyes danced in the light, her moist lips accented with pink gloss. Life was taking a turn he never saw coming. That's how it was when he first saw her all those years ago in the library. She turned his life on its head, and she was doing it again. The crazy thing was, he didn't mind.

He convinced her to order her prime rib medium rare. From her moans and half-closed eyes as she chewed, she was obviously enjoying every bite.

His T-bone was prepared to perfection. It had been years since he ate at the steakhouse. Not dating and the lack of special occasions to celebrate kept him from the valley's finer establishments. Maybe that was all about to change.

Their plates cleared, he leaned back, full, happy, and content.

Music filtered from the bar, and patrons left the dining room, moving in the direction of the country tunes.

He paid the bill and escorted Hannah into the bar where they found a small table in a back corner. He set the bottle of wine on the table and draped his coat over the chair. She folded her shawl over her chair, and he took her by the hand out to the dance floor.

They did the two-step and sauntered around with the crowd. The fast tempo of drums and searing guitar riff of a popular early-nineties rock song gave way to the twang of a George Strait ballad. Luke twirled her around the floor, caught her hand, and wrapped an arm around her waist drawing her to his side. Scraping of heels on the wood surface punctuated by the thud of boots in unison with the beat of a top 40's one-hit wonder. The band, anticipating the need for a reprieve, played a slow love song, and Luke drew Hannah snug in his arms.

With his cheek against her hair, he breathed in the sweet floral fragrance of her shampoo. Her hand rested in his while the other warmed his shoulder. He fit his hand against the small of her back. The song reminisced about losing the love of your life and having them come back. Spoke of being dead inside, going through the routine of life, but never really living. The lyrics defined the last nine years of his life.

After she had cut off all communication with him, he buried himself in work. His grandfather dead, the ranch sat vacant. He worked until the late hours of the night repairing fences, the barn, tearing down the old house and building a new one all in between hosting guided outdoor adventures.

He avoided the bars, not wanting to be bothered by women trolling such joints. They just reminded him of what he was missing, Hannah Brady.

A few times, he got sloshing drunk, but it only made the pain more intense. When getting smashed resulted in a pounding headache and him puking his guts out, he decided on another strategy. His temper made it difficult for him to hold down a job, so he started his own business. Keeping busy, working from dawn to dusk and beyond held the pain at bay.

Now things were different. Luke closed his eyes and basked in the feel of Hannah in his arms, her breath against his neck as they moved in unison. He felt more alive tonight than he had in years.

"I want to take you home," he whispered in her ear.

She nodded, and he led her off the dance floor and retrieved his coat. Hannah wrapped her shawl around her shoulders, and he hurried to the truck. They held hands on the way home. She sat in the center seat next to him. His thoughts were going places he knew they shouldn't. He had no right to do what he so badly wanted to.

If he made love to her tonight, then she'd have to stay. He'd show her how much he loved her. How much he wanted to set everything straight. She was the mother of his son. The woman he loved.

She wanted him just as much. Valentine's night proved it. But that was when she thought they were married. They're as good as married. Right? Living together, going about life together, raising their son together.

He didn't need a piece of paper giving him permission to love Hannah. He didn't need a judge or the state to ordain what he knew in his heart to be right. Hannah laid her head on his shoulder as they drove through town. Little was said—no need to verbally express what was happening between them.

Once home, he let Bear inside. Toby lifted his head from where he was sleeping curled up on the rug in front of the woodstove. Bear knew better than to challenge the cat for the premium space and resided to lying near the couch.

Luke encircled Hannah in his arms. His heart drummed loudly in his chest.

"I've been thinking." She wrapped her arms around his neck.

She could tell him later. Right now, he wasn't one for talking. He pressed his lips to hers and pulled her close. Their bodies aligned, fitting together like they were made for each other. Hannah moaned and sifted her fingers through his hair. When the kiss ended, he could scarcely breathe.

"I've been thinking," she said again. "That God used the accident to bring me back to you."

He plucked one of the barrettes from her hair, letting the silky strands cascade over her shoulder.

"And that he's giving us a second chance to do things right this time."

Luke paused from removing the other barrette. His

heart lodged in his throat.

Do things right this time. Those words struck him like a splash of ice water on his face.

"God's giving me a second chance, Luke. This time, I don't want to mess it up."

He rested his forehead to hers. She was right, God was giving them a second chance, and he couldn't mess it up this time.

She lightly set her hand on his chest, her shy smile doing crazy things to his resolve. He loosened his hold around her waist and sighed, knowing he couldn't carry out what he thought about on the drive home.

Chapter Thirty-three

Hannah parked her new SUV out front of her childhood home and stared at the house with her heart in her throat. A washed in memories of growing up in the house, the loss of her mother, and the hardship of being different, she hesitated to get out of the vehicle.

As a child of Vincent Brady, she was a member of the community, but she never did feel as if she belonged. She didn't want to be poor, forced to live on government subsidies, and wear hand-me-downs. She couldn't reconcile herself with her father's beliefs in having more than one wife. The undercurrent of jealousy, competition, and strife among his wives made her feel like she was walking between enemy camps. At times, she couldn't breathe. All she wanted to do was escape.

Sitting in her new vehicle with heated leather seats and new-car smell was vastly different from the fate of her half-sister, Jenny. The youngest of her siblings, married to Jacob Mitchell, stuck in this little town. Was Jenny his first wife?

When she became friends with Samantha, she caught a glimpse of life as she wanted. Her dream was to be the wife of one man, to have a family and a home to call her own—not to share her home or her husband with other women.

The Daniels family showed her a different way of life, a lifestyle she desperately wanted. Eloise, the perfect wife and mother, Rhett, the ideal father and husband. They were the example she strived to be someday. Maybe that's how she fell in love with Luke. He was on the inside, her ticket to the life she wanted.

Her friendship with Samantha drew her further from the life she was born into. Samantha, with her forthright manner and strong faith, had her questioning her father's ways. Samantha would open her Bible and point to Scripture and God's design for a man to be married to one woman.

Falling in love with Luke secured her dream. Until her father demanded she marry Owen Mitchell. Her father forbade her to see Luke or be friends with Samantha.

She took a deep breath and released it slowly. "Lord, give me strength to do this. Help me to show my father kindness."

Although her father wasn't the man he once was, she still felt the familiar fear rising inside. She swallowed around the lump forming in her throat. Her hands trembled, and her heart beat fast. Vincent Brady was a hard man, opinionated, passionate, and demanding. She learned early to approach him with caution, give him a wide berth, and be on her best behavior to avoid his wrath.

Rhett Daniels had shown her a different picture of a father. He hugged his sons and cherished his wife. Mr. Daniels had escorted his daughter to the father-daughter dances. Showed interest in Samantha's songwriting and, on occasion, took Sam out for ice cream or breakfast—just the two of them. How Hannah wished for a father like Rhett Daniels.

Eloise was like a mother to her, encouraging, wise, and passionate about her faith. Hannah's stepmothers were cold, distant, and verbally abusive. She hoped David was right and Katy was with people who care for her, encourage her, and listen.

Joe and Paula's compassion and love pulled her from the depths of despair and the confines of condemnation. They taught her about grace.

She got out of the vehicle and walked with heavy steps to the door. It was only right to spend time with her father, but it wasn't going to be easy.

David opened the door. "Thank you for offering to do this."

"How's he doing?" She stepped inside. A fire in the woodstove warmed the old place.

"Resting upstairs. You won't be able to get him down here. I practically have to carry him." He rested his hand on her arm. "Are you sure Luke is okay with this?"

She smiled to reassure him. "What do I do?"

Luke wasn't comfortable with her being alone in Pinegrove, but he respected her wish to help her brother. He accepted her need for reconciliation.

"If he's awake, get him to eat. There's soup and bread. Otherwise, he'll just rest."

"How long will you be?"

"Not more than a few hours. You have my cell number?"

She nodded.

After David left, Hannah climbed the stairs to her father's room. He lay propped against pillows, his breathing punctuated by a soft rattling in his chest. She pulled up a chair and sat beside the bed, hands clasped tightly in her lap.

"All my life I was afraid of you," she whispered.

The pictures of birds above the bed had been there as long as she could remember. Dust coated the old wooden frames. A cobweb stretched from the overhead light fixture to the corner above the door. The air hung stale and heavy. She approached the window and pushed back the drapes to see the back yard.

"You'd think having a couple of wives at least one would keep your room clean." She turned, and her breath caught. Her father stared at her. His gaze intense.

Hannah crossed her arms. Unsure if he was awake, she didn't move.

"You . . . came . . . back." He spoke more from his chest than moving his mouth.

Her heart lurched. She brushed her bangs from her

forehead. "Yes," she said, her voice small as if the frightened little girl inside was the one answering.

"I drove . . . you . . . away."

She swallowed hard to clear her throat. He had driven her away and Katy, too. Only David remained. Her father's confession disarmed her defenses. Hannah sat in the chair and slipped her hand over his cold one. It twitched at her touch as if he was trying to move it.

"Save your energy." She forced a smile. "Can I get you some soup?"

He closed his eyes, his breathing labored. When he opened them again, his eyes were clear and softened. "I'm dying."

"Oh, Papa." She battled the threatening tears and pressed her hand over her mouth.

"Find Katy. . ." His voice drifted off, and his eyes fluttered closed.

She nodded. Surely, David knew how to reach their sister.

He drifted into a fitful slumber.

Sensing someone behind her, she turned toward the door.

No one.

She peered out the bedroom door down the hall. "Hello, is anyone there?"

No answer.

A shadow moved across the wall at the bottom of the stairs.

Hannah hurried downstairs, her heart racing. But the

living room was quiet. The floor creaked in the kitchen. She covered her nose at the pungent scent of rank body odor mingled with acrid smoke. Goose pimples rose on her arms, and she shuddered.

She scanned the room for a weapon and grabbed the poker from the brick fireplace. Holding the iron weapon, she crept into the kitchen. Her pulse thundered in her ears. She rounded the doorway, but the kitchen was empty, the foul odor replaced by the faint scent of bacon from the grease left in a pan on the stove.

She lowered the poker and set it on the counter. *This house gives me the creeps. Maybe this wasn't such a good idea after all.*

The front door opened, and she grasped the poker, darting toward the front door.

A young woman carrying a newborn in her arms paused. Recognition sparked in her eyes. "Well, this is a surprise. Hannah Brady comes slinking back to town. Your guilty conscience got the better of you?"

Like touching a tender spot, Hannah's anger sparked. "Jenny?" Although grown, her half-sister still held the same nasty attitude.

"What do you plan on doing with that?" Jenny gestured toward the poker.

"Nothing." Hannah put the tool back on the hearth.

Jenny shifted the infant in her arms. "Where's David?"

"He's not here."

"So, he has you looking after Pa?"

"I offered to help." Hannah opted for a more gracious

337

approach. "Would you like to sit down?"

"I don't need your permission to sit in my father's house." She brushed past Hannah and plopped down on the couch.

"Congratulations on your baby.'"

Jenny's eyes flared with pride. "He's a Mitchell."

Hannah suppressed the urge to cringe.

"I hear you came back with Luke's kid." The words were flung at her.

She refused to be baited. "Luke and I have a son."

"So, I guess you ran off to have it, avoid the disgrace."

Her hands fisted. The hypocrisy of the woman! "I left to build a better life for myself and my son."

"You always did think you were better than the rest of us."

"No, Jen, you're wrong. I was just like all the rest of you. I just chose to make something better of my life." The words tumbled from her mouth before she could stop them.

Her half-sister snorted. The baby stirred, and she cuddled the child on her lap. "And now you're back to show us all."

She wouldn't be lured into an argument. "You know I don't think this is productive. I am going to have to ask that you come back when David is here. Right now, I have things to do." She slipped into the kitchen and braced her hands on the counter, taking deep breaths to calm her temper.

Jenny's acerbic attitude always had a way of getting

338

under her skin. Even as girls, they fought.

"You and Katy are cut from the same cloth," Jennifer called from the living room. "Running off just like your mother." The door slammed shut.

Hannah spun around and hurried toward the door. What did she mean running off just like their mother? Her mother grew ill and died. She stopped short of flinging the door open and going after Jenny. It didn't matter. It was just a bitter woman's ramblings. There was no truth to her words. Were there?

She reined in her conflicting emotions and went into the kitchen. Hannah heated a small amount of soup and carried the mug upstairs to her father's room. Awake, his gaze tracked her every move.

Uneasy, she offered a tentative smile. "I brought some soup and bread." Sitting beside him, she secured his hand around the mug and guided it to his mouth. As he sipped, liquid dribbled down his chin. She patted a paper napkin to his face. It brushed roughly over his whiskers.

He took a bite of bread and chewed.

Jenny's words continued to ricochet around her mind. She wished she knew more about her mother, but her father never spoke about her.

"Can you tell me about my mother?"

A spark registered in his eyes. His gaze fell upon the mug. After Hannah helped him eat more soup then take another bite of bread, she set the mug on the bedside table.

"How'd you meet my mom?"

The corner of his mouth twitched upward. "Lydia," he slurred.

"Yes, Lydia."

His eyes grew dark, and he grunted, his legs jerked beneath the bed covers. Hannah jumped from the bed. Her father's partial paralysis made it difficult for him to move, but his agitation concerned her.

"Why are you . . . back?" He spoke each word deliberately and with difficulty.

"I . . . I wanted to see you and David and Katy."

"Lydia . . ." he grunted. "Run away."

"Hannah," David called out for her. "You upstairs?"

She ran out of the room and down the stairs, leaping the last two steps, landing in front of her brother. Her heart pounded as she gasped for breath. "What happened to our mother?"

"What?" He removed his faded denim jacket.

She braced her hands on her hips. "Do you know? Do you remember?"

"Hannah, where is this coming from? Calm down."

"She got sick and died, right?"

"Yes."

"Then why does Pa think she left?"

He shook his head. "Because he's sick. He doesn't remember things."

"Then why did Jenny say I was just like my mother, that I ran away?"

David's brows drew together. "Jenny? When did you see her?"

"She came here looking for you. She said I was just like my mother."

"Have you seen the few pictures? You do look a lot like Mom."

"That's not it."

"What do you think? That Mom left? That she didn't get sick and die?"

She paced the front room. "We were young. I don't remember a funeral. Do you?"

"Of course, I . . . no. I was too young."

"You see. Is there a cemetery with a grave marking the place where she's buried?"

He held up his hands. "I don't know. Maybe she was cremated."

"Doesn't this all seem a little odd to you?"

"No. I'm sure there is a perfectly good explanation."

"What then?" She tucked her hair behind her ears. "What if she's alive? What if she's out there waiting for us to find her?"

"Now, Hannah, you're jumping to conclusions. It's probably not good for you to get this worked up given what you've been through."

David was right. She felt the beginnings of a headache. Her neck and shoulders grew tight. The last thing she needed was a full-on migraine and Luke having to come get her. She calmed her breathing and willed her heart rate to return to a more natural rhythm.

"When did you send Katy away?"

"She was a teenager. Pa was going to yank her out of

school and . . ." He stared up at the ceiling. "She wasn't safe here."

She sucked in a quick breath. "What happened?"

"Nothing. I stopped it."

"Stopped what, David?"

He turned his back and headed for the kitchen. "Just forget it. She's safe."

"I want to talk with her." Her heart sat heavy in her chest.

"Let me call, make sure she's still there."

"David, you hid her away and didn't bother to keep in touch?"

He leaned against the kitchen counter and faced her. "It was better that way. Best Pa didn't find out where she was. You of all people should understand."

She did. Still, the idea of her little sister out there living with strangers didn't make it any easier to accept. "You need to find her."

Chapter Thirty-four

Lucky opened his mouth for the spoon his mother held. She fed him the thick red cough medicine. He swallowed the cherry flavored syrup and shuddered. "Yuck." He smacked his lips and swallowed hard, trying to rid his mouth of the bitter taste.

"It will help you sleep." She screwed the cap back on and set it on the dresser then pressed her hand to his forehead. "Fever is down." She pulled back the covers. "In bed. Get some rest."

"Lots of people are sick at school." He started school three weeks ago, right after spring break.

"It's that time of year."

He snuggled under the blankets. "Will you tell me a story?"

She sat on the bed. When he scooted over, she nestled beside him. "What kind of a story do you want tonight, dragons and knights or spaceships on Mars?" Her hand poised over the two books on the bedside table.

"Tell me about you and Dad."

She lay down beside him with her head propped on her hand. "What do you want to know?"

"Dad said he met you at the library and asked you to a dance."

"He did. I worked with his mother in the library. I could read as many books as I wanted."

"Why did you want to read a lot?"

"I wanted to be smart."

"What did you think of Dad when you first met him?"

She smiled. "I thought he was cute."

Lucky snickered. "Did you want to marry him?"

"Not at first. I hung out with Samantha; she was my best friend. So, naturally, I saw your father quite often. He would offer to drive me home."

"Did he kiss you?"

"Eventually." His mother laughed. "Why all the questions?"

"'Cause, I want to know." He rolled to his side and stared at her. "Why did we leave?"

"You mean why did I leave?"

He nodded.

Her eyes darkened. "Because I was afraid of my father."

"Why?"

"Because he wouldn't have liked the idea of me seeing your father."

"Why?"

"I was supposed to marry a friend of my father's."

"You didn't want to?"

"No, I loved your father."

Lucky braced his head on his hand. "Didn't you try to tell him?"

"He threatened to hurt your father."

"Is that why I haven't gone to meet him?"

His mother nodded.

"Mom, why didn't you tell Dad about me?"

Her eyes glistened in the dim light. "I was afraid."

"Of what your father would do?"

"Yes."

"Why didn't you marry Dad?"

"I wasn't old enough."

"But you said your dad was going to make you marry his friend."

"In Montana, a parent can let you get married with his permission even if you're not old enough."

"And your dad wouldn't give you permission to marry Dad?"

"Correct." She touched his shoulder. "You know, Lucky, I am sorry for the decisions I made. I wish I could go back and change them, but I can't."

"That's okay, Mom. Now that you can remember again, we're still going to make new memories."

She laughed.

"We're going to stay, right?" He held his breath, waiting for her answer.

"Yes, we're going to stay."

He exhaled with relief. "Good. I'm glad Dad knows

about me."

"Me, too." She hugged him then kissed the top of his head. "Now go to sleep."

Luke stepped away from the bedroom door and into the living room. He hoped he wasn't playing the coward by not going into the room and offering to help in the conversation. But he didn't know what he could offer.

Hannah joined him on the couch.

"That sounded like quite the conversation in there." He crossed his ankle over his knee.

Hannah faced him, bracing her elbow on the couch and resting her head on her hand. "I guess it was time for me to explain things to him."

"He didn't appear upset by anything you told him."

"No, he's a fairly resilient little boy."

He clasped her hand. "No more thoughts of leaving?"

"No. There's nothing to fear of my father."

No, Vincent Brady was no longer a threat, but Luke still wanted to find out who torched the cabin and who cut his fence. The evidence of a liquor bottle and a broken window wasn't much to go on. Since it was the cabin closest to the street, vandalism was likely.

"I wish there was a way I could reach my father with the truth."

"What truth?"

She giggled. "The gospel, silly."

"Oh, that truth."

For a man who was supposed to be a leader in a religious community, someone who reportedly knew the Bible, Vincent Brady sure had things mixed up. Luke put an arm around her shoulder and waited to see if she'd pull away.

Hannah scooted closer and rested her head on his shoulder.

"You know, nine years ago we sat on this property, making a plan for our future."

She rested her hand on his chest, near his heart. "I remember."

He smoothed her hair back from her forehead. "How do you feel about going back to that plan?"

She lifted her head and looked into his eyes. "I think that would be a good idea."

He threaded his fingers through her hair and kissed her. The kiss deepened, and they slid back on the couch. Luke positioned himself over Hannah, careful not to crush her and rained kisses down her neck.

Her hands, moving over him, seared his skin. Until he jumped to his feet, putting distance between them. His breathing labored, his blood on fire. Hannah sat up, her lips swollen, her cheeks blazing.

"I think we better consider implementing that plan sooner rather than later."

Hannah checked in on Lucky before turning in for the night. Bear parked himself on the rug beside Lucky's bed.

The dog and her son inseparable.

She fluffed the pillow before laying her head down. Her lips still tingling from Luke's kisses. That was close. Thankfully, he had the strength to stop, because she wasn't sure she could. Just like all those years ago, her love for Luke clouded her judgment.

She longed to be his wife in every sense of the word. *I better start shopping for a dress and plan a wedding.*

The air calm outside, a stark contrast to the storm raging in her heart. There's so much to do, preparing for a wedding—set the date, order invitations, buy rings, a dress, flowers, cake. She breathed a heavy sigh.

Maybe she was getting ahead of herself. Luke hadn't actually proposed. Sure, his intentions were as clear as lightning in the night sky, but he hadn't actually asked her to marry him.

They acted like a married couple. Behaved like a family.

But she couldn't shake the sense that something bad was going to happen.

There's no need to be afraid. Fear is a lie.

Fear had caused all this mess.

"Lord, give me your peace. Help me to trust in you."

A song drifted into her thoughts, along with the memory of her and Samantha sitting on the deck, singing the old hymn.

I've got peace like a river in my soul. I've got love like an ocean in my soul. I've got joy like a fountain . . . Does Samantha still have the old book she found at an estate sale? Hannah's breathing slowed, and she drifted off with the lyrics on her mind.

The rabbit, deer, bear, and wolf stood in front of her. Fear contorted their faces, adamant were their pleas, but she couldn't figure out why they were upset. They were warning her about something, but she couldn't understand what.

The ground shook, and the trees trembled. The animals scattered. She fled through the dense forest till she came to a cliff. There was nowhere to go. The ground quaked, and she fell to her knees. A big hand came down to grab her, and she screamed.

Hannah jerked awake.

Her heart pounded against her ribs. Her nightgown clung to her damp skin. Light filtered into the room from the many nightlights—one in the hall, another in the bathroom, and yet another in the kitchen. Precautions should she or Lucky get up in the middle of the night.

It was just a dream. A silly dream. To purge the dream from her thoughts, Hannah prayed for Lucky. "Lord, heal Lucky from this cough and cold. Help David and release him of the worries for our father. Help us find Katy."

Thoughts of her father played in a loop—his illness reducing the once-strong, powerful Vincent Brady to a hunched-over, feeble man. All the years she feared him, avoided him, careful to calculate her every move as to circumvent his moods, his wrath.

Over the years, she sought counseling and read books to unwind the damage to her self-esteem. The summer after Lucky was born was a season of healing, growth, and new life. While she gave birth to Lucky, she was born anew spiritually.

Is there hope for her father?

Yes, she knew firsthand the power of God to heal the body, renew the mind, and regenerate a broken spirit.

The words of a song she heard on the radio drifted into her thoughts. She replayed the lyrics of hope, the need for grace, and for the Lord to carry her each day.

Toby lay at her feet, curled up and asleep. She gave him a quick pet before turning to her side and snuggling under the comforter. Her mind calmed, and she drifted into a deep sleep.

A man stood in the dim light, silhouetted in the doorway, his white shirt reflecting the light from the hall. "You can't have him."

"Yes, I can." She wouldn't give up. There had to be something she could say, something she could do, to help her father see the truth.

He entered the room. "You can't change him."

Her breath caught. "I can help him."

A cold, scornful laugh shivered through the room. "It's too late."

Hannah pulled the covers up to her chin.

The menacing figure approached her bedside and bent forward. "He's mine." The air crackled with his deep voice.

"No. You can't take him," she cried and bolted upright.

Toby stood at the foot of the bed, hissing toward the door.

Her heart pounded, her breathing heavy.

She stared out into the hall. Toby jumped from the bed and raced out of the room in hot pursuit. Of what?

Chills prickled her skin, and she shivered.

Footsteps descended toward her. She pressed her back against the headboard, drawing her knees up. Her pulse thundered in her ears. A figure appeared in the doorway. Her heart jumped.

She screamed.

"Hannah? Are you okay?"

Luke's voice penetrated her fear. "Luke?"

"Did you have another bad dream?" The bed dipped with his weight as he sat beside her.

She threw her arms around his neck.

"You're trembling?" He held her tight and rubbed his hand along her spine.

When her heart rate slowed enough to speak, she loosened her hold. "How long have you been down here?"

"I came down when I heard you yell."

She brushed her hair back from her face. "I'm sorry." Her pulse drummed in her ears.

Luke reached over and switched on the table lamp. "Do you want to tell me about it?"

"It was so real. A man came into my room and said I couldn't save my dad. He was . . . scary. I frightened Toby so bad he hissed and took off out of here."

Luke sat up straight. "Toby hissed?"

Lucky shuffled into the room. "What's going on?"

"Your mom had a bad dream."

Lucky climbed up onto the bed and lay beside his mother. Hannah sifted her fingers through his hair, and within minutes, their son was fast asleep.

Luke took Hannah by the hand and led her into the kitchen. He filled the kettle with water and set the burner on high.

Toby meowed at the slider wanting out.

"You're not going out, not this late at night." Hannah picked up the big cat and cuddled him. "I dreamed about the giant again. Then I fell back asleep and had this weird dream."

"I'm not sure it was a dream." Luke set a basket of tea on the counter.

She set Toby on the floor. "What could it be?"

"A premonition."

The phone rang, startling them both. Luke snatched the receiver from the wall.

Hannah held her breath. A late-night call could only mean bad news.

"Yeah, she's here." He handed her the phone. "It's David."

She cradled the phone to her ear. "David?"

"Hannah, sorry to call at this time of night."

Her throat tightened. "What is it?"

"It's Pa." He sighed. "He's gone."

She closed her eyes and swayed. "When?"

"Not long ago. I just got the call myself."

Chapter Thirty-five

At the back of the gallery, Hannah finished telling Irene and Samantha about the awful dream she had right before the call from David. Steam rose from the teacup she held to her lips. The purple liquid emanated a sweet berry scent as she sipped.

Irene sat forward. "So in this dream, a man comes into your room and says you can't have your dad?"

"And that I can't save him." Hannah set the cup down and cleared her throat. "Then I got the call." Fresh tears pierced her eyes.

Irene put a hand on Hannah's arm. "I'm so sorry."

"I don't want to attend the service. I don't want to see all those people, subject myself to their stares and ridicule."

Samantha set her cup down. "There's no need to endure their abuse."

"It's best you protect yourself." Irene patted her hand. "You can honor your father's memory in your own way."

Hannah shrugged. "Not all my memories are bad." A tear slipped free and rolled down her cheek. "I wish I could've reached him." She brushed away the stray tear.

Samantha swirled her tea. "All of creation declares his glory. If your father couldn't see that living here in this valley . . ." She shook her head.

Irene grabbed a chocolate chip cookie from the platter in the center of the table. "No one knows what happens in a heart those moments before death." She set the cookie on a small porcelain saucer. "Back to this . . . dream. Have you had anything like this happen before?"

"No."

"Are you sure?"

Samantha swiped a plump cookie. "Maybe not a dream, but something else . . . like seeing someone but then not. Or heard voices."

Hannah's mouth dropped open. "I'm not crazy."

"No, no, I didn't mean it in that way." Samantha took a bite.

Irene's eyes widened. "Are you thinking what I'm thinking?"

Samantha swallowed. "Probably."

Lost in the conversation, Hannah glanced from Irene to Samantha. "Excuse me, what are you guys talking about?"

"Demonic activity," Samantha blurted.

Hannah's breath caught. "You guys are freaking me out."

"Let us explain," Irene soothed in a matter-of-fact

tone.

Hannah squeezed her hands around the warm cup. "Wait. I remember when I was in the hospital I heard whispering and I thought I saw two little people standing in the doorway, but when I looked, no one was there."

Irene leaned forward. "Anything else?"

"When . . . when I visited my father." Hannah's fingers pinched against the warmth. "I was alone in the house, and I thought I heard someone." Chilled, she shuddered.

Samantha's eyes grew wide. "Who was it?"

Releasing the cup, Hannah rubbed the tight muscles in the back of her neck. "No one. Just this awful smell, but then it went away, and Jenny showed up."

"I remember Jenny." Samantha grimaced.

"A smell?" Irene tapped manicured nails against her cup.

Hannah wrinkled her nose, remembering the foul odor. "Yes, like bad body odor."

Samantha eased her cup onto its matching saucer. "Maybe you have the gift of discernment and can sense when they're near."

"Who?" Hannah reached for a cookie.

Irene tucked her hair behind her ears. "Demonic spirits."

Hannah dropped the cookie. "I don't think I want such a gift."

The following morning, the conversation with Irene and

Samantha still weighed heavy on Hannah's mind, but she wasn't about to broach the subject with her brother. Maybe it was being in the house that held so many bad memories. Or maybe it was knowing her father passed away in the bedroom. Whatever it was, she couldn't shake the creepy feeling. Her nerves tingled on high alert.

Hannah trudged upstairs with David behind her. "Have you called Katy?"

"No, I haven't had time to search for the phone number."

She spun around on a step halfway up the stairs. "David, you need to find her. She needs to know."

"I will. I promise."

At eye level with her brother, she gripped the handrail. He was tired. Puffy eyes accented several days' growth of whiskers shadowing his strong jawline.

Hand on her shoulder, he turned her around, urging her up the stairs. "Thank you for helping me with Father's things. I didn't want to have to do this myself."

"Nor should you." She stood in the doorway to his room. The bed, the pine dresser along one wall, his boots on the floor near the closet all suddenly seeming larger. She swayed and grasped the doorframe.

David slipped around her to the dresser. He opened a top drawer full of socks, undergarments, and T-shirts. He unfurled a black garbage bag and scooped a handful of socks into the bag.

Hannah sat on the bed. The old mattress creaked. "Shouldn't we see what we can give to charity?"

He shook a tattered sock. "Don't see any use in that. Most of these have holes."

Reaching over from her place on the bed, she pulled out a drawer crammed with papers. "This is going take time."

"Looks like that may need to be gone through. Let's pull it out and set it on the bed." Easing it from her hands, he hefted the drawer to the foot of the bed.

She crossed her legs, then sifted through the papers— old utility bills, expired contracts, sales receipts for tools and car repairs. She removed a crinkled photograph folded in two.

Her breath caught when she unfolded it. Her father stood holding David. Their mother held her. Her parents were smiling. "David, look." She held up the photo.

"Wow, that's us."

A lump rose in her throat. She turned the photo over and read a faded date written in blue ink. "We were only three years old."

"Let me see that." David extended his hand. He caressed the weathered and creased photo then eyed her before returning the photo. "You look a lot like Mom."

She tipped it to the light. "We have her hair and eyes."

"Wonder where that was taken. Doesn't look like this house."

She shrugged. "Do you remember if we lived anywhere else?"

"No, do you?"

Shaking her head, she set the photo off to the side.

David continued to dispose of the contents in the other drawers. Then opened the bottom drawer. "These seem like they might be important." He removed several manila envelopes and set them beside her.

She opened one and found her and David's birth certificates. "This is weird. Did you know your first name is Jesse?"

"Let me see that." He took his certificate. "Jesse David Brady. Why have they always called me David?"

Hannah shrugged. She read her certificate. "Hannah Ruth Brady. My name is correct." She remembered how difficult it was to get her driver's license without her birth certificate—she'd had to write the county to get a certified copy. "Didn't you have to present your certificate when you got your license?"

"No. Pa filled out the paperwork and signed it." David opened another envelope and gasped. His eyes wide, his mouth dropped open.

"What is it?"

"Look." He held up a stapled document. Divorce Decree, in bold black ink, glared back at her.

She inhaled with a shriek.

The document shook in his hand. "Mom filed for a divorce."

She pointed to the date. "David, this was filed the year she died."

"That's impossible." He dropped onto the bed.

Her mind raced. "David. Oh, David." She grasped his arm with a surge of adrenaline. "What if she didn't die of an illness? What if—"

"Don't say it!"

"But . . ."

"He didn't kill her."

"I wasn't thinking that." She jumped off the bed. "Maybe she's not dead. Maybe she's alive. Maybe she ran away like I did." She snagged the papers and waved them in the air. "That's what Jenny meant."

"Look at the date." David nodded to the document. "We were eight years old. That's when she got sick and died."

"No, that's what we were told." Hannah shook her head. "David, I think Mom is alive."

"That's impossible." David snagged the papers, set them on the dresser, and stared at the smattering of greeting cards on the bottom of the drawer. "Odd. Why would Pa save all these?" He grabbed one and read the address. "From our aunt and uncle in Hood River. That's who I sent Katy to live with."

"Hood River isn't that far."

He removed the card and flipped it open. "A birthday card?" He presented it to Hannah. A check floated and landed at his feet.

Dear Jesse and Hannah, happy tenth birthday. We would love to have you come for a visit soon.

With love, Aunt Audrey and Uncle Lawrence.

Hannah's heart slammed against her ribs. "David, I don't think this is from our aunt and uncle. Why would Pa hide it from us?"

"Who else would it be from?"

"Mom." She picked up a card. "David, this is proof. She's alive, and she's in Hood River." She seized the divorce papers and read the address on the letterhead, Hood River, Oregon. "This attorney is in Hood River."

He took the letter from her. "Maybe . . ." Disbelief widened his eyes.

She grasped her brother's arm. "Please, find Katy."

Chapter Thirty-six

Hannah held Luke's hand as they walked into the county courthouse and down the long hallway to the clerk of records.

"I'm so nervous," she said as they waited in line.

Luke squeezed her hand. "Why are you nervous?"

"What if we can't find anything? Then what do we do?"

"Let's wait for David to call Katy."

Hope waged war with uncertainty. "What if there is a death certificate?" Her throat constricted.

"Then at least, you have an answer."

What answer did she really want—did she hope to find? That her mother did die all those years ago? Sure, that would make it simple. Or to find out her mother abandoned her and her siblings? That opened a whole host of questions.

How could a woman leave her three children? Why would a mother do such a thing?

"Next," the clerk behind the counter called.

Luke nudged her forward with a hand on her back. Was she doing the right thing?

"Hello." She clasped her hands together on the counter to keep them from shaking. "I need to find out information on my mother who may have died when I was young."

The clerk with the nametag Debbie offered a sympathetic smile. She tapped on the keyboard then turned to retrieve a document from the printer. "I'll need you to fill out this form. If you want a death certificate, we'll need proof of your relationship to the deceased."

"I do not need a death certificate. Just to confirm the date of her death and possible cause."

"We'll need this form completed." Debbie handed her a long legal form.

Luke took the clipboard, pen, and the form to a chair. "Date of death," he read.

"That's why I'm here. I don't know for sure."

"You were eight?"

She nodded.

He counted on his fingers and filled in a year, leaving the month and day blank. "Reason for the request?"

"To prove if she is dead."

He wrote, "For health records." Luke shrugged. "We need your driver's license or photo ID."

She pulled out her wallet and handed him her new Montana driver's license.

They returned to the line and waited. Once called,

Hannah handed the form to the clerk who reviewed it. "You don't know what month she died?"

Hannah shook her head, tempted to remind the clerk she wasn't convinced her mother was dead.

"Well, a year is helpful. This may take us a few weeks to search our records. We will contact you once we have something."

Her heart sank. What was she expecting? That the clerk would type in a name, a year, and tell her something today? That was too much to hope for. "Thank you for your assistance."

They walked back to the truck. Luke opened the passenger door for her before climbing behind the wheel. "One way or another, you'll have your answer." He reached across the seat and squeezed her hand.

Hannah craved an answer. Waiting drove her to distraction so much so she left a load of towels in the washer for three days till they turned musty and she had to wash them again. She misplaced her keys to her car and forgot her cell phone at home.

This morning was the worst when she fed Bear a can of Friskies turkey in gravy and dumped a scoop of Alpo in Toby's dish. Bear looked at her as if to say, Is that it? While Toby turned up his nose and yowled.

No matter what the answer, she needed to know. Was her mother alive? She sat in the back of the gallery, sipping tea with Irene and Samantha. "I just can't help but wonder what if my mom is alive?"

"I know one thing for sure," Samantha said. "If there was any hope that my mom or dad were still living, I'd do anything to find them."

Irene reached across the table, placing her hand on Samantha's wrist. "We know where they are. And someday, we'll see them again."

Samantha held her teacup to her mouth. "What does Luke think of all this?"

"Much the same as David. That it's the ramblings of an old man. That the divorce papers were filed the same year she died."

Irene stirred a little honey into her cup. "But he did go with you to file the papers. That shows he supports you and wants to help."

Yes, Luke had been supportive of her.

Deep compassion softened Irene's eyes. "If you don't find a death certificate then the difficulty will come in trying to find someone who may not want to be found."

Her heart constricted. "But why?"

Irene shrugged. "Desperate people often have to do desperate things to protect themselves and those they love."

"Irene knows what she's talking about," Samantha said.

"But today, the Internet makes it much easier to find people." Irene tried to offer some encouragement.

Maybe that's what she should do—search the Internet. Hannah braced her chin in her hand. "If she is alive, then why didn't she take us with her?"

Irene leaned forward. "Maybe she tried, or maybe she couldn't."

Samantha reached for a slice of lemon pound cake. "Maybe she was going to use the divorce to gain full custody. Do everything legal like."

Her friends had good points. "Maybe I'm getting ahead of myself, and she did get sick and die." She took a deep breath and released it slowly. "How did everything get so messed up with my family?"

After eyeing Samantha's plate, Irene helped herself to a piece of pound cake. "Have you heard from Katy yet?"

Hannah shook her head. "I'm not sure David has called her. She might not be living in the same place. A lot of time has passed. She could have moved, gone off to college, maybe even married."

Samantha washed down a bite of cake with a sip of tea. "Have faith, God will see you through this."

"No matter the outcome," Irene added.

Hannah glanced at a framed picture of a lighthouse shrouded in thick fog. Its white beam of light pierced the darkness. A brass plate at the bottom of the photograph read, "The Lord is my light and my salvation: whom shall I fear?"

Samantha caught the direction of her gaze. "I took that picture on the Oregon Coast."

Plagued by the uncertainty of what happened to her mom, Hannah couldn't see her way out of the fog.

Luke took a break and chugged down a bottle of water before wiping the sweat from his brow. The steadily pounding hammers and occasional high-pitched whine of the saw music to his ears.

Better was to see all those who came to help rebuild the cabin. Jared supervised the team as they erected the walls. With the walls up, Trent and Gabe worked on the roof. Inside, Wade strung electrical wire, cutting in the electrical boxes and switches.

"Dad?"

"Yeah, son?"

"We're blessed with good friends, aren't we?"

Gratitude swelled Luke's chest. "We sure are."

"Will we be ready by Memorial Day?"

"Doubt it. That's next weekend, but we don't need all three cabins until mid-June. So, we're in good shape."

He handed Lucky a water bottle. The boy chugged a good portion down before letting rip a belch. "Excuse me."

Luke suppressed a laugh.

Lucky wiped his mouth on his flannel shirt's sleeve before running back across the yard and into the cabin.

Hannah drove into the driveway, and his stomach growled right on cue. Lunchtime. He gave Irene a helping hand from the passenger side.

"Brownies." She brandished a pan of dark chocolate squares.

Samantha pushed open the back door and reached inside to remove a large bowl.

He approached his sister. "What's that?"

"Potato salad." She carried the bowl to the picnic table.

Hannah lifted a small cooler from the back seat and handed it to him. "Sandwiches—ham and chicken salad."

Lucky raced out of the cabin and skidded to a stop in front of her. "Can I help?"

"Get the bag of chips from that back seat, please."

The banging and sawing silenced as word spread that lunch had arrived.

As everyone sat on the unfinished porch or found a log to sit on, Luke glanced around the circle of family and friends. Even his sister and Jared sat together, sharing a bag of chips. A mixture of gratitude and pride swelled in his chest. The sense that all was right with the world set his mind at ease.

For the first time in his life, Luke could truly say he was content.

Hannah's eyes flew open. Did she hear something? She lay still, listening to the quiet. The ticking of the bedside clock mingled with the low hum of the refrigerator down the hall. She rolled to her side and closed her eyes.

A flash of light and swoosh made her bolt upright. A shadow of a man moved outside her bedroom window. She scrambled out of bed and peeked through the blinds.

Voices broke the silence. Two shadows darted past.

An orange glow illuminated the yard. She wrapped her robe around her and hurried into the living room. Her breath caught.

"The barn!"

Flames spread up the barn's west side.

"What is it, Mom?" Lucky bolted out of his bedroom and skidded in his slippers.

"Hannah?" Luke called from the top of the stairs.

"The barn, it's on fire." She grabbed the phone and dialed emergency. "Lucky, put your jacket on, hurry."

Luke jogged down the stairs, fastening his jeans, and shoved his feet into his boots at the door. He thrust his cell phone in Lucky's hand. "Call Wade."

Lucky fumbled with the cell phone as Hannah gave the dispatcher their address.

She rushed down the hall and dressed then slipped into a pair of sneakers. "Lucky, get your shoes on."

"Branson, Lightning," Lucky yelled, gawking at the flames.

Hannah knelt in front of Lucky and held his shoulders. "I need you to be brave."

He nodded as tears streamed down his cheeks.

She wrapped his jacket around him. "Go to the front yard by the light and watch for the fire trucks."

"But Branson and Lightning . . ."

"Your father's taking care of them. Do as I say." Hannah handed him his sneakers then led Lucky out the front door and pushed him toward the yard light. There, her son would be safe, out of harm's way.

She ran to the back of the house.

Fire engulfed the side of the barn and climbed up to

the roof. The hay stacked near the wall provided fuel.

A lone figure stood with a hose leading from the well house and sprayed the barn. David? What was her brother doing here? Never mind, he was doing what little could be done to hold back the flames while Luke opened the stalls. Cattle groaned and called in the evening night. Horses screeched in fear. Luke's voice barely rose above the roaring blaze.

Hannah backed the truck out of the garage, parking it at the side of the road. Then she pulled the SUV to the front.

Bear lunged to the pasture barking, moving the livestock farther from the barn.

At the back of the house, Luke turned on the hose and sprayed the siding and the roof.

She hurried beside Luke, and he shoved the hose in her hand. "Get it wet. If the flames get anywhere near here; I want you out."

Her heart hammered. She nodded her understanding.

Luke retrieved a shovel from the garage and scraped back the bark dust she had laid along the flowerbeds, around the purple pansies she had planted. They worked together to protect their home from the flames and burning embers sparking in the night sky.

Grabbed by her arm, she spun around. "Find Lucky."

"David!"

"Find your son. You have to protect him." He snatched the hose from her hand and continued to spray the house.

"What are you doing here?"

369

"Hannah, do it. Find Lucky."

Behind her, the barn's west wall crumbled.

Luke raked chunks of burning debris off the deck. She sprinted toward the garage. An explosion rocked the ground. She stumbled and covered her head. Sirens wailed in the distance.

"Lucky." She ran to the front yard light, but he wasn't there.

She scanned the side yard for her son. "Lucky!"

Why didn't he listen?

Fire trucks arrived and whirred around the SUV. Hannah scrambled to the truck and searched inside, but no Lucky. She ran to the SUV and yanked open the doors.

"Lucky, where are you?"

She sprinted into the house through the front door. "Lucky." Her heart pounded.

No response.

"God, please. Where is he?"

Outside, Wade arrived in his truck. She bolted out the front door and leaped off the porch. "Have you seen Lucky?"

"No, I just got here."

"I can't find him."

"When was the last time you saw him?"

"Luke gave him his phone and told him to call you."

"I never heard from him. I saw the glow and heard the sirens. I came as fast I could."

Her heart plummeted. "Help me find him."

"Did you check inside the house?"

"Yes, he's not inside."

"Where is Bear?"

Her stomach twisted. "I don't know."

"Find Bear, you find Lucky."

Wade limped toward the pasture. "Lucky," he called. "Bear. Come, Bear."

"Lucky," Hannah cried.

Luke raced toward her. "Where is he?"

"I don't know. I can't find him."

Luke searched the pasture, the front yard, calling for his son. "Lucky!"

Panting heavily, Bear loped from the road toward Wade. "Bear, where is he?" He bent and grabbed the dog by his collar.

Hannah pressed her hand over her mouth, unable to believe Bear would leave Lucky if he was in trouble. "Where did Bear come from?"

Wade pointed toward the road. "Maybe he's on the road on his way to my house."

"That doesn't make sense." Hannah brushed back her hair from her eyes. "Bear wouldn't have left him."

David sprinted up to her. "Where is he?"

"I don't know. I can't find him."

David raked his hand through his hair and cursed. "Are you sure?"

"Yes, I checked the house. David, what's going on?"

But before David could answer, Luke grasped her brother by the arm, spun him around, and punched him in the jaw.

371

David hit the ground.

"No, Luke. Don't." She grabbed Luke's arm, but he wrenched it free. She stammered backward.

"What have you done, you no-good—"

David scrambled to his feet and wiped the blood from his lip with the back of his hand. "We don't have time for this."

"How dare you come on my property and threaten my family."

"She's my family, too."

Luke glared.

"Stop it. Stop it." She faced her brother. "Please, David, if you know what's happened to Lucky . . ."

"Owen and his son, Gene, started the fire. They burned down your cabin, too." His dark eyes held a plea. "I overheard them talking, and I've been watching them, waiting for them to strike again." He closed his eyes. "I think they have Lucky."

"No, David. Please, God, no." Her legs buckled, and she crumpled to the cold hard ground.

Chapter Thirty-seven

Sitting between the two men, Lucky folded his arms in an effort not to touch either one. Tears streamed down his cheeks. "Where are you taking me?"

The one to his right rubbed his hand where Lucky had bit him in an attempt to break free. "Shut up, kid. I ought to—" He raised his hand as if he was going to strike Lucky.

Lucky shrank in the seat and kept his head down.

"You'll do nothing," the older one snarled driving the loud truck.

A sinking sick feeling gripped Lucky. He shoved his hand into his coat pocket and wrapped his fingers around his father's phone. How could he make a call without them seeing? Maybe if he knew more about these men, he could trick them and get away.

"Do you know my mom and dad?"

"Yeah, kid, we go way back." The old man steered the truck through a curve, causing Lucky to lean into the younger one.

He didn't believe either of these men were friends with his dad. His dad wouldn't have friends like these.

"There was a time your mother was going to marry me." The old man sneered.

This must be the man Mom was supposed to marry. The reason she ran away to Walla Walla. Lucky shivered. He looked mean, smelled bad, and acted scary.

Dark outside, he couldn't see where they were going. The road turned rough and bumpy, and by the pings against the truck, he guessed they were on a gravel road. Guessing from the slant of the truck, they were going up in elevation, and his ears popped.

"Ever see an emerald, kid?" the younger one asked.

"No, sir," he mumbled.

"Well, they're right pretty. Ain't they, Pop?"

"Shut up, you idiot."

"Just sayin'."

"Aren't they green?" Lucky asked, remembering details from his geology class.

"Yeah, real pretty green. Just like money."

"Gene, I won't warn you again."

So the younger one's name was Jean. That was a girl's name.

He could only hope by now his parents realized he was missing.

Luke paced the dining room as Trent and Sheriff Traeger gathered information from David. Officers filed into his home, and one set up her laptop on the table.

David dabbed a wet washcloth to his swollen lip. "My guess is they took Lucky to a cabin just south of Cougar Mountain."

The sheriff spoke into his radio. "I want all roads in around Cougar Mountain blocked." He faced David. "Think they'll demand a ransom?"

"Yeah, but it will be for information, not money."

Trent leaned against the kitchen counter. "What kind of information?"

David spread his hands, and then lifted his gaze across the table to Hannah and Luke. "This isn't about you, Hannah. They want the emerald mine."

"Emeralds!" Luke snapped. "They burned down my property to get to you?"

David hung his head. "With Hannah and Katy gone, they had nothing to get to me. No bribery, no threats. I'm not married, no kids, not even a girlfriend."

Liar!

Luke braced his hands on his hips. "I saw you with a woman at the grocery store."

"Jenny, my sister. She's married to Jacob." David crossed his arms. "I help her out, take her to the store, and she tells me things. That's how I knew they let your cattle loose and burned down your cabin. That's how I knew they were planning worse."

"Why didn't you tell us what was going on?" Hannah said, her voice hoarse from crying.

"I found out a few days ago. I thought if I could catch

them in the act, I could make sure they were put away for good. In jail, where they belong." He braced his hands on the table and leaned forward. "No cop in this county will touch a Mitchell without real proof." David pinned the sheriff under his gaze. "Right, Sheriff? We don't bother you; you don't bother us. It's an unspoken rule in this county when it comes to Pinegrove."

The sheriff didn't respond.

But Luke knew it to be true.

Trent cleared his throat. "I know that area. Three hunting cabins are up there. Which one will they be in?"

"It faces east. No porch, just a green metal roof and windows on all four sides."

"I can have a handful of men up there by morning light, sheriff." Trent pushed to his feet.

The sheriff nodded. Trent stepped away and made a call from his cell phone.

"I don't understand." Hannah pressed her hand to her forehead. "Why would they take Lucky?"

"Because when you came back, you gave them the opportunity they needed to get at me. They want the mine."

Luke ran his hand over his eyes. "Why the fires?"

"Revenge I guess. Pa traded Hannah for the deed to the mine."

Hannah gasped. Luke knew Brady was a monster, but to purchase a mine with his daughter's life . . . He clenched his hands into tight fists.

"When we saw Luke and Lucky at the grocery store

and Jenny insisted on talking with Lucky, she knew you came back. Jenny told Gene you were back and had a kid with Luke."

Trent came back to the table. "I have to go. Sheriff, I'll keep you posted."

Luke jumped from the table. "I'm going with you."

"Don't think that's wise." Trent put a hand on his shoulder. "You need to stay here with Hannah."

"I'm not taking no for an answer."

Trent sighed. "All right, but you follow my orders. I don't want anyone getting hurt."

Luke ran upstairs and yanked his heavy canvas jacket from the closet. Then from his office, he retrieved his pistol and the extra clip and shoved a box of 9-mm shells in his coat pocket.

Hannah handed him Lucky's gloves and scarf. "Take these." Her hands trembled. "He's probably cold."

Luke's gut twisted, and he closed his eyes. The vision of his son shivering and cold haunted him.

"It's going to be all right." He hugged her. "You hear me? He's going to be fine."

She clung to him.

He cupped her face in his hands. "Pray for us."

Nodding, she wiped her tears from her cheeks.

Outside a fire engine remained, dousing the glowing embers of what was left of the barn.

Gabe walked up to them with a pair of shoes. "I found these by the yard light."

Luke's stomach dropped. "They're Lucky's. I'll take

377

them."

"Is there anything I can do to help?" Gabe asked handing him the shoes.

"Pray." Trent glanced back at the house. "And if you can, check in on Hannah."

"I will."

Luke climbed into his brother's truck, David sat in the back seat behind him, and they headed west into the Bitterroot Mountains.

Cold, Lucky shivered. Along the trek from the truck to the cabin, moisture penetrated his slippers' thin soles. His wet feet ached, and his flannel pajama pants couldn't keep the cold away. The sharp smell of smoke mingled with mildew stung his nose.

The fire Gene built in the woodstove had yet to warm the cabin.

He wrapped his arms tight around himself. "What are we doing here?"

"We're waiting," the old man grumbled.

"For what?"

"To be contacted."

"By who?" Lucky coughed.

"You ask too many questions, kid."

Lucky shrank back in the hard chair. "Just curious." He had to find a way to call his dad without them seeing. "I have to go to the bathroom."

"Well, there isn't a toilet in this place," the old man

said.

"Just the wide-open outdoors," Gene snickered. He picked up a pack of cards and shuffled them.

It was still too dark to see. But that might be what he needed to escape. Then again, his slippers weren't going to help. If he had his shoes, he could probably outrun them. But in his slippers?

Plus, he didn't want to catch hypothermia. So, he'd best stay put for now. Maybe his dad had the phone company pinging the phone. He saw that on a show once. One of those cop shows he and Uncle Dane watched when Mom was at a client's late.

"Can I at least go outside and pee?" He covered his mouth and coughed.

The older one glared at him with narrow eyes. He was mean.

"I'll take ya." Gene stood, leaving the cards laid out in a row on the table.

Lucky followed Gene outside to a tree. "Can you stand over there, please?"

With a grudging huff, Gene stepped back a few paces. Lucky turned his back and slid the phone from his coat pocket and dialed home then set it against the tree. He stepped a few feet away and did his business.

The phone rang once, and Hannah snatched it from the wall. Her heart in her throat. "Hello." No answer. "Is anyone there?" Hannah pressed the phone tight against her ear. "Lucky, is that you?"

"Stay on the line, ma'am. We're tracing the call," a female officer instructed from the dining room table.

"Lucky, honey. I love you so much. If you can hear me, know that I love you. Your daddy loves you. He's so proud of you." Her voice cracked.

"A little longer," the officer said.

Fear sliced through her. "Sweetheart, don't be afraid. Be brave for Mommy." She trembled. "God is with you. Jesus is watching over you, sweetie. We're going to get through this."

"Got it." The female officer stared at the laptop open in front of her.

A thin thread of hope wrapped around Hannah's heart. "You have his location?"

"Yes," the officer said without raising her eyes from the screen.

Samantha clasped her hands and raised her eyes. "Thank you, Jesus."

Irene turned from staring out the dining room slider and offered an encouraging smile.

"Lucky, can you hear me? Are you there?" Her heart shattered into a thousand pieces. "Please, honey, say something. Let me know you're okay."

Crackling and what sounded like footsteps came across the connection, then Lucky's voice. "I'm coming." He coughed several times.

From a distance came the voice of a man. "Hurry up, boy!"

Her stomach dived.

"Hold your horses," Lucky grumbled.

"Lucky!" She grabbed Samantha's hand. "I heard him. He's okay."

"What did he say?"

"I'm coming. Hold your horses." She giggled.

"Let me listen." Samantha took the phone.

Irene stood beside them. "What do you hear?"

Samantha shook her head. "Nothing."

Hannah wiped a stray tear from her cheek. "But I heard him."

Sam handed Hannah the phone.

She faced the female officer. The computer screen reflecting blue and green in the lens of her glasses.

"Did you hear my son?"

"Yes, ma'am."

"What do think it meant?"

"We don't know. But we think your son dialed home and put the phone down someplace outside."

Her heart plummeted. "He's outside?"

"The phone is. We hear someone walking and crickets."

Her heart sank. "He's outside. He must be cold." Her son is out in the wet and cold, and his cough is back.

The officer pressed an earpiece tighter to her head. Silence hung heavy in the air until she finally spoke. "We're analyzing the call, but we think your son was outside briefly and made the call."

Hannah breathed a sigh of relief. "He dialed home."

She cupped her hand to her mouth to suppress the cry rising in her throat.

Samantha stood with her arms crossed. "Smart kid."

Hannah's legs faltered, and she grabbed the back of a chair.

"The call has ended. We need you to hang up the phone while we wait to be contacted by the kidnapers."

Chapter Thirty-eight

David led them to a cabin in the mountains nestled at the bottom of a hill and surrounded by thick forest. Luke rubbed his sore knuckles, wishing he hadn't hit David. He grimaced at seeing the strawberry on David's chin and swollen lip. It was a gut reaction. How was he to know David had followed Owen and Gene Mitchell to the house? His reaction pure adrenaline and fear. There was no time to think, only to react.

Dawn broke, and a ribbon of light appeared in the eastern sky. Trent peered through binoculars at the cabin below.

"Think they're armed?" Luke asked.

David nodded.

"Best to assume they are." Trent lowered the binoculars.

Luke pulled his gun from his holster beneath his coat and dropped the clip to see how many rounds were in it. It was full. Ten rounds in the clip.

"Put it away," Trent whispered.

Luke pointed down the hill. "That's my son."

"Yeah, and I have five guys surrounding this place. I don't want anyone hurt."

He shoved the clip in place with a click and slipped the gun back beneath his coat.

Trent held his finger to the earpiece. "Apparently, Lucky went outside and dialed home. The phone is still somewhere outside."

Pride swelled in Luke's chest. "That's my boy."

David sat against a tree. "I know both are armed. And there might be a rifle or two inside."

Trent listened again through his earpiece then confirmed their location.

"What's the plan?" Luke crouched beside a ponderosa pine.

His brother leaned against another tree. "I've got a negotiator getting into place."

"A negotiator," Luke whispered loud.

Trent pressed his finger to his mouth.

Down the hill, a man scurried from tree to tree, working his way closer to the cabin, a rifle slung over his shoulder. Then he dropped on his belly and crawled to the truck. What in the world?

The truck rocked from side to side as the tires deflated.

Owen Mitchell met his match. If he thought he could mess with the Daniels family, he was sorely mistaken. The man on the ground waved for the others to close in.

"Stay put," Trent ordered David and Luke.

Luke stood. "I'm not staying here."

His brother rose to his full height. "You are."

"That's my kid."

"Yeah, and he needs to be raised with a father. Stay put." Trent pointed at the ground.

"Or what?"

Trent leveled a warning glare. "Don't tempt me, little brother."

Luke raised his chin to meet Trent eye to eye, even as his brother stood a good three inches over him. His hands fisted and loosened. He needed to do something. "He's my son," he repeated the only words that made sense.

"I know. Trust me. When I get your kid out of there safely, he's all yours. In the meantime, watch your temper."

David bowed his head and clenched his hands together as if he were praying. He lifted his head. "Hannah needs you."

Defeated, Luke slouched against the tree he'd been hiding behind. "All right, I'll stay put."

"Watch him." Trent eyed David. "And if he tries anything, knock him out."

David nodded.

No doubt, David would like an opportunity to repay him for that swollen lip and sore jaw. Luke winced. He should probably apologize for hitting David, but he couldn't bring himself to do so.

Trent ducked low, sprinting down the hillside. In the

surrounding trees, Luke caught movement. He wiped his hand across his eyes and over his mouth. "Jesus, that's my kid down there. Please, Lord, protect him."

There was a lot of firepower down there. If things went nuts and bullets started flying, his kid could get caught in the crossfire.

He leaned his forehead against the rough bark and closed his eyes. "God, please." Compelled to pray, but he couldn't find the words. Besides, why would God listen to him? He made a mess of his life, turned his back on God. Made horrible decisions.

What had his father used to say? "Be sure of this, your sin will find you out."

Now he's reaping what he sowed.

"Please, God, protect my son." The words squeezed through his tight throat.

At the rustling of leaves and twigs, Luke opened his eyes and peered around the tree.

David scrambled down the hillside to Trent. They exchanged words, and then David rose and walked up to the cabin.

Luke stood, ready to run down the hillside and save his son. Trent stared him down, shaking his head. Luke's knees weakened, and he crumbled to the spongy ground.

"God, that's my boy down there. Please, don't take him." Thorns of regret pierced his heart. "Take me instead."

Hannah paced the kitchen with her arms crossed. When the door opened, her heart lurched.

Gabe entered, wearing his yellow firefighter jacket, a helmet tucked under his arm. "The fire is contained."

Over her shoulder, in the predawn light, the red glow was gone. In the fire engine's headlights, smoke curled from the barn's ashen remains. The air hung heavy with acrid smoke.

Wade entered behind him and closed the door. "The horses are safe, and the livestock are in the north pasture."

But their reassurance meant nothing. She needed to know if they found Lucky.

She wiped the tears seeping from her eyes.

The officer sitting at her dining room table provided little comfort. She pressed the earpiece to her ear then glanced up at Hannah. "They found the cabin and the phone."

Hannah swayed and would've collapsed if it weren't for Gabe. He held her upright, guiding her to the couch. "You better sit."

"They have the cabin surrounded."

As Hannah tried to make sense of the words the officer spoke so calmly, Irene sat beside her and took her hand. "Trent's with them. He won't let anything happen to Luke or Lucky."

Samantha handed her a glass of water and sat on her other side. "Maybe we should pray."

Gabe and Wade joined them. Each taking turns

praying for Lucky's safety. For Luke to be strong. Praying for the officers and that no one would get hurt.

Gripped in deep sorrow, Hannah prayed, "Lord, I'm sorry for keeping Lucky from Luke. I'm sorry for not trusting you. For being afraid. Please, God, forgive me. Give me a chance to make it right."

Samantha put her arm around her shoulders. "Jehovah is a God of second chances."

The words familiar, Hannah gawked at her friend.

Samantha shrugged. "That's what Mom used to say."

Irene squeezed her hand. "Do not fear, Hannah. Fear is a lie."

She gaped at Irene.

Her friend lifted a shoulder. "Another one of Eloise's sayings I found to be true."

Hungry and tired, Lucky wanted to go home. The old man dozed off in the ugly brown chair, while Gene played cards at the small table. Lucky sat in the rocker pushing it with his foot. The hardwood legs squeaked in rhythm as he rocked back and forth. The faint musty smell receded as the sharp scent of wood smoke filled the cabin. The fire snapped and crackled, chasing away the cold.

"Hey, Mitchell. You want to know where the mine is, give me the boy," a voice shouted outside.

The old man sprang to his feet.

Gene jumped up, knocking the chair over. "All be, he showed up, just like you said he would, Pa."

"Hush, we need to make sure he's alone." Mitchell snatched a rifle off the rack near the small kitchen and then pressed his back against the wall and cracked the door. "You alone?" he bellowed.

"Yeah, I'm alone. Let me see the boy."

Lucky's heart beat fast. He sat forward in the chair. "Who is that?"

Mitchell cocked his head for him to come to the door. "Your uncle. Now show yourself at the door. Then you get back in the chair. You hear me, boy?"

Lucky nodded. Slowly, he stood and walked to the door. His breath caught when he saw the man he now knew to be his uncle David.

Gene lurked behind the door, with a gun pointed outside.

When Gene snagged Lucky by the arm and yanked him back, Lucky stumbled and fell against the old man.

"Get off me, kid. Now go sit and be quiet."

Lucky did as he was told.

Was his dad out there?

"I need to talk to him, Gene. Make sure he's okay."

"You don't need nothin' of the sort. Now here's what we want. We want the deed to the mine, signed over to us. Then you can have the boy."

Mitchell grinned at Gene, seeming satisfied with his show of who's in control. His teeth yellow from behind his gray stubble.

"That's going to take time," David responded.

"You have an hour."

"That's impossible. I can't get off this mountain in an hour."

Mitchell rubbed his wrinkled hand along his jaw, his whiskers rasping like sandpaper.

Gene stared with bug eyes. "What now, Pa?"

"I'm thinking."

Lucky paused the chair's rocking. "We could get the deed later if he wrote up a letter." His chest tight from his cough. He needed is cough medicine.

"Shut up. Who asked you?" Old man Mitchell glared.

"He's got a point, Pa."

Seeing Gene was open to the idea, Lucky continued, "He can write up a letter of intent."

"What kind of a letter?" Gene loomed closer.

"An intent to sell the mine." Lucky's voice grew froggy, and he coughed several times.

"I'm not paying for the mine. It's rightfully ours. David's old man stole it from us."

"A letter of intent to sell is as good as having the deed. My Grandpa Joe did that, and it worked." He wasn't sure of the details, but if he could make them believe getting a letter would get them the mine, then they'd let him go.

"Tell us more." Mitchell lowered his hand from his jaw.

Lucky cleared his throat. "Well, my Grandpa Joe had some land, and he wanted to sell it to a guy he met in Portland, but he didn't have the deed with him. So he wrote up a letter of intent to sell, and once home, he sent the deed and sold the land." He rubbed his sore chest.

"What if David backs out?" Gene leaned so close his stinky breath fogged in Lucky's face.

Lucky sat up a little straighter. "Then you can take him to court."

Mitchell stuck his head out the open door. "Okay, draw us up a letter of intent to sell the mine to us and a map. Then we'll release the boy."

"I don't have any paper on me."

Gene groaned. "Now what?"

"Is he armed?" Mitchell asked.

Gene yanked Lucky to the door. "Ask him."

Lucky stood in the doorway. "Are you armed?" He covered his mouth and coughed twice.

"No." David held up his hands.

Mitchell grabbed a pen and a small pad of paper from a kitchen drawer. He handed the paper and pen to Lucky. "Take this to him." The pad had been used for keeping score of some sort.

Lucky shuffled outside and walked toward his uncle. Moisture seeped up through his slippers. His breath fogged. He shivered, keeping his eyes on his uncle. He held out the pad of paper and pen to David. "They want you to write up an intent to sell the mine and a map."

"Are you okay?"

"Yeah." His throat tightened. "I want to go home."

"You will. I promise." David knelt in front of him. "Where are you sitting?" he asked in a hushed tone.

"In the corner by the woodstove."

"I want you to stay there. You hear guns; you hit the

391

floor."

Guns? He gulped. "I thought you weren't armed?"

"Hey, get back here, kid," Mitchell yelled.

"I'm coming," he hollered over his shoulder then coughed.

"Don't look, but your daddy is up that hill behind me, and there are officers behind the trees. We'll get you out."

Hope surged.

"Get back here, boy!" Gene hollered.

David cupped Lucky's shoulder, holding his gaze, reassuring him. "You better get back inside."

Lucky scrambled to the cabin. His slipper came free, and he paused to get it back on then hurried inside. The old man slammed the door shut.

Chapter Thirty-nine

David climbed the hill and sat beside Luke.

Luke's nostrils flared. "Why didn't you grab him?"

This was not the time for dangerous heroics.

"Because I had two rifles pointed at us." David rested his back against the tree and drew a map of mountains, a stream, and a rocky crag.

"You're not seriously going to give them a map to the mine?"

"Nope." He added a few more details to make the map look legitimate. Drew an arrow pointing up for north. Wrote in a fictitious forest service road number and a few mileage indicators. That should do it.

Across the top, he wrote *Intent To Sell.*

Luke stared at the document. "They're not going to buy into that."

"They already did. This is what they want in exchange for Lucky."

"They're idiots."

David chuckled. "The Mitchells aren't known for their brains."

Trent hunkered beside them. "Here's the plan. You give them these papers but not before you get Lucky. Once you get Lucky, get behind the truck. We'll go in after that."

Got it. For his nephew's sake, David prayed the Mitchells would give up. It wouldn't take much to outsmart them. Their request for a map and a so-called contract testified to that. If he had to, he could bust down the door and take Owen out with one punch then deal with Gene. But that could get messy. David stood.

"No heroics," Trent warned them both.

Luke drew in a lungful of air and forced a tight nod.

Trent stayed crouched. "I'm hoping we can get out of this without using bullets. But my men have their orders. If the Mitchells threaten Lucky or my men, they'll shoot."

David placed a hand on Luke's shoulder. "I won't let Lucky get hurt."

Luke swallowed hard.

"Let's get your son." Trent moved into position two hundred yards from the cabin and hid behind a tree with his pistol drawn.

David trotted down the steep embankment, past Trent, and into the open. He raised the pad of paper over his head. "Owen, I have what you want." This better work.

The door opened. "Toss it inside."

His jaw clenched. "No, I want the boy."

What'd they take him for a fool?

"I'll set it right here." David set the pad on the ground.

"Let the boy come to me."

He waited. Voices drifted from the cabin, but he couldn't make out what was being said. The door sat ajar. His hands clenched into fist, and his heart sped. Come on, Owen, do the right thing. Don't let this escalate into a shootout.

Luke scrambled down the hillside and leaned against a tree. Maybe twelve feet from his brother, he pulled his gun and aimed at the door. One Mitchell as much as pokes their head out that door and he'll shoot.

Lucky appeared in the doorway. He glanced back and nodded.

Lucky walked up to David and picked up the pad of paper. David grabbed him and ran behind the truck.

"Hey! Get back here." Mitchell appeared in the doorway, sporting a hunting rifle.

Guns drew, clicked, and Trent gave the order. "Put your guns down."

Owen froze, the firearm at his side.

Luke's hand trembled as he aimed the pistol at Owen Mitchell's head.

In robotic-like motions, Owen set the rifle down and raised his hands over his head. He stood there with his eyes the size of cow pies. Luke held Owen's head in his sight, his jaw clenched, his trigger finger ached.

"Gene Mitchell," Trent shouted. "Come out with your hands in the air. You're surrounded."

Gene stepped out of the cabin and stood beside his father. His hands held over his head, and his knees knocked. He paled, and his mouth hung slack.

Luke took aim. He was a good shot, and at this distance, he'd have no problem hitting his mark. He stared through the sight at Owen's head. His hand shook. Sweat beaded on his forehead. Luke took a deep breath. His finger tightened on the trigger. His son coughed, drawing his attention from the cabin. Down behind the vehicle, his son peered up at him with innocent eyes.

Anger diffused, Luke released his breath.

He lowered the pistol.

Let the law deal with the Mitchells. He flipped the safety on. Trent approached with his hand extended, and Luke relinquished the gun.

"You did the right thing. Now go get your son."

Luke slid down the hill and ran to Lucky. He scooped his son up in his arms and drew him close. Relief flooded his veins.

"Dad!" His son clung to him.

"Thank you, God." Luke kissed the side of Lucky's head and squeezed him tight. The feel of his little arms clinging to his neck was unlike anything Luke had ever known.

"I knew you'd come for me," Lucky said against Luke's neck.

"I'd never let anyone hurt you. I love you so much."

"I love you, too, Dad."

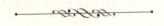

Hannah stood in the driveway and tore open the envelope from the county clerks' office. Anticipation and trepidation warred in her heart as she read the typed document.

No record of death for Lydia Brady. . . . Her breath rushed from her lungs. She read the line once more to be sure. There's no record of her mother's death in Ravalli County nor all of Montana.

Her hands shook, and tears blurred her vision. Raising her face to the clear blue sky, she breathed a sigh of relief. Hope infused her veins, and she ran to the garage where Luke and David were working on the drift boat. Wade set down a fishing rod on a table next to several others.

"I got it." She waved the letter in the air.

The three men turned toward her.

"There's no death certificate on file for our mother."

David took the letter and read it. "I called that attorney, but they couldn't tell me anything. I left them my number should they find something."

Hannah's lips trembled. They weren't any closer to finding Katy or discovering what happened to their mother.

"The number for our aunt and uncle was for some orchard."

Luke wrapped her in a tender embrace. "We're not going to give up. Don't lose hope."

Pride swelled in Luke's chest as he watched his son sitting

on the wood floor tying his high-top shoes.

"Where we going?" Lucky asked.

With his heart in his throat, Luke struggled to keep his voice even. "For a hike."

Behind him, Hannah put her hand on his back. "Sandwiches are packed."

He sprang from the couch like a wound-up toy. "Okay. Well, let's get rolling."

Lucky sprinted past them. "Come on, Bear."

The dog followed him outside.

On the way to the trailhead, Luke's nerves zinged like a reel with a hooked trout. He resisted the urge to feel for the ring in his pocket. It was there—the diamond poking him in the hip. To keep his hands from shaking, he kept a tight grip on the steering wheel.

"You all right?" Hannah asked.

She knew him too well.

"Yeah, why wouldn't I be? We're going for a hike, it's a warm spring day, and I'm with my two favorite people."

Lucky stuck his head between the seats. "Is there fishing where we're going?"

"Sure is, but the water is running too fast right now."

"But it's almost June."

Luke glanced up in the rear view mirror. "A few more weeks, son."

They parked in the small lot, and Hannah smiled sexy-like.

Luke's heart leaped. "Ah, you remember this place."

She unlatched her seatbelt and scooted across the

seat. "How could I forget?"

He met her in the middle, cupped her face in his hand, and moved in.

"Oh, yuck. Come on, you guys." Lucky opened the door behind his mother. Bear's tail thumped against the back of the seat.

They chuckled, but Luke wouldn't be dissuaded by an eight-year-old boy. He pressed his lips to hers, and her sweet little sigh was almost his undoing.

Lucky and Bear jumped out of the truck.

"I think we better get going," Hannah whispered against his lips.

He groaned.

They followed the trail. Lucky and Bear setting the pace.

"Lucky, don't get too far ahead of us," Hannah called.

Stopping at the waterfall, he took Hannah by the hand and led her to the water's edge.

She sighed. "The water is so clear." A butterfly flitted from one pink towering foxglove to another as a bumblebee dove deep within a blossom for the sweet nectar. "Look, a butterfly."

"Aren't they good luck?" Luke asked.

Her smile brightened her eyes. "There's no such thing as luck. Only God's grace."

"Sounds like something my mother would say."

"Maybe that's where I first heard it."

He fished the ring from his pocket, making sure he could see Lucky, and then bent on one knee. "Hannah."

He cleared his throat.

She faced him. Her eyes grew wide. "Luke?" She covered her mouth.

"Will you do me the honor of being my wife and making me the happiest man on earth?" He struggled to breathe as his pulse raced.

She nodded.

"Is that a yes?"

Hannah pressed her hand to her heart. "Yes, yes!"

He stood. "May I have your hand?"

Hannah presented him a trembling left hand. Luke took her hand, sliding the ring in place.

She launched into his arms. "You surprised me."

"What's going on?" Lucky ran at them.

"We're going to get married." Hannah's voice quivered.

Lucky wrapped his arms around them. "God answered my prayer."

Luke laughed. "What prayer is that?"

"That I'd have a mom and dad."

"Yes." Hannah's eyes shone. "We're going to be a family."

Acknowledgments

First and foremost, I want to thank my husband, Gary who encouraged me to write. Thank you for being my cheerleader. You are my inspiration to write romances.

This book is dedicate to my mother-in-law Marge who shares my love for books and God. Thank you for your encouragement and support.

Thank you to Romance Writers of America and Oregon Christian Writers for their excellent writing conferences that taught me the craft of writing.

I am thankful to my many critique group partners who are too numerous to list.

A huge debt of gratitude is owed to Deirdre Lockhart for her amazing gift of editing and coaching.

Most important, I thank the Lord for planting in me the dream to write. For going before me and opening doors and ushering me through. Thank you for giving me the ideas, strength, and vision for each story. Thank you, Lord for being the ultimate author of love.

For future releases visit www.wendyholley.com

Dear Friends,

In preparing to write A Matter of Hope, I did quite a bit of research on head injuries. Each year in the United States, 1.7 million people sustain a traumatic brain injury TBI.

The leading causes of TBI are:
- Falls 35.2%
- Motor vehicle traffic crashes 17.3%
- Struck by something 16.5%
- Assaults 10%
- Unknown or other causes 21%

The Center for Disease Control and Prevention estimates that at least 5.3 million Americans currently have a long-term need for assistance to perform daily living activities as a result of a TBI.

TBI can cause a wide range of functional changes affecting thinking, language, learning, emotions, behavior and/or sensation. For those who have experienced a TBI an increased risk for such conditions as Alzheimer's, Parkinson's, dementia, and other brain disorders which become more prevalent with age.

Drawing from my personal experience with a TBI, I applied memory loss, panic attacks, and balance issues to Hannah.

If you suspect a friend or family member has sustained an

injury to the head, seek medical care as quickly as possible.